SALINA PUBLIC LIBRARY
1701 9100 225
P9-BAT-977

FALSE STEP

Further Titles by Veronica Heley from Severn House

The Ellie Quicke Mysteries

MURDER AT THE ALTAR
MURDER BY SUICIDE
MURDER OF INNOCENCE
MURDER BY ACCIDENT
MURDER IN THE GARDEN
MURDER BY COMMITTEE
MURDER BY BICYCLE
MURDER OF IDENTITY

The new Bea Abbot Agency mystery series

FALSE CHARITY
FALSE PICTURE
FALSE STEP

FALSE STEP

An Abbot Agency Mystery

Veronica Heley

This first world edition published 2008
in Great Britain and in 2009 in the USA by
SEVERN HOUSE PUBLISHERS LTD of
9–15 High Street, Sutton, Surrey, England, SM1 1DF.
Trade paperback edition published
in Great Britain and the USA 2009 by
SEVERN HOUSE PUBLISHERS LTD

British Library Cataloguing in Publication Data

Heley, Veronica
False step. - (Abbott Agency mystery series)
1. Abbot, Bea (Fictitious character) - Fiction 2. Widows - England - London - Fiction 3. Women private detectives - England - London - Fiction 4. Entertainers - Death - Fiction 5. Murder - Investigation - Fiction 6. Detective and mystery stories
I. Title
823.9'14[F]

ISBN-13: 978-0-7278-6708-7 (cased)
ISBN-13: 978-1-84751-101-0 (trade paper)

All Severn House titles are printed on acid-free paper.

Typeset by Palimpsest Book Production Ltd.,
Grangemouth, Stirlingshire, Scotland.
Printed and bound in Great Britain by
MPG Books Ltd., Bodmin, Cornwall.

One

Thursday, noon

Bea Abbot, sixtyish and widowed but coping pretty well with life, answered the phone by saying, 'Abbot Agency. How may I help you?'

The voice at the other end quacked away.

Bea recoiled. 'We are not that kind of agency. We do not supply girls for . . . no, certainly not!' She put the phone down with some force.

Oliver, her teenaged assistant, turned a guffaw into a cough. Prompt on cue, the builders started hammering away downstairs.

Bea winced. How much longer were the workmen going to be? 'You can take that grin off your face, Oliver,' said Bea. 'We are a reputable domestic agency, supplying staff to reputable clients. We are not, repeat not, in the business of supplying girls for A-list parties.'

Oliver was feeling chirpy. 'But we have dealt with the odd murder.'

Bea took off her reading glasses to glare at him. 'That's different. That was an accident.'

'Two accidents, and we got well paid for each of them.'

'Never again.' Bea replaced her glasses and picked up the top letter of the morning's post. While the agency rooms in the basement of her Kensington house were being replumbed and rewired they were trying to work in her living room, surrounded by banks of office furniture, filing cabinets, printers and computers. Highly inconvenient.

The phone chirruped, and this time Bea listened to the excited babble without interrupting. 'Calm down, Florrie. Yes, of course it's distressing to find someone dead. Where are you?' Bea scribbled an address on the back of the topmost letter in the pile before her. 'I can get to you in five minutes. Just keep calm, right?'

She set the phone down, took off her reading glasses and put them in her handbag. What else did she need? Mobile phone, car keys, purse.

Oliver cocked his head. 'Florrie in trouble? The unflappable Florrie Green of the Green Girls Cleaning Company?'

'She's found her client dead to the world. No, what I mean is . . . he's dead!'

'Another murder,' said Oliver, full of glee.

'Certainly not! Natural causes, I'm sure.' Was it raining? Did she need her umbrella?

'Can I come, too? I like murders.'

'You'll be the death of me.' Bea checked that it wasn't raining, picked up the letter on which she'd written the address, and left. There were days when young Oliver was morose and couldn't be prised away from his computer, and others when he was overly bright and cheerful. Bea didn't know which was worse.

It wasn't murder, exactly. It was suicide. Sort of. The note proved it was suicide, anyway. Things hadn't exactly gone to plan, no. But with some improvisation here and a little imagination there, the outcome was satisfactory. Or it would be in due course.

They were still short of cash. It hadn't been advisable to remove all the money from his wallet, or the police might have suspected a burglary. Fifty pounds each wasn't much to keep them going. They'd have to sell the car. The key was on his key ring which now resided in her purse.

It was annoying that they hadn't found his spare set of keys.

The address Florrie had given Bea was not far away in the tangle of small streets which echoed medieval Kensington. Her own house lay in a terrace of early Victorian property, all cream stucco and large sash windows. The one she'd been directed to was a higgledy-piggledy sort of house, with a front door tucked into a recess, and windows of all shapes and sizes. There was no front garden, but there was a light well to a basement and, possibly – here she craned her neck to see – a roof garden?

Early nineteenth century, with later additions? It was a one-off in a road of what had once been workmen's cottages but which were now so gentrified as to command prices that only a millionaire could afford.

Bea had half expected to find a doctor's car in front of the house, but there wasn't one. Only the usual residents' cars, neatly ticketed to show they had paid for the right to be there. And Florrie's Mini.

Bea drew her jacket close around her throat. She ought to have picked up a scarf since the day was decidedly chilly. She pressed the doorbell.

Florrie must have been waiting for Bea to arrive, since she opened the door without delay. A spacious hall, panelled and painted magnolia with curving stairs on the left going up to the first floor and down to a basement. A not-too-modern landscape in oils on the wall over an oak chest.

Florrie Green was sixty, aimed to look forty and succeeded reasonably well. She had short, dyed blonde hair, a strong, muscular frame and dressed for work in teenage and boys' clothing. Today she was wearing a bright green cropped T-shirt over a slightly longer red one. Her jeans were low slung, showing a hint of red thong.

'Sorry to trouble you,' she said, ushering Bea into the living room. 'I totally lost it when I saw him.' She was nervous, her hands fussing with two fine gold chains around her neck.

Bea looked around but there was no corpse to be seen in the slightly over-furnished room. The day was overcast and though there were small windows front and back, the place seemed dark. 'A terrible shock. Did you get yourself a nice hot cup of tea before you rang for the medics?'

'I didn't bother. They came and said he was dead, which of course I could see for myself, and then they said they didn't take bodies away, which I knew, really, only I'd forgotten for the moment. Then I looked by the phone and there's his telephone book open with a number for his daughter and I rang her because she'll have to make all the arrangements only there was no answer so I left a message on her answerphone. There's no mobile phone number for her. Then I remembered I was due to meet the girls at the Mansfields' up the road at twelve, and although I texted Yvonne to say I'll be late, it's a big house and it has to be the four of us or we'll never get it done in time.'

Florrie Green and her three friends had formed themselves into a cleaning company known as the Green Girls. They undertook contract cleaning for schools, office blocks and large premises of all kinds.

Florrie wasn't meeting Bea's eyes. 'So I thought, seeing as how you've got the builders in, you might be happy to get away for a while, just till the daughter turns up . . .'

It was understandable that Florrie didn't want to hang around in the old man's house while paid work was waiting for her, but Bea was taken aback by the assumption that Bea had nothing better to do than hang around waiting for a dead man's family to surface.

The day-to-day business of running the agency could of course be left in Oliver's hands; a computer geek who knew more than most IT professionals, he was more than capable, even if he was only eighteen. Her other live-in assistant, Maggie . . . Well, Maggie might not be gifted at office work, but she had turned out to be a good project manager with a gift for dealing with workmen. At the moment she was overseeing the redecoration of a client's flat, supervising the work downstairs in the agency rooms, and running the household with a twitch of her little finger.

But sit with a corpse? No way.

'Couldn't Yvonne or one of the others stand in for you here?'

Florrie gave Bea a look, indicating exactly what she thought of foolish people who didn't know what they were talking about. 'Like I said, we need four of us to get through the work in time. We have to start cleaning the school at five, remember.'

'Perhaps I can find someone else to help you out?'

Florrie wasn't waiting around for Bea to find another solution to the problem. She shrugged herself into a blue denim jacket, and picked up the canvas bag in which she toted around her belongings. 'I've left the keys on the table. He's upstairs on his bed and won't be needing anything. The daughter's number is in the phone book. The page is open and her name underlined.'

'Florrie, no!'

'See you, Mrs Abbot. Can't let the girls down, can I?'

Florrie whisked herself out of the room and Bea heard the front door bang.

'Well!' On the other hand, would it be a hardship to be out of the office for a bit? It was so confoundedly noisy there. Bea switched on the centre light, which didn't do much to repel the gloom. She tried a couple of side lights. Yes, that was better.

There was indeed an address book by the phone, open to a page where 'Daughter: Damaris' had been pencilled in, with a West London number. Bea tried it. There was still no reply. She left another message, not doubting that Florrie had done the right thing but, well, making sure.

She set her handbag down on a nearby table, and dropped into an elderly Chesterfield chair which had seen much use in its time. Its rounded arms and thick cushions enfolded her in comfortable fashion. The left-hand arm was stained; coffee, probably. Or dirt from the garden. She thought of its dead owner, who would never sit in his chair again, and nearly found another, but didn't. He was past caring, and she wasn't going to stand up for an hour, or however long it took.

The room was large and oddly shaped with unexpected recesses and niches. It had character. She decided she rather liked it. But oh, for a cup of coffee!

She got out her mobile phone and rang home. Oliver must deal with the morning's post himself. The phone rang and rang, and it wasn't Oliver who answered it, but happy-go-lucky Maggie.

'Hi, Mrs Abbot. Did you want Oliver? He's having a row with the electrician, something to do with the computers. I don't know what, but I do know I can't sort it. Will you be back for lunch? I thought I'd make a chicken and mushroom pie with the leftovers from the roast last night. Will that do you?'

'Can you take a message, Maggie? Tell Oliver I'm held up here but he can reach me on my mobile if anything happens. Don't bother with anything else. I may be some time so we'll have the chicken pie tonight, right?'

'Oh, Mrs Abbot, before you go, there was something Oliver said before he disappeared downstairs . . . now, what was it? Oh, I know. He said you'd turned your mobile off and Mr Max had rung, wanting to speak to you, but he's going to ring back later. I think that's everything.'

Now what did her self-important – though of course very much loved – son want? Max was inclined to think he could call on her to sort out every trivial little crease in the rose petal of his life, despite having successfully managed to get into Parliament and to marry a blonde trophy of a wife. Max could wait.

Bea left her mobile switched on, just in case.

Somewhere in her files at the office – now stowed in piles around her living room – there was a leaflet telling you what to do when a person died. She must look it out sometime. But Florrie seemed to have taken the right steps, so she might as well relax. Try the daughter every half-hour till she answered. Make herself at home.

She took off her jacket and went in search of a cup of coffee. A door at the end of the room let her through into a modern kitchen, where French windows gave on to a large, flagstoned patio. There was no garden as the patio was enclosed by the backs and sides of other houses, but the walls had been painted apricot, a wrought-iron Edwardian bench sat on the tiled floor and there was an elegant sufficiency of plants sitting around in tubs. Scarlet geraniums cascaded from pots on the walls. The geraniums were still in full flower even though it was now autumn. In that sheltered position, they might well survive the winter.

There were no breakfast dishes in the sink; the man must have died some time in the night.

A hoover had been left half in and half out of a broom cupboard. Bea shook her head. Florrie should have put that away before she panicked and rang for help.

Bea filled the kettle and stood admiring the pretty patio till it boiled. Tea bags were on the counter, as were tins of sugar and coffee. Milk – she sniffed at it to make sure it was fresh – in the well-filled fridge. She made herself a cup of instant, pushing aside an unwashed mug half full of cold coffee. Florrie must have had a drink after all, before she went upstairs and found the corpse.

Odd, that. Florrie never usually stopped for a coffee break. She toted her own flask of special tea around with her, and occasionally sipped from that. So whose coffee mug was that on the side?

Oh, it must have been Florrie who'd had it. She'd been in shock. Hadn't known quite what she was doing. Or maybe it had been a late night cuppa for the man upstairs. Only . . .

Bea took her coffee into the sitting room and drank it, letting her eyes rove around. The furniture in here was not new, not valuable antique, but anything up to a hundred years old and in good condition. There was that quintessential piece of twentieth century furniture, an upright piano, in one corner of the room – if you could call it a corner when there were only angles between walls. There were William Morris tiles around a simulated log gas fire. The carpet was one of those all-over Turkish patterned affairs that didn't show the dirt but there was a distinctive trail of cigarette ash on the floor by the fireplace, although there was no ashtray in sight.

Ah, yes. One was on the floor under a Parker Knoll chair, upholstered in a good quality, but rather worn moquette. 1960s style. Bea sniffed the air. Was that a trace of cigarettes she could smell? Had the man been a smoker? Two cigarette butts, no lipstick. As the man of the house would presumably sit in the big Chesterfield, the man who'd sat in the Parker Knoll chair opposite would have been a visitor.

He was going to get a shock when he discovered what had happened, wasn't he?

There were some faded photographs on the mantelpiece, family pictures, snapshots. Two faded pictures of elderly people – presumably his parents? – and some snapshots of a nice-looking fair-haired man with friends and family. No dust. Or hardly any. The television set was not new but still in use to judge by a copy of the current *Radio Times* sitting on top of it.

There was a well-filled rack of DVDs and CDs nearby and a pair of speakers which were rather too large and modern to blend into their surroundings. Music, presumably, had been important to the occupant. And books, lots of them. Mostly travellers' tales. Sea stories. A lot of them looked Victorian and might or might not be valuable.

A china cabinet held some porcelain figures which again were not new, but might fetch a good price at auction. Everything was slightly shabby. Dated, but comfortable.

An elderly gentleman, then? Possibly living with inherited furniture?

Bea looked at her watch. Time was passing. She tried the daughter's number again; still no reply. She finished her cup of coffee and thought she might like to visit the loo, which meant finding a bathroom. She explored the hall – no loo. She didn't really feel like going upstairs but needs must, even if it did feel as if she were invading the dead man's privacy. Which was absurd, of course.

The house was very quiet.

She held on to the banister, as the stairs curled up to the first floor. This was a surprisingly large house for its narrow frontage; an estate agent might describe it as 'characterful, needing some modernization'. The ceilings were low, and there probably wasn't a straight wall or right angle anywhere.

On the first floor landing sat a large plastic box containing cleaning materials, with several aerosols sticking out of it. Florrie must have brought it upstairs meaning to do the bathroom and on discovering the corpse, had forgotten to remove it.

The room straight ahead was a double bedroom, the window overlooking the patio below. More magnolia paint, cupboards built into the wall. Light and airy, Laura Ashley and Sanderson furnishings. A guest bedroom, not often used by the look of it.

The door to the master bedroom was on the right. It was ajar, but Bea avoided looking at it as she went into the bathroom on the left. Again, everything was dated, but functioned. There was an old-fashioned, claw-footed bath but the owner had installed a shower. Towels had been thrust at the rail, wedged in rather than folded and hanging free. There was a noticeable rim around the bath and one around the washbasin as well. The soap was dry.

Bea washed her hands, thinking it was a shame that Florrie hadn't got around to cleaning the bathroom before she discovered the body. A selfish thought, perhaps.

The stairs went on upwards and Bea, bored with waiting, ascended them up to the second floor. Another double bedroom, also painted in magnolia, furnishings ditto. A small bathroom. Then came a tiny square room which contained nothing but garden furniture, including a table and a parasol. This room's windows were barred. There was a locked door, whose window was also barred, which led out on to the roof garden. Presumably the bars were to protect against burglars getting in over the rooftops. Sensible.

Bea peered out of the window. The roof garden was laid out with apricot tiles on the floor, more tubs, and a hammock shrouded against wind and rain. The sun was out, for a miracle. The rooftop must be a regular sun trap in the summer.

Oh well. What now? She wished she'd brought something

with her to read. Perhaps she'd borrow a book from the shelves below while she was waiting.

She went down to the ground floor and then, having nothing better to do, continued down into the basement. Opening a door at the bottom of the stairs, she got the shock of her life, as a ghostly figure swam out of the darkness to meet her.

She pulled the door shut and fell back, hand to heart. Who . . .? What . . .?

There wasn't anyone else in the house, was there?

Ridiculous! She'd have heard, if there had been.

Dear Lord, from ghosties and gremlins and things that go bump in the night, please deliver us. Or words to that effect. She couldn't remember exactly how the prayer went, but the sentiment was spot on. *Dear Lord, deliver us.*

Calming her breathing, she told herself that what she'd seen was just a trick of the light. There was nobody else there. Full stop.

She thought of going back upstairs and waiting till the daughter could be contacted. She shouldn't have explored, anyway. It was not right.

She took a deep breath, pushed the door open and called out, 'Hello there?'

Silence.

The ghostly figure was still there, one hand holding open the door, facing her. It was dressed in a pale-grey trouser suit, and had short, ash-blonde hair. In other words, she was looking at herself in a mirror! The relief was so great that she sagged at the knees. She told herself that this was all very amusing and some time or other it would make a good story.

The room was in darkness. There ought to have been a window in it, because she had noticed a light well for the basement when she arrived. She found a light switch and shut her eyes momentarily as glaring neon strips came on overhead.

Whatever she'd expected – a playroom with billiard table, a junk room? – it wasn't this. The window had been blacked out, and all around were wardrobes and cupboards, some of metal, some of wood. She took one step more into the basement and recoiled again, for every wardrobe door had a mirror, and everywhere she looked, she saw herself. The room was cavernous and she experienced a moment of disorientation.

She shaded her eyes against the dazzling strip lights. Opposite was an up-to-the-minute computer set-up, with an adjustable typing chair in front of it. Laptop, printer, fax, telephone . . . everything that a man might need to run a small business. A set of large speakers, a 'desk' such as DJs use, with microphone, etc. Had the man been in the music business?

Nearby was a mirror surrounded by light bulbs with a wide ledge under it, and a stool in front. An old-fashioned tin box sat on the ledge, next to a box of tissues. She'd seen something like that before, somewhere. But where?

What was this place? As she stepped forward, a floorboard shifted, and one of the mirrored doors swung open. A sunburst of colour met her eyes. And glitter. Women's clothes, not men's.

What . . .?

She pulled open the door of the nearest cupboard, to reveal ranks of shoes in a large size. The following cupboard was dedicated to wigs of all colours and lengths; some on stands, others on what looked like balloons.

She realized that the 'desk' was for theatrical make-up. The box would contain the tools of his trade, perhaps.

Whatever had been going on here?

There was one way to find out. She put her head out of the door to listen for the noises of someone arriving, but there was nothing. She told herself that curiosity killed the cat, but yes, she was curious. Who wouldn't be?

She went to the computer desk and pulled out drawers till she found some business cards. All had 'Magnificent Millie' written on them. A woman? Bea had formed the impression that Florrie's client had been male. Whatever was going on here? Ah, underneath the flourish of the words 'Magnificent Millie' was some small print. 'Matthew Kent', followed by a phone number, website and email address. Was Matthew Kent the same person as Magnificent Millie? Did he do a drag act for the clubs, perhaps?

Bea pocketed a card, switched off the lights, shut the door to the basement, and climbed the stairs to the first floor, to the master bedroom. She really must catch a glimpse of the man or woman who had owned all this. Was he a transvestite, perhaps? Getting his kicks out of dressing as a woman?

She pushed the door of the main bedroom open but all was

dark within, so she groped for a light switch . . . and took a hasty step back.

In front of an enormous old mahogany bed were a pair of shoes such as Bea had never seen out of the theatre or cinema. They reminded her of Dorothy's shoes in *The Wizard of Oz*. They were bright red, with a small heel. They were covered with sequins and finished off with stiff bows, also in red.

Bea blinked. Was she really seeing what she was seeing?

She lifted her eyes to a tide of scarlet and gold. Spread over the bed was a travesty of a woman's eighteenth-century costume in red and gold. The overskirt was of scarlet satin, frilled, ruched and garnished with gold bows. The padded petticoat was of gold silk, trellised with black ribbon. The bodice was of scarlet satin, low-cut in front with sleeves to the elbow, finished with falls of lace.

It reminded Bea of the costume for the Pantomime Dame in the last act, where he-cum-she descends the stairs to thunderous applause from the audience. It covered the body on the bed almost completely. The corpse wasn't actually wearing it, but was covered by it, as it were by a blanket.

Was it a man, or a woman? If it was a man, then he'd been made up to look like a woman, with lipstick and rouge, eye shadow and grotesquely painted-on eyebrows. A wide hairband such as tennis players wear was around his or her head, almost completely covering the hair, waiting for the wig to be fitted. The wig was still on a stand beside the bed.

Man or woman? There was only one way to find out. Bea twitched up the dress to inspect the body beneath. So it was a man after all.

Hand to throat, Bea said, 'I don't believe it! I simply cannot be seeing what I am seeing.'

She looked around the rest of the room. The walls were a pale grey-green. The blinds and curtains, closely drawn, had been made to match. Restful. The rest of the furniture matched the bed, being Victorian and well-polished. On the bedside stand was a bottle of wine, an empty glass, and a packet which had once contained sleeping tablets. Plus a note.

This wasn't – couldn't be – a death by natural causes. Bea's mind whirled around what Florrie had told her about her client having died of natural causes. What had Florrie actually said? Not much, really.

Natural causes, my foot!

Florrie had taken one look, realized this must be a suicide, and . . . and what? Had she even phoned for the medics? Because if she had, wouldn't they have done something else, phoned for the police, the doctor . . . whatever?

Bea leaned back against the bedroom door, which shut with a click, startling her. Getting over the shock, Bea began to get angry. How dare Florrie drop Bea in it like this!

That note . . . what did it say? The whole set-up screamed of suicide, but . . . perhaps a closer look . . .? She unglued herself from the door and rounded the bed, careful not to brush against the overhanging dress.

The note was a mere scrawl. It said 'Sorry.'

So it was a suicide after all. It must have been, mustn't it? Hadn't Florrie seen the note? What on earth was the girl playing at?

Bea went downstairs to phone the police.

Lunchtime

She took her sandwich to the tiny staff room in the basement, and made herself a cup of instant. The rest of the salesgirls knew enough not to talk to her when she didn't want to be disturbed. She ran through a mental checklist. Clothes; disposed of. Broken wine glass; wrapped in paper and put in the bin. Diary; removed. Blood stains; cleaned up. Files on computer; deleted. Publicity flyers taken away. Telephone book left out with her number prominently displayed. She didn't think they'd missed anything important.

She glanced at her watch. Time to get back to work. She wondered how soon the police would track her down in order to break the sad news?

Two

Thursday evening

By the time Bea got back home, she was both exhausted and angry. A bad combination for digestion. Maggie, who was not a particularly good timekeeper in some respects, could time a meal to perfection. Half past six, on the table. This allowed the two youngsters to go out for the evening and allowed Bea time to relax, chat to friends, watch telly or just sit and think.

She looked at her watch as she let herself into the house. Nearly six o'clock.

Oliver appeared like a jack-in-the-box from the basement. There was no sound of banging and crashing; presumably the workmen had departed for the day. Just as well. In her present mood, Bea would have been quite capable of yelling at them to get lost and never darken her door again. She knew in her head that it was entirely necessary for the agency quarters to be rewired, replumbed and redecorated. She just hated every minute of the disruption and noise and fuss concerned. And the cost.

Oliver said, 'Oh-ho! Don't tell me it really was a murder!'

'Certainly not!' Bea glared at him. 'Suicide. And no, I don't know why. But I do know that if you don't get me Florrie Green's mobile telephone number at once, I shall . . . I don't know what I shall do, but I'll think of something! I need to speak to her before she finishes cleaning at the school and goes home.'

Maggie appeared from the kitchen, followed by the sound of the telly. Maggie was tall, skinny, noisy and lacking in self-confidence. She was on her own mobile, but on seeing Bea, took it away from her ear long enough to ask, 'Is there something, Mrs Abbot? I'm afraid the plumber's got bad news. He's found a patch of damp so we shan't be back downstairs for quite a while. We'll have to get the computers working on the ground floor, somehow.'

'Sorry, both of you,' said Bea. 'I know I'm in a foul temper, but this is not directed at you. Oliver, if the computers are down, can you still find me Florrie's mobile phone number?'

Oliver, computer geek that he was, had his laptop up and running. 'Just a sec . . . I think . . . yes, here it is. I've got this programme now which asks all our clients to keep their mobile numbers updated. Yes, I've got it. Shall I get her on the land-line for you?'

Bea told herself that he was worth his weight in gold and she ought not to be cross with him. It didn't do any good. If he'd come within reach of her hand, he'd have got his ears boxed. Maggie, too.

Oliver handed the phone to Bea but stayed close, listening. Maggie cut off her own phone and draped her length against the doorway, also anxious to hear what had made the usually calm Mrs Abbot lose her temper.

'Florrie Green,' said Bea, grinding out the words, 'you dropped me right in it, didn't you? I want you here, at my house, within ten minutes.'

Florrie had had time to think what line she should take. 'I don't know what you mean, Mrs Abbot. What am I supposed to have done?'

'The police want to interview you about finding the body. Naturally I cooperated, told them everything. I gave them your home address but just in case you can come up with a good explanation for your actions, I said I wasn't sure where you'd be working this afternoon, so you'd better get over here and brief me properly before they get round to you.' She crashed the phone down.

Oliver narrowed his eyes. 'Florrie found the body and told you it was natural causes. She left you there and went off to work? You found out it couldn't be natural causes and called the police. Is that right?'

'There was a pack of pills, empty, at his bedside. Ditto a dead bottle of wine. A note saying "Sorry." That enough for you?'

He was still hoping. 'Not murder?'

Bea told herself she was not going to scream at him, but perhaps the look in her eye informed him that he'd better make himself scarce. Which he did.

Maggie went into mother hen mode. 'You poor thing. Shall I get you a cup of coffee, some herbal tea? Oh, by the way, Mr Max rang here again and sounded quite cross that he couldn't get hold of you. He's out for the evening but will ring you again tomorrow, if that's all right.'

'Did he, now? Well, it can't be anything very urgent. As for tea; no, thank you. I made tea for the police. I gave a statement. I was totally helpful, and calm and . . . I could kill Florrie! She knew perfectly well that it wasn't a natural death.'

Maggie said, 'A cuppa is definitely called for.'

'Grrr,' said Bea. She knew she needed to calm down. But how? She raged about her pretty sitting room, stepping around the piles of files and equipment which had been brought up from below. Backwards and forwards she went, from the dining table in the front window overlooking the road, to the card table and chair at the back of the house where her dear husband used to sit and play patience in the evenings.

Seated in his own big chair, he would look out over the garden below, see through the branches of the sycamore at the far end, to the spire of the church beyond. That view always seemed to give him pleasure. Normally, it gave Bea pleasure, too.

But not tonight.

She got the patience cards out and dealt to play Spider. Hamilton always said that the rhythmic slap of the cards kept the forefront of his mind occupied while the little men at the back of his head worked on whatever problem was bugging him. She didn't, herself, find it so helpful. *Slap, slap*, went the cards.

Playing patience didn't do anything for her.

The front doorbell rang and Oliver ushered Florrie into the sitting room.

Florrie looked around her. Usually her business was conducted in the offices downstairs, and she hadn't been up here before.

'Well, Florrie?' Bea continued to lay out her cards, *slap, slap, slap*. This game was not going to work out.

Florrie seated herself, unasked. With an appearance of candour, she trotted out a prepared excuse. 'Well, it was like this, Mrs Abbot. I'd never seen anything like it. It spooked me, completely. I couldn't get out of there fast enough. I thought you'd handle it better than me. With the police, I mean.'

Slap, slap went the cards. Silence.

Florrie fidgeted, her eyes touching everything and resting on nothing. She cleared her throat. 'You've got some nice furniture here. Was it Mr Abbot's, rest his soul?'

Bea put the rest of the cards down. 'Florrie, if you saw your client and realized he was dead, you also saw the packet of pills and the note. Right?'

Florrie coloured up, unzipped her jacket, and zipped it up again. 'If I don't work, I don't get paid. I knew if I called the police they'd keep me there for hours and I needed the money from the Mansfield cleaning job. I know what I did wasn't right, but I wasn't thinking straight. It was a shock, see.'

'Oh, I see all right. What time did you get there?'

Florrie's nose seemed to sharpen as she drew in an audible breath.

Bea raised her voice. 'Oliver, shut that door properly, and find yourself something to do.'

The door eased to, very quietly. The handle returned to its normal height.

Florrie looked shocked. 'He was listening?'

'He may be young but he's pretty good at knowing when people aren't telling the truth.'

'I *am* telling the truth.'

'But not the whole truth. You didn't tidy up well enough before I got there. You left a half-drunk cup of coffee in the kitchen. There was no scum on the top, and the contents hadn't had time to dry out so it must have been poured that morning. You don't make yourself coffee when you're working. You told me yourself that you hadn't made yourself a cup this morning. So someone else did. Who?'

Florrie reared her head. 'Are you calling me a liar?'

'Also,' said Bea, 'you don't use aerosol polish on good furniture. You use a vinegar and water mix every week, and a good beeswax preparation once a month, yet the box of cleaning materials on the first landing contained aerosols. How do you account for that?'

'Sometimes I have to be quick, like. Beeswax takes time.'

Bea swivelled around to face her. 'Shall I ask the other members of your team what your first job was this morning . . . and what time you left them to do this one job on your own?'

Florrie swallowed, but was mute.

Bea abandoned her game to go and sit beside Florrie. Time to play soft cop, instead of hard. 'Florrie, if the police weren't involved I could let it go, but as it is . . . if they start questioning you about what time you got to the house, what are you going to say?'

'Do they have to know?'

'Tell me the truth, and we can take it from there. I don't think you were the usual cleaner at that house. You've got enough and more than enough work, organizing the Green Girls. But you were greedy—'

'Short of money. Donny lost his job a while back, can't seem to get another, you know how it is, he's on these pills but they don't seem to do much good.'

'I know how it can be. I think you applied for the job as cleaner to that house but subcontracted the job out, taking a rake-off for your trouble. How much did you pay . . . whoever it was you got to do the job for you?'

'She's Polish, was desperate for the job. I pay her every week in cash, and keep a bit back for arranging it. She hasn't complained.'

'In that case, why did you panic this morning and get me to front for you to the police? You knew perfectly well that the death wasn't natural. You didn't want to be asked questions, did you?'

'I haven't done anything wrong. He was dead and . . . ugh! If I'd known he was one of that sort I'd never have gone anywhere near him.'

'You think he was a transvestite, a man who only feels right in women's clothes? No, Florrie. He was an entertainer of the old-fashioned variety. Stand-up comic, singer, that sort of thing. The flamboyant clothing was part of his act.'

Florrie shrugged.

Bea said, 'The Polish woman. Is she a student?'

Florrie shrugged again. 'How should I know? She advertised for a job in the newsagent's.'

'If she's Polish, she's got every right to be here and work here. Did you employ and pay her properly, or was it cash in hand?' Florrie's face gave Bea her answer. 'Oh, Florrie.'

'No need to "Oh, Florrie" me! I got her some work, didn't I? I paid her on the dot every week, didn't I? My nose is clean.'

'If so, then why did you get rid of her before you phoned me for help?'

Silence. Florrie pleated her jacket, fiddled with the zip.

Bea sighed, reaching a long arm for a pencil and paper. 'Give me her name and mobile telephone number. The sooner I speak to her, the better.'

'You won't tell the police about her?'

'How can I avoid doing so?'

'She knows nothing, saw nothing. She likes to work from the top down, so as soon as she arrived, she went upstairs to do the bathroom out and found him. She didn't touch anything, didn't know what to do, was too scared to phone a doctor, and definitely too scared to phone the police. I can't say for certain why she's scared of the police but maybe in Poland things are different. Or maybe she isn't Polish, but from one of those countries where they've got no right to be over here, taking the bread out of our mouths. I didn't ask. Maybe it was in her mind that if she got mixed up with the police, they'd send her home. All I know is, she rang me and I got over there straight away. She'd gone by that time, left the keys in the front door. I let myself in, saw what she'd seen and phoned you. At least I stayed till you arrived.'

Bea deplored Florrie's racist attitude but now was not the time to say so. 'Her name and contact number.' Bea handed Florrie pencil and paper. Florrie pulled a face, but wrote down a name and – after consulting a little book in her bag – also a mobile phone number. 'That's all I know. I don't know her last name. Something unpronounceable. If you tell the police about her, she'll do something drastic, I'm sure she will. Throw herself under a train, maybe. Disappear, anyway.'

'I'm sure she's no need to fear the police. If she's that scared, perhaps you can offer to go with her to see them.'

'Count me out. I'm due for a holiday, anyway, and no, I don't know where I can be contacted. Donny and I'll be taking the camper van, travelling around.'

Well, that was a surprise! Bea wondered what Donny had been up to, that Florrie couldn't risk drawing the attention of the police to herself. 'I have your mobile phone number and—'

'My mobile phone is running out of credit. Which reminds

me' – she took an envelope out of her bag – 'her wages that I was going to give her after she'd finished this morning. You can tell her she won't be needed at the other places after this.'

'What other places? You mean, you've subcontracted other jobs to her as well? How many?'

Florrie wriggled. 'Four. I pay her at the end of each week, never miss. But I'll have to stop doing it now you know. Won't I?'

'Yes, of course you will,' said Bea, mentally trying to work out how much money Florrie had been creaming off the Polish girl's wages each week. 'I take it she's a good cleaner, worth her money?'

Florrie shrugged. 'Better than most. She turns up on time, leaves a room tidy, doesn't mind cleaning the oven, empties the waste-paper bins and doesn't leave early. Yes, she's all right. I was even thinking of letting her join the Green Girls, when we need an extra hand and to cover holidays and that. But . . . well . . . you see how it is.' She stood up. 'No hard feelings?'

Bea shook her head. She didn't like what Florrie had been doing, but she understood it. If she had a husband who was virtually unemployable due to clinical depression maybe she, too, would be looking for ways to rake in extra money.

'And you'll still think of the Green Girls when cleaning contracts come up?'

'Probably,' said Bea. 'But only if you let me have a list of the jobs you've subcontracted out to this girl so that I can get them covered by another cleaner.'

Florrie pulled a face. 'All right. I'll give the names and addresses to that young man of yours on the way out. You won't let on to the police about what I've been doing, will you?'

'Not unless they ask, no. But if they do ask, I shall have to tell them you've had a sudden desire to leave town and they won't like that.'

'But you won't tell them, will you?' Florrie regained her usual bounce. 'All's well, then. And, er, I suppose, thanks.'

Only after the front door had banged to, did Bea realize that Florrie had 'forgotten' to give Oliver the names and addresses of the other subcontracted jobs. Shaking her head at herself, Bea dialled the mobile phone number she'd been given for the Polish girl. The phone was switched off. Bea left a message for the girl to call.

Time to eat. Over supper in the kitchen, Bea brought her two assistants up to date with what had been happening. '. . . and I'm sorry if I was a bit short with you two when I came back, but it was worrying. It's still worrying me. I keep seeing . . .' She passed her hand over her eyes. 'Hope I don't get nightmares.' She tried to laugh. Almost made it. The sight of that painted face sticking out from under the grotesque red and gold dress was something she wasn't going to be able to forget easily. And those red shoes!

The Polish girl failed to ring back that evening. Oliver went out to the gym as usual, and Maggie went to meet a new boyfriend in the pub. Maggie was the victim of a managing mother, who'd pushed her into a marriage doomed to failure, so nowadays she fell in love at regular intervals with men her mother would never have liked.

Bea descended to the agency rooms to see what had been done that day, and to wonder if they'd ever be straight again. Carpets had been taken up and stacked against walls, her big settee and visitors' chairs ditto. The replumbing had left their tiny kitchen and loo looking like a bomb site. There was dust and rubble everywhere, seeping up the stairs into the rooms on the ground floor as well. A dust sheet had been hung over the stairwell to contain the problem, but wasn't really up to the job.

Bea fell over a stack of files in her sitting room; she moved them to one side of the fireplace, and then moved them back again. She could settle to nothing, and eventually went to bed early, hoping she wouldn't dream of pantomime dames.

Friday morning

In the morning things seemed no better. Florrie Green was not at work; Bea checked. Kasia failed to ring. Bea forced herself to deal with routine matters, and succeeded fairly well until Max rang.

'Sorry I missed you yesterday,' Bea said, trying to focus on what her son might want this time. 'I had to do a site visit.'

'You'd switched your mobile off.'

'Only in the morning. Yes, sorry. So, how are you getting on?'

Heavy breathing. A long sigh. Bea realized she was expected to show sympathy, to rush with plasters and band aid to clean up the grazed knee, or whatever it was this time. She assumed his troubles were trivial; overspending by his almost-anorexic wife, Nicole? Being omitted from the guest list of some function or other?

'The thing is . . .' he started and then stopped. 'Well, Nicole's going through a bad time, health-wise. It makes her hypersensitive.'

Bea's eyebrows peaked. To her mind Nicole was as hypersensitive as a piledriver. 'Oh dear,' was all she could say.

'I've tried reasoning with her. I've bent over backwards to reassure her . . .'

Bea's tone sharpened. 'She needs reassurance?'

'The fact is . . . you'll laugh when you hear this . . . but she's jealous of . . . of my research assistant. And honestly, there's nothing in it.'

Bea rolled her eyes. 'I suppose the girl's young and blonde?'

'You've met her?'

'When would I . . .? Never mind. Sack her, obviously. Not Nicole, the research assistant.'

'I wish I could.' He sounded eight years old and tearful. 'The thing is, Mother, Nicole's thrown me out. Would it be all right if I moved back home for a few days, just till she calms down?'

Bea closed her eyes, sending up an arrow prayer for patience. 'You realize Oliver now lives in your old bedroom, and pays me rent for it? Plus we've got the builders in. I'm not sure you ought to be flying back here so quickly. Why can't you sack the troublemaker?'

'She's Nicole's younger sister. It was Nicole's father – the chair of my local constituency party – who asked me to take the girl on. She's his favourite, you see. I couldn't refuse since he's helped us so much, buying a place for us in the constituency. I didn't realize the girl was, well, like she is. I have to talk to him, try to make him understand, but I'm afraid he might still take her part. It's no wonder, really, that Nicole's jealous.'

Bea sighed. 'All right. Just for a few days. Use the guest bedroom. When will you arrive?'

'As soon as. I'll be at the House most of the time, will eat there, and so on.'

'You're very welcome, Max.' She put the phone down, thinking that of course it would be lovely to see him, but she wished he were better at handling his relationships.

He must have been sitting in his car outside, for he arrived within five minutes, lugged a couple of suitcases up the stairs to the guest bedroom and disappeared for the rest of the day. Bea informed Maggie that they had a guest for the week, and left it at that. She was not, definitely not, going to get involved in her son's problems.

Late in the afternoon there was a call from the Polish girl, asking about money due to her. Bea coaxed her to come round that evening, after she'd finished her cleaning jobs for the day.

Friday afternoon

Going home in the rush hour seemed worse than usual. Everyone bad-tempered, closely crammed into the Tube.

She got out at Ealing Broadway and trudged up the stairs in a moving queue of people. The formal identification had gone well. She'd even managed to weep a little. Poor old man. He'd been in a lot of pain with his arthritis . . . a merciful release . . . the autopsy would prove how he died . . . there'd be no problem with the death certificate . . . then she had to register the death . . . inform the solicitor.

They'd been understanding at work and given her some time off. So they jolly well should. How she hated that manageress. Well, soon she'd be able to tell her what to do with her piddling little job.

The family were over the moon at the news. The boys, bless them, wanted a monster telly. Well, why not, eh?

It was a pity that the pot of gold would have to be divided between two. If she'd had sufficient time to think, perhaps there might have been another way to do it. But the best laid plans, et cetera. Best not tell the boys the prize had to be shared.

She was a little concerned about the Polish girl. They'd planned that Kasia should report the death to the police, but apparently she'd chickened out and involved someone from the agency she worked for. They must have a word with the girl. For one thing, she had a set of keys, and they needed them.

Three

Friday evening

Bea had been expecting some young Polish student, but Kasia was perhaps forty, a pretty woman dressed in a modest black top and well-cut trousers, not jeans. She was carrying a large leather handbag, wore good shoes and looked nervous. As Bea let her in, their eyes met and in that moment they recognized certain things about one another. When a woman has watched someone die, the knowledge stays in her eyes.

'Come in,' said Bea. 'I'm afraid we've got the builders in, so can't use the agency rooms at the moment. Tea, coffee? A soft drink?'

'Thank you, but no.' Kasia held on to her handbag with both hands, but Bea thought that in ordinary circumstances this woman could have held her own in any stratum of society. She was definitely a cut above Florrie by birth, and possibly also by education. Bea told herself that she was a snob, but knew enough of the world to understand that different backgrounds created different expectations and patterns of behaviour.

Kasia moved with grace, looking around her at Bea's pretty sitting room just once and then concentrating on Bea. 'I am so sorry. Yesterday, I did not behave good. It was bad to run away, but I was afraid. My papers are all right, but in my country . . . it is different here, the language, the police.'

'Mrs Green has given you a good reference. How long have you been working for Mr Kent?'

'A year. I put advertisement in window of paper shop. Mrs Green rings me and arranges.'

'She collects the money from Mr Kent, and pays you?'

'For that and for some other jobs. I am happy for this. It is hard to begin here. Then one of my ladies say, can I take on another job and another. And so is good now. I am, how you say, full up?'

'I understand, but . . .' How to tell this nice woman that she had to stop working for Florrie? Was there any way around it? Bea handed over the envelope Florrie had given her. 'This is from Mrs Green, for yesterday. I realize she has been giving you jobs to do which she could not spare the time to do herself, but this must stop. Oh, don't look so alarmed . . .'

Kasia half-started to her feet, then sat down again. 'Something is wrong?'

Bea thought of the problems facing people who worked in the black economy; the paperwork, the difficulty of getting free medical care, the likelihood of there being no holiday pay or insurance. She decided not to talk about that for the moment. 'It seems that Mrs Green didn't pay you the full amount each time. She was taking a rake-off.'

Kasia was resigned, not bitter. 'Same like Polish agency. One big rake-off for people who need to work.'

'If you will give the details of the other jobs you got through Mrs Green, I will contact them and arrange for you to continue with them, the money going direct to you. All of it. Have you ever considered getting a full-time job, maybe as a live-in housekeeper, for better pay? Our agency does this all the time.'

'You will charge me a fee?'

'There will be a registration fee, yes. But once you are on our books you will soon recover it, because you will be paid the proper rate in future. Everything will be legal, if you do it through us. We will help you with all the forms, getting a National Insurance number, everything. You understand?'

Kasia seemed to have heard it all before. 'I will think about it.'

'You do that. Now, tell me exactly what happened yesterday.'

Kasia stiffened. 'Is bad. I not like to talk about it.'

Bea started again, trying to put Kasia at her ease. 'What was Mr Kent like?'

Kasia relaxed. 'So high, like my husband.' She got up to mime a man taller than herself, perhaps five foot ten. 'His hair going away in front of his head. He laughs, I laugh. Nice man. Always kind, say I must have coffee, biscuits, some cake he makes, sit in the sun on the patio, take your time.'

'You liked working for him. What time did you usually get there?'

'Nine o'clock. Mr Kent say not to worry if bus is late, but I am there at nine o'clock, just right. Many times he is still in bed when I come because he works late, in the clubs, at parties. He is entertainer, you know. Dressing up, singing, telling jokes. But for some time not so much smiling, for he was sick in his stomach.' She shook her head. 'I not like his look. But the last time he was, how you say, chipper? He say everything is all right. All smiles. So I come as usual on Thursday morning. I use my key to go in, and I say, "Hello", like always. But he is quiet. I think maybe he sleeps.

'I get out my box of things to clean, and out comes the hoover, which is wrong. I take my box and I go up the stairs to the bathroom. Every time, the bathroom first so it is clean for him when he wakes up. I see the bedroom door is open. That is not right. If he is in bed, the door is closed so I know not to go in. He is . . . what you say . . . careful? Not to show me when he is bare?'

'Modest?'

Kasia nodded. 'I think this is strange. He is not downstairs and there is no music from the studio at the bottom. So I look in the room and it is still all dark, so I turn on the light and I see . . .' She hesitated.

'The shoes. You saw the shoes first?'

'Yes. Is very odd. The shoes, the dresses, all live downstairs. They are for work, not for every day. Then I see the dress and I go close up and I look at his face which is now so small . . . and I am afraid.'

'There is nothing to be afraid of,' said Bea, who had also been distressed by the sight.

'I say to myself, out loud I say, "This is not right." I sit down on the floor, bump. I hold myself like this' – and she hugged herself. 'I say, "This is very bad." I am looking at the shoes. His shoes that go with the red dress. I lift up the dress and there are his feet in black socks. I put the shoe on, and it is the wrong fit!'

Bea looked at her in bewilderment. 'Wrong fit?'

'Wrong fit! Wrong fit!' Seeing that Bea still didn't understand, Kasia took off one of her own shoes, leaned over and took off one of Bea's. She tried to put her own shoe on

Bea, who had a much bigger foot than Kasia, so the shoe didn't fit.

'Wrong fit! See?' said Kasia, shaking her head.

Bea repeated. 'Wrong feet. The shoe didn't fit?'

'Too big. Wrong fit. I put the shoe back on the floor, and I pull the dress down, and my heart is coming quick, quick, and I turn off the light and I get down the stairs quick, quick, and I phone Mrs Green to come, help, help! And I run away.'

Bea couldn't make head nor tail of this. 'The wrong feet? But . . . I don't understand. Would you be prepared to tell the police about this?'

The woman drew back. Bea could see her working it out. It was better for her to say she'd been mistaken than to insist something was wrong. If she did that, it opened up all sorts of trouble . . . police, investigations, the legality of working for cash in hand, the language barrier.

Finally Kasia said, 'I know nothing. I went up there. Was big shock. I made mistake about the fit. I phoned Mrs Green. I came away.'

Bea swept her fringe slantwise across her forehead. Did she need a haircut soon? Probably. She wasn't sure what to think. Kasia had seemed convinced that the shoes were wrong at first, but now she wasn't. Bea knew that shock could skew people's perception of an incident. Look how many different versions of the 'truth' were given by witnesses to an accident.

Besides, if Kasia had spoken the truth . . . no, her story was so unlikely that if Bea hadn't seen the body for herself, she would have dismissed it out of hand. As it was, Bea didn't know what to think.

The phone rang, and Bea took the call.

A woman's voice, well-educated but sharp. 'Good evening. Is that Mrs Abbot, of the Abbot Agency? The police gave me your name. I believe you found my father yesterday. It must have been a shock for you, though not for me, of course. Oh, my name is Frasier, by the way, Damaris Frasier.'

'Mrs Frasier. How can I help you?'

'I only heard of my father's death when the police came round after work yesterday. I gather someone tried to phone during the day but both my husband and I were out and our son was at school, of course. Looking back, I suppose I ought to have suspected he was up to something. He knew the pain was only going to get worse. I believe the pills he took would have given him release very quickly. A bizarre way to go but he was an eccentric, wasn't he?'

'I'm afraid I never met him in life.'

'Didn't you? Well, I suppose you drew certain conclusions, seeing the body—'

Bea shuddered, remembering. 'I gather he was an entertainer and used to dress up in extravagant clothes.'

'Least said, frankly. The family are not exactly anxious to have that side of his life appearing in the tabloids, which is why I have to get rid of all those disgusting garments first off . . .'

Kasia made as if to go, but Bea signalled that she should stay put.

'The police say you found him, or that someone in your employ found him and called you. I'm not clear what happened.'

'His cleaner found him and was so shocked that she phoned the agency to take over from her. Which is how I came into it.' It did no harm to cut Florrie out of this story, did it?

'I see. Well, what's done is done, and we have to move on, don't we? Now the police told me you run an agency which supplies domestic staff, clears houses, that sort of thing, which is a stroke of luck, for of course the house will need to be cleared before it can be sold. Do you still have the keys? If so, I suggest we meet there on Monday morning at ten o'clock sharp.'

Bea said, 'Isn't it a bit soon to—?'

'Not at all.' Briskly. 'Time is money, I've a job and a family to look after, and I don't believe in hanging around waiting for things to happen. I made the formal identification last night, and they are rushing through the autopsy, though of course we know exactly how he died. I shall have the death certificate by the day after tomorrow at the latest, and after that I can register the death. It won't take long. I'll fix up the funeral for as soon as possible. It will be private because the family don't want any jokes about dressing up in women's clothes on such a solemn occasion, and he will be cremated, which is what he wanted. I've been in touch with his solicitor. Everything comes to me so the sooner the house is cleared and on the market, the better. Till Monday morning, then.'

The phone clicked off.

Bea looked at the receiver, before putting it down. 'Well, that settles it. Kasia, that was Mr Kent's daughter on the phone. Have you ever met her? No? She sounds very . . . positive. She was out at work, which is why we couldn't get hold of her earlier. She's identified the body as that of her father and is making all the necessary arrangements. So that's that.'

The two women stared at one another. Bea tried to make sense of what had happened. 'We were both badly shaken when we saw the body. The body on the bed was definitely that of Mr Kent. I suppose people look smaller when they're dead.'

Kasia nodded. She got to her feet, her expression remote. 'I was upset. I didn't see straight.'

'Me, neither. The daughter wants to tidy him away without a lot of gossip about his dressing-up in women's clothes. I can understand that. She wants the agency to help her clear the house and put it on the market. If I get the job, would you like to put in some hours on it?'

Kasia refused to meet her eyes. 'Maybe.'

Bea walked Kasia to the front door. 'You will register with us tomorrow, so that we can get you better jobs and put your present ones on a proper footing? You should get more money that way.'

Still Kasia refused to meet her eyes. 'Thank you. That would be good.'

Bea hesitated, holding the front door open. 'Kasia, if you ever have a problem, at any time, you know where I am?'

A wooden look. 'Thank you.'

'Stay in touch, right?'

Kasia inclined her head and walked down the steps, turning left to the High Street and the Tube station.

Bea watched her till she was out of sight, then closed the door quietly. She was not happy about what had happened. Suppose the shoe really hadn't fitted?

Oh, ridiculous. There could be a thousand reasons why it hadn't. He'd bought them, knowing they would slip off, but hoping to be able to fix the problem. Bea had done that a couple of times, buying shoes which were a fraction too big, lining the inside of the heel or stuffing the toes with paper . . . and finally throwing them away because no matter what she did, they wouldn't stay on.

Of course. She shook herself. 'Brrr.' No need to make a drama out of it.

So, she was due to go out that night, a theatre date with an old friend. Well, not an old friend, really, for she was meeting her long-time-divorced ex-husband, Piers, who had somehow managed to reinstate himself in her life as a friend. What was she going to wear?

Not scarlet and gold, that was for sure. Or red shoes.

Friday evening

As arranged, she phoned her friend late that night.

'So far, so good. I should get the death certificate tomorrow some time. The Polish girl won't answer her phone, so I got in touch with the agency . . .'

'Why on earth did you do that?'

'I wanted to be sure she got the picture. The police said that it was someone from the agency who actually reported the death. Apparently Kasia saw the body, lost her nerve, called in her supervisor and ran away. No backbone. Anyway, we need someone to make an inventory of the house contents, so that we know exactly what we're getting. The agency can do that. Also, if I put an advert for the car in the papers, they can field the replies. Neither of us wants to sit at the end of the phone all day, do we?'

'I suppose you're right. Where is the car, by the way? I looked around this morning, and couldn't see it. If I'd got keys, I could have gone in and checked through his paperwork. I'm sure there's still some stuff that needs shredding.'

'I could let you have his keys, I suppose. As for the car, it must be around. It's residents' parking only. In the next street, perhaps? I'll have a look tomorrow.'

Saturday evening

Bea had no illusions about her ex-husband. He was never going to be faithful to one woman until the day he failed to perform in bed and, though he was now in his sixties, he was as attractive as ever in a rumpled, charmingly ugly sort of way, and showed no signs of slowing down. Sometimes she wondered why he'd ever chosen to marry her, a priggish child fresh out of school. He certainly hadn't kept his marriage vows for long or, as a struggling portrait painter, provided enough for her and little Max to live on. She'd gone out cleaning for other people to make ends meet, eventually finding herself a job helping dear Hamilton in his domestic agency . . . then marrying him . . . and living with him contentedly until cancer had struck.

No, thought Bea, struggling into and then out of strappy shoes which were a trifle too tight. I'm not going to cry. Piers hates seeing women cry, and he won't like it if I do, even though he and Hamilton became good friends over the years, and Piers' portrait of Hamilton is my most precious possession.

She inspected herself in the long mirror; a short dark-green satin sheath, sparkling with jet around the low neckline. Luckily her figure was still good enough to pass, with help from a sensible bra. Black satin pumps with a heel. Luckily Piers was a tall man. A brilliant-green jacket to go with it? No. Too harsh. A dark-green silk with splashy pink roses on it. Yes, that was better.

She took a cab to the theatre where she was to meet Piers. There was no point in taking the car in, as they were to have a meal afterwards. Bea suppressed the thought that it would probably give her indigestion to eat after the performance, but there . . . Piers had suggested it and she'd not thought quickly enough to argue. But then, few people did argue with Piers. Women didn't, anyway.

He made it to the theatre at the very last moment, so they had no time to talk beforehand, and in the interval they met up with some friends of his. Bea tried to concentrate on the play, which in her opinion was too depressing for words and didn't deserve the nearly full house it was attracting.

Piers noticed her moments of abstraction of course, but didn't comment on it till they were seated at an Italian restaurant in Covent Garden, and had ordered.

'What's up, Bea?'

She made an effort. 'Sorry. Poor company tonight, I'm afraid. It was just that something bizarre happened. There was a perfectly rational explanation to it, but I keep getting flash-backs.'

'I like bizarre. Tell me about it.'

'Well . . .' She tried to make a funny story out of it, the

shock she'd got when she opened the studio door and saw herself in the mirror, the red shoes, the body on the bed.

Piers suspended operations on his osso buco. 'What did you say his name was?'

'Kent. On his business cards it says "Magnificent Millie".'

Piers looked shocked. 'Not Matthew Kent!' He took a gulp of his wine. 'Are you sure? I know him. Everyone knows him.'

'I don't.'

'That's because you don't get out and about enough. One of the last of the old-style entertainers. Surely you've come across him at a party or . . . no, you hardly ever go out at night, do you?'

She shook her head. Not since Hamilton had started to die, no.

Piers patted her hand. 'Of course. I forget you were tied up for so long. I didn't mean to sound callous. Well, well. I did hear that he was thinking of retiring when I last saw him, must be eighteen months or so back. He wanted to concentrate on doing something else, writing for television, something like that. He couldn't be that old. Late fifties, early sixties, I suppose. Was it his heart?'

Bea shook her head.

Piers pushed his plate aside. 'I must have missed the notice in *The Times*. I'm amazed no one's mentioned it.' He glanced around the restaurant, but for a wonder didn't seem to recognize anyone there. 'I suppose there'll be a memorial service? I must try to go.'

'I don't think there's going to be a memorial service. His daughter wants to keep the funeral quiet. Apparently she finds the dressing-up side of him rather embarrassing.'

'Didn't know he had a daughter. Wives, yes. Two at least.'

Bea blinked. For some reason she'd imagined that Mr Kent might not have been too interested in women. 'Someone called Damaris Frasier rang me, said she was his daughter and sole heir.'

'Damaris?' He shook his head. 'Name doesn't ring a bell, but then I only knew him well for a short time, a couple of years back, when I was painting him. In full fig, reflected in a mirror; real life man this side, his version of a number of women looking back at him. A bit corny, I thought, doing a reflection in a mirror, but the critics say it's one of my best.

It was still in the Portrait Gallery a while back; I'll have to check, see if it's still there. On loan, of course. Must be worth a bob or two now.'

'Two wives? I wonder what they feel about his daughter taking over.'

Piers was looking at his watch. 'Sorry to rush you, but I'm due in the Midlands tomorrow afternoon, to paint another quango billionaire. Animal, vegetable or mineral; he's got a stake in all three. Must get an early start. You don't want a pudding or coffee, do you?'

No, she didn't, but she would have liked to have been able to refuse. Instead, he called for the bill and hustled her into her jacket. At least he settled the bill himself. Piers was doing well, nowadays.

'Poor old Matthew,' he said, summoning her a taxi. 'Let me know when the funeral is, won't you? I'll pass the word around, get some of the lads together. He deserves a good send-off.'

Four

Sunday morning

Hamilton had long ago decided they wouldn't work on a Sunday. Sometimes he went to an early service at St Mary Abbots church nearby. Sometimes – more often as his illness wore him down – he'd just sit in the garden, or at his table overlooking the garden, and . . . well, just sit, really.

He hadn't had a lot of pain, for which Bea was profoundly thankful. It depended where cancer struck, didn't it? The last few months had been tiresome for him because of increasing weakness, rather than pain. They'd delayed the start of their round-the-world trip, because it had seemed a new drug was actually holding the cancer at bay, but finally he'd said they should go as he wanted to see India before he died. And he had.

Lucky old him.

Now that Bea was back in London, she often thought about going to the early morning service at church, but rarely did so. It wasn't so much that she thought it a waste of time, but rather that she wasn't sure she believed enough. Hamilton had said that acquiring faith was a journey, that you took it one step at a time, consulting the travel guide when in doubt as to the right road to take.

That Sunday Bea overslept. She stood at her bedroom window looking up above the sycamore tree to the spire of the church behind. The bells were calling her to worship, but she hadn't got dressed yet, and . . . no, she didn't feel peaceful enough to go to church. Dear Max had come in late and to judge by his wayward footsteps as he climbed the stairs, he'd been drinking. Oh dear. All was quiet now. Presumably he'd sleep it off and then . . . what?

Bea found herself praying for him. *Please, dear Lord, help Max to sort himself out. I don't hold any brief for Nicole, who is a hard, self-centred woman – although I suppose I ought not to say that – but, well, she is! Oh, all right, I'll say a little prayer for her, too. Perhaps, if her younger sister were the pet of the family, she's got some cause to be bitter, and if Max kissed the sister . . . no, he didn't say he had. That's just me wondering what triggered the explosion. Oh, I don't know. I feel miserable for him, and for them. Any ideas?*

Maggie and Oliver both had plans to go out for the day. That was right and proper and just as it should be. They didn't need to stay at home to look after Bea. Goodness gracious, no. Of course not. Especially with Max around.

Bea made herself a cafetière of good coffee and took it on a tray into her sitting room. Still no sign of Max. The bells had ceased. She opened the French windows and stepped out on to the curling iron staircase which led down into the garden. Then stepped back inside. There was a cold wind blowing, and a spit of rain in the air.

She turned on the radio. Turned it off.

She was restless. She could ring up one of her friends, ask them if they'd like to go out for the day to Kew, or Richmond, or . . . anywhere. She realized she was waiting around for Max to say whether or not he wanted her company for the day, just as if he were still a teenager.

She looked for the address book she kept in her handbag and couldn't find it. She'd laid it down somewhere, but where? She looked around the piles of office paperwork that had drifted up into her living room; at the boxes of redundant floppy discs and the fireproof case which contained all their memory sticks, and still couldn't find it.

Oliver had left his laptop out. If he had the agency address list on his computer, then she might be able to find her friends' details, too.

She booted up but couldn't find her friends' telephone numbers anywhere. Idly, she rolled down the lists of agency contacts. Oliver had them in alphabetical order, and then in categories. Housekeepers. Nannies. Silver Service. Theatrical agents.

She was amused to see that Oliver wasn't infallible. He still had dear old Sylvester listed, but she was pretty sure he'd now retired, and let the Superstars Agency pass to one of his sons.

Superstars. Sylvester. An old-timer who might well have

known Magnificent Millie. Yes, of course he would. If he was retired, he might be at a loose end and perhaps willing to gossip about him?

Sylvester's home number was there. Max probably wouldn't want her company even when he did surface. She was at a loose end. Well, why not?

She pressed buttons and heard the unmistakable rasping voice of a confirmed sixty-a-day cigarette smoker. The Abbot Agency had been using Sylvester's agency for years, and she was on easy terms with him.

'Sylvester, my old friend. Bea Abbot here. How are you finding retirement?'

'Boring, boring. So what can I do for you today?'

'I was wondering if you were free for lunch today? I'm pining for a run out into the country and a lunch which I haven't cooked myself.'

'Pick me up in half an hour, but we won't go far. I've got the grandkids coming for tea.'

There was still no sign of Max so Bea, feeling rather daring and a trifle guilty, put a note for him on the kitchen table and left the house.

Sylvester was a large man who fitted himself into her car with some difficulty. Listening to the bubble in his breathing, Bea wondered how many more years, or perhaps months, he had to live. But there, Sylvester had always preferred to live life to the full rather than cut down his smoking. His choice.

He directed her to a pleasant pub by the river, where they could sit inside by a simulated coal gas fire and choose dishes from an extensive menu. Sylvester said his life was being made a misery by the new laws about smoking in restaurants, and how was she doing nowadays?

'The agency is doing well,' said Bea. 'Both my young assistants are worth their weight in gold, but I do miss Hamilton.'

He nodded, patted her arm, and said, 'He was something special.'

'Occasionally, when I meet up with something unusual, I say to myself, "I must tell him about that." Then I remember that he's gone and it's as bad as it ever was. You know?'

He sighed, felt for a packet of cigarettes, took one out, shook his head at it and returned it to the pack. 'Can't say I miss my old lady the same way, except when it comes to steak and kidney pudding. No one else can make it like she used to. So what do you want an old man's company for today, eh? You wanted to tell Hamilton something, and I'm the next best thing, eh?'

'Thank you, Sylvester. Yes. I do need to consult an older, wiser head about something that's happened. You've heard of Matthew Kent's death?'

'What?' He gaped. 'You don't mean Magnificent Millie? Dead? No, I don't believe it.'

'Was he on your books?'

'It must be twenty years since he started with me, although he's not done much lately. Dead? Are you sure? He was one of the best things ever to hit the club circuit. Never got into the big time, but always delivered. Remarkable voice, alto or bass as required, enormous repertoire. One thing that made him stand out from the rest, he wouldn't do smut. Said it upset his stomach. We used to joke about it; I said he was a closet Christian, and he didn't deny it. A kind man, clever with it. He wrote, too; gags for other comedians, sketches.'

He rumbled out a laugh. 'We used to go horse racing sometimes, not that he was a betting man, but I am . . . *was*. He did a sketch making fun of me talking to my bookmaker, apologizing because I'd won instead of losing as usual. Ah, me. Happy days. He's dead, you say? When did that happen? How come I haven't seen it in the papers?'

'Let me tell you what I know.' She recounted the events of the previous week. Their food came, but he hardly touched his, though she did justice to hers.

Once more Sylvester pulled out his cigarettes and this time got as far as putting one in his mouth before recalling where he was and shoving it back in his pocket. 'Suicide? You're sure?'

'Pills, a bottle of wine, and a note saying he was sorry.'

He was abstracted. 'I suppose it does make sense. He hadn't worked much lately, stomach problems. Also, you know what they say, those who make other people laugh, are often manic depressive . . . though I wouldn't have said he was. Manic depressive, I mean. Perhaps a little melancholy at times? Yes.'

'Damaris thinks it was his arthritis, making him realize he had to go into a home soon.'

'Who's Damaris? Arthritis? It's the devil, is arthritis. I didn't know he had that.' He blew out a giant sigh.

Bea said, 'He wasn't that old, was he?'

'He said he couldn't do the late nights any more, but would try to make up for the loss of income by doing scripts for radio. He'd sold a lot of gags in his time, and we thought he'd do well. I said we'd happily represent him for that – or rather, my son would, since he's running the agency nowadays. Matthew said I ought to be taking things more easily, too, and of course he was right because the doc told me to cut down or fall down. Well, well, poor old Matt. I didn't think I'd see him out. When's the funeral?'

'Now that's what I don't know. I was contacted by his daughter—'

Sylvester frowned. 'Didn't know he had any children.'

'She calls herself Damaris Frasier.'

'Damaris Frasier? Never heard of . . . Damaris. Now, let me think.' He clicked his fingers. 'Got it. Matt's second wife had a daughter with a fancy name – might well have been Damaris. Gail, that was her name. The second wife, I mean. He liked his Gs. All three of his wives' names began with a G. He said it was his lucky letter. Well . . . not so much good luck as bad, in my opinion. Gerda was the first, yes. Backing singer, not bad. My, that's going back a few years. Killed in a train crash in the Sixties. Then it was Gail . . . or was it Gladys next? Not that she used the name Gladys. Goldie, she called herself. A trifle too bright for my taste, but she did well enough as a dancer – Tiller Girls, Bluebell Girls? Tiller girls. Got too old for it and married a magician called The Great Daley, some name like that. Acted as his assistant, all legs and sequins and hair piled up high. That was after she split with Matt, of course. Don't know what she's doing now.'

'So Matt didn't have any children of his own, but you think his second wife—'

'Gail. An English teacher. Can't imagine where they met or why he hitched up with her, it was never going to work. Only lasted a few years. He paid her off with a lump sum to divorce him, bought her a flat or something, and she went back to teaching. I'm not sure she ever stopped, come to think of it. Bossy boots with a cut-glass voice. Drove away all his friends, looking down her nose at them. After they divorced, he used to make fun of her in some of his sketches, not being nasty, you know, but . . . Lord, he used to bring the house down.

I can hear him now. He would dress up as a cleaning woman, and she'd be his employer, giving him a hard time. Makes me laugh, just to think of it.'

Bea grinned. 'No wonder her daughter's not keen to promote his memory. She's a chip off the old block. Anal retentive? Shocked that he used to dress up in women's clothes.' She thought of the red shoes and dress, and shuddered.

He pushed his plate away, having eaten next to nothing, and ordered coffee.

She thought about what she'd learned about Matthew Kent from Kasia, from Piers and now from Sylvester. They'd painted a picture of a man she would have liked if she'd ever met him, a man who made his cleaner take a coffee break on his patio, a man who Piers had respected, a man Sylvester had valued as a friend. She accepted that there was a streak of melancholy in most comics, and she could understand – just – why failing health had driven Matthew Kent to kill himself. It was just the manner of his death which she still found disturbing. That over-the-top dress, make-up and shoes.

The more she learned about the man, the more she worried about His Final Tableau. It really wasn't like the man she'd been hearing about. But perhaps that was the whole point? That a man whose living had been made by entertaining others, had put on a show for his death?

'Tell me,' she said, 'when he was on stage, did he dress like the pantomime dame, or . . . how?'

Sylvester blew his nose with some force. 'Panto? Never. When he was all got up in one of his slinky outfits, he was more of a woman than any woman you'll ever meet. Stunning! In real life, of course, he wasn't a handsome man but nice-looking, if you know what I mean. He laughed a lot; at himself most of the time. His hair was receding, which worried him, but he wouldn't wear a toupee. Hey, but I'm going to miss him.'

Bea added this to her knowledge of him, thinking that yes, the over-the-top deathbed scene had been just that. A final gesture, two fingers up. Or perhaps – and here she smiled to herself – he'd done it knowing how it would shock dear Damaris?

Sylvester blew his nose again, folding his handkerchief over and over. 'We'd arranged that we'd meet up every couple of months, his place or mine, sink a pint, have a good gossip. I'm going to miss him something chronic.'

'He wasn't a smoker, was he?' Bea remembered the trail of cigarette ash under the visitor's chair in Matt's house.

'Never. Said it would damage his lungs. He was always on at me about it. Poor old Matt. I never thought to outlive him. I'll come to the funeral, and there'll be a memorial service, of course. I'll pass the word around. A lot of his old friends will want to attend.'

'I'll tell Damaris when I see her, but I must warn you, she's hoping her father's—'

'Stepfather's.'

'—demise will pass unnoticed by the press. She's embarrassed by the way he earned his living.'

'Tcha!' He invested the sound with so much disgust that she had to laugh. Walking back to her car, he took her arm, and she noted with a thrill of sorrow that his gait was unsteady and his breathing far too loud.

With downcast eyes, she adopted her creamiest, most innocent tone of voice. 'I wonder how many more people ought to be told about Matt's death. His wives? The press, maybe?'

Sylvester began to laugh, which turned into a cough. Spluttering, he produced his handkerchief again. Leaning on the car, he whooped and coughed, eyes streaming.

Bea was alarmed. 'Sylvester, are you all right? Silly question. Of course you're not. Is there anything I can do?'

His breathing slowed to a grumble. 'You do me good, Bea. When I saw you last – at my retirement party, wasn't it? – I thought to myself that you were far too quiet. I wondered if you'd ever get back to your old self after, you know, Hamilton, rest his soul. Now, you just keep on poking us into action, do you hear? I'm pretty well done for as you can see, but I liked Matt and I don't like to hear of his daughter trying to wipe out the memory of a great gentleman. Yes, I'll contact his ex-wives, both of them. Goldie will be easy to find. The teacher . . .? I think she kept his name after the divorce. She shouldn't be hard to locate. And yes, I'll get the press involved, too.' He began to laugh, his stomach wobbling. 'I'm looking forward to this. One last ploy for Sylvester!'

'Now you've got me worried. Perhaps I shouldn't have said anything.'

'Yes, you should. Let's go out with a bang, right? All I need from you is the date of the funeral. Leave the rest to me. Now take me home. I'd better rest up a while before the grandkids come for their tea. My son and daughter-in-law think they're doing me a favour by bringing them over on Sunday afternoons, but to be frank, although I love them dearly, after ten minutes I'm wishing them gone.'

'Just don't die before you've rearranged Matt's funeral.'

'Trust me for that. And when it comes to my turn, you can read a poem at my memorial service. You've got a beautiful voice. Did you never think of radio?'

Bea was laughing as she inserted him into her car, and clipped his seat belt on. 'Shut up, Sylvester. Let's get you home in one piece.'

Bea parked the car outside her house but instead of going in, she walked down to the bus stop and made her way to the National Portrait Gallery. Tomorrow morning she had an appointment to meet Damaris Frasier, and she was not easy in her mind about it. Was Matthew Kent the good friend and employer she'd heard about, or was he a cross-dressing man with grubby tendencies, as Damaris had hinted and as Bea's own view of his body had indicated?

Yes, his portrait was still there, as were a couple of other portraits painted by Piers over the years. Nowadays Piers charged such high prices that only the most important or wealthiest people could afford him. The portrait of a prime minister from the previous decade, for instance, was so justly acclaimed that it defined people's memory of him.

Matthew Kent's portrait was, as he'd said, a composite one. A slender man in his late fifties, wearing jeans and a grey silk shirt, sat in front of a mirror framed in theatrical light bulbs. He had turned his head so that he was three-quarters on to the viewer. A nice-looking man, with cornflower-blue eyes, and a high forehead from which fair but greying hair was receding.

Piers had an uncanny knack of presenting his sitters on two different levels; the surface might, for instance, show a man of wealth but if you looked hard enough, you could catch a glimpse of the inner person, greedy, sensual, or cruel.

This man wasn't greedy, or sensual, or cruel. He looked . . .

Bea sought for the right word . . . sad? Thoughtful? There was humour in the twist of the lips, the slant of the eyebrow. A knowledge of human nature in the lines about eyes and mouth. He looked . . . again, she had to seek for a word . . . trustworthy. A man of inner strength..

That made her frown. Trustworthy? Humorous? Strong?

Then what of the image in the mirror? Ah, but there was not one image, but several to be seen.

The first was that of Matthew Kent transformed into a beautiful woman, not young, but luscious; the twist of the lips and slant of the eyebrow indicated a quizzical turn of mind. The make-up was only slightly over the top, the bronze wig not too obvious. The high-cut dress was also in grey silk, matching the grey of the man's shirt, but slightly less strong in colour. In fact, the image of the woman was altogether less colourful than Bea had thought it would be. And behind her were more women, each one wearing a different wig, make-up and clothes, and each one less distinct than the one in front. It was as if Piers were saying, 'The man is real; the women he plays are not.'

As Piers had admitted to her before now, he didn't always know what he had revealed about a sitter in his paintings, even when he'd finished.

Bea tried to overlay what she was seeing in the picture with her memory of the body on the bed and still couldn't make sense of it. Why had he made up his face in such grotesque fashion, when he used a subtle make-up for his nightclub appearances? Why had he chosen that pantomime dame dress, which was so unlike his usual taste? Or was it? Perhaps Piers had failed to read the man correctly? Was that extraordinary deathbed appearance a deliberate slap in the face for everyone who'd known him in life?

Bea didn't think she had enough pieces of the jigsaw to complete the puzzle. But perhaps that was the point. Perhaps the man had been an enigma in life, and remained so in death.

Perhaps she'd find out more on the morrow. She turned for home, acknowledging that she'd made excuses to stay out all day rather than talk to her son. She also acknowledged that she hoped he'd have gone out for the evening by the time she got back. A spat with his wife over her younger sister . . . surely that wasn't grounds for divorce, was it?

Well, her inner voice said, it might be, if the younger sister wanted to take Nicole's place as the wife of an MP. And if the parents backed the younger against the older sister, there might well be difficulties for Max, whichever way he jumped.

Sunday evening

The two women heaved the last of the black plastic sacks into the elderly car, and got in. The driver said, 'I'll be glad when we can get shot of this old wreck. Buy something new. Now remember, the paperwork has all got to be shredded, not just put out for the dustbin men to take.'

'It's going to take time. You know I have to let the machine cool down every few minutes. Have you put the advert in for his car?'

'Done. It can't be far away. Tomorrow I'll get the agency started on the clothes, bag them up, dispose of them.'

'I wonder if they're worth anything.'

'Shouldn't think so. I gave you the details for the funeral, didn't I? Private. No flowers. Just the usual crematorium minister to take the service, canned music, press the button and away we go. Then on to the reading of the will.'

'Divided two ways. I have your word on that?'

'You do, indeed.'

Five

Monday morning

Max had gone from the house by the time Bea returned from the Portrait Gallery, and he only returned after midnight. There was no sign of him at breakfast, and the workmen were due to arrive before nine, so over her second cup of coffee Bea briefed her assistants in peace and quiet.

'Maggie, I don't know how long Max will be staying, but I don't suppose he'll need much feeding. Can you cope?'

Both Maggie and Oliver were obviously dying to hear why Max had moved into the guest room. Their eyes were wide with questions but Bea was not about to enlighten them.

'Now,' she said, 'on the Kent front, things have been happening. Let me tell you what I did yesterday . . .' She told them everything that had happened, after which both looked thoughtful. 'And no, Oliver, it's not a murder case and it's none of our business.'

'Fraud? A dicey will?'

'What an imagination you have, Oliver. I haven't the slightest reason to think either of those things.' She struggled with herself and lost. 'All right, I admit to being curious about the manner of his death. So, would you go on the Internet – he's got a website – see what you can find out about Matthew Kent? Presumably he owned his house; you can check that, too. I could also bear to have some information about his marriages; one wife died early on, and the other two marriages ended in divorce.'

'Have we any names for the divorcees?'

'They were all Gs. Gail Kent, who was – or maybe still is – a teacher. Goldie, née Gladys, subsequently married a magician whose name is something like The Great Daley. Don't ring Sylvester; I've got him on the trail already.'

'If it really isn't murder, then who's our client?'

Bea pulled a face. 'Damaris Frasier wants me to meet her at ten to discuss clearing out the house prior to selling it. I'll make sure she understands our terms.'

'You could send me to meet her,' suggested Maggie, licking the honey spoon before popping it into the dishwasher. 'I'm not bad at that sort of thing.'

'She says she's the sole heir and I've no reason to believe she's lying. The fact that I took against her is . . . no, I really must not prejudge the woman. She may be perfectly straightforward for all I know. And before Oliver reminds me, I know we can't right all the wrongs in the world.'

Oliver was interested. 'But you do think there's been a wrong done? To whom?'

Bea shrugged. 'Wish I knew that, too.' Well, she did have a niggling fear that she'd overstepped the mark yesterday, prodding Sylvester into action. Did she feel guilty about that? Er, yes. She did. She was perfectly aware that she wanted to discover something dicey about the daughter to justify her action.

She looked down at the cream silk shirt and designer trousers that she was wearing. Maggie often borrowed Bea's clothes. Perhaps it was time to return the compliment? 'Maggie, I need to borrow the white shirt you bought off a market stall, the one with the badly fitting collar.'

Maggie gaped. 'What on earth for? You hated it.'

'I'm not going in disguise but I'd like to appear not exactly badly dressed, but as if I didn't know where to buy good clothes.'

Oliver guffawed. 'Isn't that disguise? Misrepresenting yourself?'

Bea grinned. 'Possibly. I want Damaris Frasier to underestimate me.'

Maggie was looking serious. 'Mrs Abbot, you understand people and what makes them tick, better than anyone. If you think there's something wrong—'

'I've absolutely no reason to think so.'

'But you feel it?'

Bea nodded. 'So let's hedge our bets, shall we? Oliver, you know what to do. Maggie, apart from keeping the workmen up to scratch, I want you to try to contact Florrie and Kasia, get them in to talk to me again. I tried phoning both last night, and neither got back to me. Florrie said she was thinking of taking the camper out on the road. She wouldn't tell me where she was going, but she's probably briefed her second-in-command, Yvonne. If you can't get Florrie, see what you can get out of Yvonne. I think Kasia's scared of getting involved, but if we offered her another job? We can always find something for her to do, can't we? And we do need to regularize the jobs that Florrie gave her.'

Maggie swilled round the sink, and hung the dishcloth up to dry. 'This Damaris sounds really narrow-minded, trying to pretend her father—'

'Stepfather.'

'Whatever, didn't dress up for work. Why is she so ashamed of him? Would she feel the same if he'd been a Shakespearean actor?'

Bea said, 'To be fair, he does seem to have made fun of his ex-wife after the divorce. That might well make the daughter feel sour.'

Oliver said, 'Odd that she should inherit everything, if she felt like that about him.'

As usual, Oliver had put his finger on a sore point.

The first of the workmen rang the bell as Bea checked over the contents of her handbag, ready to depart. Oliver was already glued to his computer screen. He had the tenacity of a bull terrier and she'd no doubt that if there were any information to be found on Matthew Kent through a computer, he'd find it.

Max still hadn't surfaced.

Matthew's house looked just the same as she turned in to his road. She wondered which of the cars parked there might be his. There was only one car nearby which didn't have a residents' parking permit on it. Would that belong to Damaris? It was an elderly family car with nothing much to recommend it. Red in colour, not particularly clean, with a dent in one back wing.

Bea rang the bell, checking her watch. One minute late.

'You're late,' observed the woman who opened the door. 'I'm a busy woman, you know. I really can't afford to hang around waiting for people. Oh, don't dilly-dally on the doorstep. There's a cold wind, and I'm not putting the central heating on, wasting money. You know your way, I take it? And if that's dog poo on your shoe, will you kindly ensure it doesn't stain the carpet.'

Bea scraped the heel of her shoe backwards and forwards on the mat. She hoped she looked the part of a downtrodden employee, but feared her skirt was too good a fit. The blouse was right; the collar sat awkwardly, and she had to tug at it now and then to stop it gaping down the front. She'd brushed her fringe downwards instead of sweeping it across her forehead as she usually did. No eye make-up. Lipstick the wrong colour. She looked and felt frumpish.

Damaris Frasier was a hectoring blonde in her early thirties, perhaps not all that intelligent? She had hard, light-blue eyes, and wore a permanent frown. She had a tall, bony figure on which clothes sat well; Bea guessed that Damaris shopped at a Second Time Round or charity shop. Her shoes were from a chain store. Her voice had the sort of harsh clarity which would cut through a crowded room. Her manner was impatient, aggressive. Bea couldn't imagine Damaris making friends easily, or being an easy person to work with.

Damaris continued, 'I collected your cleaner's keys from the police, and I'm asking you to sign here for them, before I hand them over. That way we know precisely who has the right to be here.' She produced a clipboard and waited while Bea put on her reading glasses, read and signed the handwritten note. 'Good. Now you're responsible for the contents of this house, understand? I can't be taking time off work and running backwards and forwards all the time to check on what you're doing. I've written out a list of instructions in duplicate . . .'

A couple of sheets of A4 were taken off the clipboard, and handed to Bea. 'One copy for you to sign, one for me to keep. I shall be advertising the sale of the car myself. Enquiries for it will go through to your agency. I can't be pestered with all that at home. I've removed all the paperwork that I shall need to apply for probate, and I will be responsible for cancelling his credit cards, direct debits and so on. In the meantime I require your agency to prepare a detailed inventory of the contents of this house, and in due course to arrange for valuers to appraise the furniture and furnishings. Is that clear?'

Bea realized that all she was expected to do, was to nod. So she did.

'You will ring me every evening between six and seven – the telephone number is on my instructions – to report on your progress, and you will post your inventory to me as soon as you have completed it. How long do you think you will take?'

Bea contrived to be a little clumsy, extracting a folder of agency information from her bag. She handed it over in silence.

Damaris cast a hard blue eye down it. 'You charge far too much. I will pay you two-thirds, which I imagine is more than you're worth.'

So the camouflage was working? Bea opened her mouth to object, knowing that this was what Damaris would expect and was cut off, exactly as she'd thought she would be.

'Not another word. You can start work now, this morning. I've cleared out the fridge and I'll turn off the electricity at the meter before I go, as I don't expect you to loll around having coffee breaks on my time. Now, is there anything else?'

'Would you like me to send a notice to the papers about the funeral?'

'That's all taken care of.'

'If anyone enquires, when and where shall I tell them the funeral is to be?'

'Not yet fixed. Anything else?' She answered her own question. 'You can forget about getting someone in to value the house itself, because I'll be attending to that. We need a valuation but I'm told I can't put it on the market till after probate is granted.'

'Do you want us to dispose of his clothing?'

'I've taken some away already. Bag the rest up and dump it in the nearest charity shop.'

'Er . . . his professional work clothes? They may be worth something?'

Damaris pinched in her lips. 'The same. Get rid of them.'

'But . . .' Bea made her eyes wide and innocent. 'Wouldn't the Theatre Museum . . . perhaps? Or someone in the trade? A couple of thousand, maybe?'

Damaris looked undecided. 'As much as that?'

Bea tried on a nervous little cough. 'Should I ask around, perhaps? The agency has some contacts in the trade.'

'I'll let you know.'

'And' – another little cough – 'I think there's a picture in the National Portrait Gallery. Wouldn't that be worth something? Should I enquire?'

Damaris's eyes gleamed. Money, money, money. The bait was taken. 'I'll see to that. You've got enough to be getting on with. Now I don't expect you to know much about antique furniture, but after you've— What was that?' Someone was leaning on the doorbell. 'Who . . .? I'm not expecting . . .'

Bea thought, Is this Sylvester's work? Is that an ex-wife at the door? If so, let battle commence. She made herself sound tentative. 'Shall I see who it is?'

Damaris said, 'Tcha!' and strode to the front door herself, letting in a gust of keen wind and spit of rain, plus not one but two blondes. Both were in their early fifties but one had been more successful than the other at hanging on to her youthful figure.

'Mother?' That was Damaris. 'What on earth are you doing here?'

A better dressed version of Damaris swept in, removing a cashmere wrap and shaking raindrops off it. Her shoes alone must have cost as much as the whole of Damaris's wardrobe. 'Nice to see you, too, daughter. You remember my successor? Gladys, say hello to my daughter.'

Damaris's mother had the same light, piercing tone of voice and pale-blue eyes as her daughter, but was finer cut and looked more intelligent. She had good skin and wasn't wearing much make-up. There were grey shadows under her eyes; had she been crying recently? She seemed on edge, her eyes restlessly quartering the room.

The other blonde was a different matter. 'Well, well, so this is little Damaris, all grown up. Call me Goldie, dear. Everyone else does.' This blonde had turned to peroxide for assistance and there was a slight but definite sag to cheeks, chin and boobs. Her eyes were china blue, and her black suit had been chosen to suit a formal occasion. The skirt was a trifle short for someone of her age, but her legs were still good. Her laugh would be throaty and she looked as if she might be fun for a night out at the pub. She ran a finger along the top of a bookshelf, looking for dust. 'Well, well. Nothing much has changed over the years; except us. The dear old place looks just the same.'

Bea stepped back into the doorway to the kitchen, thinking this was going to be worth watching.

Gail shivered. 'Brrr, it's cold in here. Has the heating broken down?'

Damaris's lips moved. She seemed to be searching for words to express her displeasure at this intrusion, and discarding them as soon as they leaped into her head.

'Cat got your tongue?' Goldie bent down to switch on the simulated gas coal fire. 'No sense in catching cold, is there? Got any coffee on the go? Who's that in the kitchen? A cleaner? Will you put the kettle on, dearie?'

Bea filled the empty kettle, and set out some mugs on a tray. The fridge had been emptied but the contents were in a couple of large shopping bags on the table. Bea dived into the bags to locate coffee, sugar and milk. And listened.

'How sweet!' That was the alto voice of Goldie. 'Look, he kept the little china shepherdess I got him for his birthday one year. I gave a fiver for it in a stall on the Portobello Road but told him I'd paid a fortune for it in an antiques shop and he believed me, silly old fool. And here's the little silver jug I used to put violets in, in the spring.'

'Putting flowers into silver does the silver no good.' Damaris, acid in her voice.

'It's all right if you put a glass jar inside it,' said Goldie, batting the criticism back, honey-sweet.

The kettle boiled, and Bea put her head round the door. 'How do you like it, ladies?'

'Black,' was the response all round.

Damaris was clutching her arms, either because of the chill in the room or, more probably, from temper. She spat the words out, 'You both divorced him long ago, so why are you here?'

'Do take that frown off your face, Damaris.' Her mother speaking. 'It's most unbecoming. His agent rang me this morning, wondering if I'd heard. He said you were arranging the funeral. I'm amazed you didn't tell me.'

Goldie's turn. 'Sylvester rang me, too. To put it bluntly, dear, I need to know if he's left me anything. This house must be worth a couple of million, I suppose. So, who's his solicitor?'

Bea passed round mugs of coffee, keeping her eyes down. She'd noticed long ago that if you don't make eye contact with people, they discount your presence.

Damaris rolled her neck to relieve tension. 'I was the only person who gave a toss about him in his last months. I kept in touch, made him feel valued and part of the family. He made his will a couple of months ago, and left everything to me.'

Bea retired to the kitchen, leaving the door partly open. Why not make herself a cuppa while she was at it?

Frost crackled in Gail's voice. 'Just don't let that husband of yours get his hands on it.'

'You never liked him, did you? And you never understood how Matthew felt about me. Because he couldn't stand the sight of you, it didn't mean he hated me. He loved me, and once you two were out of the way, he could show that he did.'

'Come off it,' said Goldie. 'You'll be having us believe he liked little girls better than he liked women, and I know for a fact that's not true. He was everything a man should be, not like that apology for a man you chose to marry.'

'How dare you! Get out, both of you! You've no right to come here and insult me, with him barely cold in his bed. And tell me this, if you thought so much of him, why weren't you around to comfort him when the pain got too much for him to bear? Why didn't you give him something to live for? Oh no, you let him commit suicide, and then you come round like scavengers, to see what you can pick from his bones. I despise you both!'

Silence.

Bea edged one eye round the door. Gail was standing in front of the fireplace, eyes closed, clutching her shoulders. Was she in pain?

Goldie's colour had risen, and she was biting dark-red lipstick off her mouth.

Gail opened her eyes to consult a tiny watch. 'Let me have the details of the funeral and I'll leave you in peace.'

'I'm arranging everything as he wanted it to be. Private. No church service. At the crematorium. No flowers.'

Goldie set her empty mug on the table beside her. 'No flowers? He always liked a good show of flowers. Red in particular. Who's the funeral director? I'll arrange for a floral tribute to be put on the coffin. And I'll take that china shepherdess and the silver jug with me now, to remember him by.'

Damaris made as if to stop the woman but restrained herself.

Goldie took out a packet of tissues, wrapped each keepsake carefully and stowed them in her handbag.

'Very well,' said Damaris. 'You've had your pound of flesh, and that's it . . . understand? I'm having an inventory done of everything in the house and if one single cup is missing after this, I shall know who to come after.'

Gail smoothed her already smooth hair, checking her image in the mirror over the fireplace. 'I'll be round later to choose a keepsake or two. All right with you, Damaris?'

'I suppose so.' Through gritted teeth.

Goldie applied another layer of lipstick to her mouth. 'You are overreacting, Damaris dear. Should have been on the boards. I'll have to think about what else is due to me, but all I need for now is the name of the funeral director.'

Damaris put the back of her hand to her forehead. 'I think I must be going down with something. The strain . . . I can't think. The doctor arranged it. I'll have to phone him, get the name from him, and then get back to you.'

'Ring me with the details.' Gail arranged the folds of her wrap around herself.

The two women let themselves out of the house, both being very polite about it. 'After you,' and, 'No, after you.'

Bea busied herself in the kitchen, washing up her own mug, and then went through to the living room to collect the mugs used by the others.

'What are you grinning at?' asked Damaris. If she'd been a cat, she'd have been lashing her tail. 'Turn off that fire. No need to waste gas.' She picked up her mug and threw it with all her might at the fireplace, where it shattered.

Bea froze.

Damaris clenched her fists. 'I could murder that agent of his. I can do without those two shoving their noses in. If I could find out who told him . . .' She switched her eyes to Bea. 'You didn't tell him, did you? Because if you did, I'd sue the living daylights out of your piddling little agency, understood?'

'Tell who?' Bea tried to act nervous, and there wasn't much need for acting. Damaris was truly terrifying. She wasn't that big a woman, but she seemed to expand with rage.

Damaris relaxed a trifle. 'No, of course you didn't. How could you know?' She picked up her handbag, looked round the room. 'Well, what are you waiting for? You'd better get on with it before the light fails, hadn't you? And clear up that mess before you do anything else. I don't want coffee stains marking the carpet.'

Her mobile phone rang and she answered it, with a terse 'Yes?'

Bea returned to the kitchen to find a dustpan and brush, only to have the kitchen door slammed in her face. Despite this barrier, Bea could still hear Damaris's clear voice. Good diction had its points. Bea pressed her ear to the wood, to hear better.

'Yes, I'm still here. How are you getting on with the shredding? . . . Yes, well, we knew it would take time. The agency sent a fool of a woman to do the inventory, but I suppose it's better than nothing. The only problem is that the news has leaked out . . . how do I know? That agent of his. But how he knew . . . what? No, I certainly didn't . . . Well, yes, it does matter. My mother turned up, would you believe? And Gladys. You remember her? His third. Vultures. Wanted to know when the funeral was to be but . . . no, of course I didn't! . . . Look, I'm running late. Ring you this evening.'

So Damaris had a confidante? An old friend, by the sound of it.

Bea moved away from the door as Damaris threw it open. 'Get a move on, why don't you? And you needn't think I'm paying you for this morning, either. Understood? I must go.' She glanced at her watch – not an expensive one – and collected the bags of food she'd taken out of the fridge on her way out. There was to be no chance of the hired help making herself a cuppa in her absence.

Bea went to the window to watch Damaris leave. She sincerely hoped the woman would never find out who had informed wives two and three about Matthew's death. Damaris meant it when she'd said she'd sue. Although what grounds she might use . . .? Well, even if she were on shaky ground, some solicitors would sue just to get the work and the agency needed to be convicted of leaking confidential information like it needed a hole in the head.

When Damaris's car was out of sight, Bea got out her own phone.

'Oliver, how are you doing?'

'Not bad. Got a load of stuff from the Internet. Matthew Kent was a well-known entertainer, clubs and pubs, mainly. I've got some pictures of him in drag, a list of television and radio credits, and some odd items about his third wife. Nothing about his second.'

'How are the workmen doing?'

'Noisy.'

'In that case I think I'll stay up here for the time being. Mrs Frasier wants an inventory done. Would you look through our files and find someone to do it for us? But before that, would you check when and where Matthew's funeral is taking place? Damaris says it's a cremation and private, but pretends she's forgotten the details. I think we should find out, don't you? Sylvester wants to know for a start. There are only a few crematoria around. It's probably at Mortlake, you could start there. Or you could start at the other end with local funeral parlours. Or . . . come to think of it, Damaris gave me a list of instructions as to what she wants done at the house and . . . yes, yes. We've got a telephone number for her. The telephone prefix is 8997. Do we know where that might be? Outer London, yes?'

'West London, somewhere? I'll check. You think she might have used a funeral director local to her rather than a Kensington one? Why would she do that?'

'Why has she done all sorts of things?' said Bea. 'And Oliver, try to keep our name out of it, will you? Damaris is already threatening to sue whoever leaked the news of Matthew's death to his ex-wives. And she means it.'

Oliver thought that was amusing. 'How can she do that?'

Bea hissed at him. 'It's not funny!' and shut off the phone as the front doorbell rang. Now who . . .?

Bea peeped out of the window. Not Damaris's car. She went to open the door.

Six

Monday midday

Gail Frasier sailed into the hall, unwinding herself from her cashmere and silk wrap. She spoke in a rush, in a high voice, sweeter-toned than her daughter's.

'It seems to have stopped raining, thank goodness. I'm afraid my daughter didn't introduce us properly. I'm Gail Frasier. I was married to Matthew Kent for five years. Damaris is my daughter.'

Gail was turning on the charm. Bea had to admit the effect was good.

Gail didn't actually push past Bea into the sitting room, but somehow managed to get there, dropping her wrap and a handbag on the nearest chair and looking around her. 'I always had flowers around when I lived here. They liven up the room, don't they? It seems so much darker and colder than I remember . . . I see you've switched off the fire. Oh, a small accident here?'

Bea went on her hands and knees to sweep up the pieces. Now what had Gail come for?

'So,' said Gail, turning on her heel to take everything in, 'what's your name? You work for a local agency, do you? That's nice. And what instructions has my daughter given you?' She was talking mechanically, not paying attention to what she said.

Bea swept up the pieces, and got to her feet. 'I'm Bea. I work for the Abbot Agency. Your daughter has asked me to bag up the deceased's clothing and professional costumes, and to make an inventory of what's in the house.'

'Of course.' Gail had never once met Bea's eye. Just as well, perhaps.

Close to, Bea saw that Gail's originally blonde hair was now grey, but expertly cut. She must be in her early fifties and though she'd made little attempt to hide the destructive effects of time, her complexion and bone structure were both good and she could probably pass for forty with the light behind her. Except for those dark stains under her eyes. And her hands were shaking. Was she ill?

Bea took the shards of the coffee cup out to the kitchen and put them in the bin, which was almost full. She would empty it later, perhaps. She ran hot water, found carpet shampoo, and returned with it to the sitting room to get rid of the coffee stain.

Now, what was Gail after?

Gail was after the photographs on the mantelpiece. There were a half-dozen or so, all in silver frames. She picked them up one by one, took them to the light. Sighed. Sank into a chair by the window, eased off her shoes. 'You couldn't rustle up a cup of good coffee, could you, Bea?'

'I'm afraid not. Mrs Frasier took the coffee with her when she left.'

'Typical. Oh, do carry on with whatever you're doing. Take no notice of me.'

As if Bea could do that. Bea got down on her hands and knees to deal with the coffee stain, keeping her head down. So far her 'disguise' seemed to be working. But this coffee stain was not coming out easily. And there was red on her cleaning rag. Something other than coffee had been spilled here recently.

Gail sighed, rubbed one of the silver frames with her hand, and then with her handkerchief. She put them both down, looking about her. She said, to herself rather than to Bea, 'As Gladys said, hardly anything's changed. You'd think that . . . after all this time. Oh dear . . .' She put her hand to her mouth. Her colour was bad. 'I need to use the loo. Don't bother to show me. I know where it is.'

Bea watched from the bottom of the stairs to make sure that Gail was indeed going to use the bathroom. Yes, she was. Bea could hear retching sounds, and then running water. The loo was flushed.

When Gail came out, instead of descending the stairs she went across the landing. Bea crept up two, then three steps and craned her neck to see what Gail was doing.

Gail was standing in the doorway to the master bedroom

looking, not touching. Bea knew the body had been taken away, and wondered if the red dress were still there. She shuddered. There was something about that red dress which gave her goose-pimples.

Gail turned her back on the bedroom and Bea prepared to scramble back into the sitting room but no, from the creaks on the floorboards she could tell Gail was moving around upstairs, probably checking on each room in turn . . . yes, going up to the top floor . . . looking around.

It was understandable; after all, she had lived here once. Hadn't she? Or would that be jumping to conclusions? After all, Gail hadn't actually said she had lived here, only that not much had changed over the years.

Gail didn't spend much time above but came down the stairs, moving heavily, probably feeling her age. Bea scuttled back into the sitting room, scooped up her cleaning materials and made it to the kitchen before Gail reappeared.

'Bea . . .?' Gail came to the kitchen door, holding one of the silver framed photographs in her hand. 'I'm going to run off with this photo if you don't mind. Tell my daughter, by all means. I'm sure she won't object, since it's not one of his studio portraits which presumably have some value. See?'

It was an informal snap of a youngish Matthew, aged forty, perhaps? He looked just like the man in Piers' picture, except that in the photo he had more hair. He had his arm around a fair-haired girl of perhaps twelve years of age. Was that Damaris? Both were relaxed, smiling.

Gail said, 'I'll take it out of the frame, if you like. Surely she can't object to that.' Her mouth twitched, and her eyelids contracted. 'It's a good one of him. We all four went out for the afternoon to Windsor. Matt had heard of a good bookshop there. He collected Edwardian travel stories, you know. He bought me a pendant. I've still got it somewhere. I think it must have been half-term because Damaris was with us, and he bought her a silver bracelet. Perhaps she has some happy memories, too. Perhaps she really did care about him.'

She recollected who she was talking to. 'Sorry. Rambling.' She took the photo out of its frame and put it in her handbag. 'You can tell my daughter what I've done.'

'Would it be a good idea to sign for it? I mean, Mrs Frasier has made me responsible for everything, and she might . . . might . . .'

Gail grimaced. 'Yes, she very well might.' Scrabbling in her handbag, she produced a small notebook, wrote on a page, tore it out and gave it to Bea. 'That's my address and phone number. If my daughter happens to remember where the funeral is going to be and when, will you let me know? I wish . . . if only . . .'

Bea made her voice soft. 'You have some regrets?'

Gail brought her mind back from whatever black hole she'd been looking into. 'Oh, perhaps. We both stepped out of our comfort zone to marry. I didn't fit into his world, and he didn't fit into mine. He was often out in the evenings, just when I wanted to relax after work. I was a teacher, you see. Primary school. Then along came Gladys. You wouldn't think it to look at her now, but she was a raving beauty in those days.'

'You were a teacher?' Bea maintained her soft, enquiring tone. She didn't think Gail realized how much she was saying. Gail was almost in a trance, reliving the past. But it was one question too many.

Gail snapped back to the present. 'I made head teacher eventually but took early retirement a year ago. Got knifed by a teenager when I tried to break up a fight. Stupid of me. I should have let them get on with it. Ah, well. I was glad to go. Everything's changed. I liked teaching but I didn't like having to cope with new laws every minute.'

She turned on her heel, imprinting everything in the room on her memory, then left, letting the front door bang to behind her. The wind was getting up.

Bea replaced the rest of the photograph frames on the mantelpiece, wondering who'd come calling for a keepsake next.

Now, what was it that Damaris had said about shredding paper? Something of Matthew's? Bea wondered if she were getting paranoid, thinking that everything Damaris did was suspect.

Gail had said something interesting. Four of them had gone out to Windsor for the afternoon. Four? Matthew, Gail and Damaris made three. So who was the fourth? It was the fourth, presumably, who'd taken the picture, or Gail would have claimed it as hers.

A pity that Bea hadn't had a chance to look at the photographs properly herself.

She caught sight of herself in the mirror and twitched at the collar of that awful blouse in an effort to make it lie straight. She hugged herself for warmth. Why hadn't she thought to bring something warmer with her to wear? She turned the fire back on, and the side lights. What luck that Damaris had forgotten to turn off the electricity at the meter as she'd threatened to do. She would be cross when she remembered. Tough! thought Bea.

She got out her make-up bag, and attended to her face and hair. There! She looked more like herself. Now she felt up to tackling anything. Well, almost anything.

She got down on her hands and knees to inspect that stain on the carpet, and while she was there, she sniffed at the stain on the arm of the Chesterfield. That one was wine. Yes. But the one on the carpet . . . was that wine, too? She manoeuvred one of the side lamps from where it sat on a bookcase behind the big chair, and held it at an angle to examine the tiles, the grate and the carpet more closely. There was a brass fender around the fireplace . . . goodness, you didn't see those often nowadays. The top rail was shiningly bright, but underneath . . . sloppy cleaning . . . there was a long dark stain.

She moistened her forefinger, pressed it to the stain, and sniffed. Not wine. Blood? But how could that be?

The light now shed on the carpet revealed two lots of dark stains. One was coffee. Yes. That had come about when Damaris had thrown her mug at the fireplace.

One looked like – and tasted like – wine.

Bea sat back on her heels to consider this. She could see Matthew sitting in his Chesterfield, a glass of wine at his elbow, balanced on the arm of the chair. A sudden movement and over goes the wine, staining the cover, splashing over on to the fireplace and the carpet. Dear me. And tut.

She let the scene run on in her head. Matthew is not the sloppy type who might leave the stain for his cleaner to deal with. So he gets up to find something to clean up the wine and . . . what happens next? He falls and hurts himself, cuts himself . . .? Yeees. Sort of.

She ran that past her brain once more. Matthew cleans up

the mess. Did the glass shatter on the tiles? Yes, it probably would have done.

Bea squinted along the tiles, moving the table lamp to catch sight of any fragments of broken glass that might remain. Saw them lodged in the base of the fender and in the slot of the ash can. So yes, he broke a glass, and cleaned it up. He went out to the kitchen to fetch the hoover, and he got a cloth and wiped down the top of the fender. But he didn't do a very good job of wiping the rail down, and he didn't put the hoover back properly.

As for the blood, he must have cut himself on the broken glass when he was cleaning it up.

Good. Everything explained. She put the table lamp back and stood up, dusting down her skirt.

Her brain went on thinking, and she couldn't stop it. After he'd cleaned up the mess, he went downstairs to make up his face and select a wig. He took the dress, the wig and slippers back up to his bedroom, lay down on the bed, took the pills, drank a bottle of wine, scrawled a suicide note, and died.

A tingle ran down her back. A little voice at the back of her head said, 'And if you believe that, you'll believe anything!' She rubbed her hands down her skirt, violently, trying to rid herself of her suspicions.

What of the cigarettes in the ashtray, and the ash on the carpet? Why didn't he clean that up while he had the hoover in his hand?

Because . . . because his guest was still there? No, no. Of course not. His guest must have been here some other time, perhaps the previous night. At any time since Kasia's last visit. Quite simply, Matthew must have missed the ash and ashtray when he was cleaning up. He was a tidy man. He left everything neat and tidy before he committed suicide.

And he didn't even see the ashtray? He might have missed the ash, but surely not the ashtray?

It would depend if he were standing beside the chair or not. If he were, he wouldn't have caught sight of it, because it was tucked right under the chair, wasn't it? Bea bent over the chair to check. Couldn't see it. Peeped under the chair. It wasn't there. And at that moment a musical note twanged through the air.

She shot upright, breathing rapid. Was she beginning to hear things as well as see them?

The note rang out through the room again. The piano? No, the lid was down, and there was no one sitting on the stool in front of it. Superstition rules, OK? She shifted her feet and again the note resounded.

She stifled a laugh. Really, she was becoming unhinged.

She rocked to and fro, and the floorboard beneath her feet shifted. A loose floorboard. When you trod on it in a certain way, the far end of the floorboard moved under the piano and a sensitive string on the piano responded. She giggled. First the mirror and now the piano. Anyone would think . . .

No, she did not, certainly not believe in ghosts.

Dear Lord, I'm not going crazy, am I? I do not believe in ghostly manifestations. If we're not talking uneasy spirits, coming back to haunt the living – and we're definitely not, are we? – and if I'm reading clues subliminally – if that's the right word – then something is very wrong. Do you want me to do something about it, because if so, I'd be obliged if you'd point me in the right direction?

No voice answered her, but the air in the room seemed to settle down around her with a sigh of . . . relief?

'This is ridiculous!' said Bea, and went out to the kitchen to investigate the contents of the rubbish bin, and the hoover. The hoover bag did contain tiny shards of glass, but the rubbish bin under the sink contained nothing but the usual household and kitchen refuse. She investigated further. There was a black bin bag tied up and ready to be disposed of, sitting on the patio in a sort of lean-to. On top of it was a small cardboard box marked 'Glass'. She opened it with care to see the remains of a broken wine glass.

Just at that moment the phone rang. By the time she got back inside and had traced the phone to where it sat on the floor at the side of the Chesterfield, an answerphone had clicked in. It gave Bea more goosebumps to hear Matthew's voice.

'I'm afraid I can't come to the phone at the moment, but if you'll leave a message, I'll get back to you as soon as possible.'

Well! thought Bea. He might have cancelled that before he committed suicide! Whoever was ringing, hadn't left a message. The answerphone light was blinking. There were six messages, unanswered.

She got out her pad and pencil, and listened to them. An enquiry as to whether Matthew could entertain a senior citizens do after Christmas; a voice confirming that they wanted Matthew on a certain date and would he please confirm the cost. Three hang-ups. A woman with a breathy voice wanting to know if he'd be able to judge a children's fancy dress parade for the church, same as last year.

Business as usual, thought Bea. There was a leaflet from St Mary Abbots church stuck into the bookcase at the side of Matthew's big chair. Bea wondered why the funeral wasn't taking place there. Obviously he was known there, and had attended a service recently. Bea wondered if she'd ever been at the same service as him. She might well have done. Hamilton, of course, had attended regularly . . .

She veered her thoughts away from Hamilton as the front doorbell rang.

This time it was Oliver, sheltering from the rain under an umbrella – one of Hamilton's, by the look of it – and carrying a laptop plus a bulging shopping bag.

'Maggie thought you might be a bit peckish, since you missed elevenses. Also she made me bring one of your good sweaters since the weather's turned colder. And she's put up some sandwiches and a Thermos of hot soup for our lunch.'

'Oliver, you're not supposed to leave the office unattended.'

'Couldn't resist. I got your old bookkeeper in to hold the fort. She's such a dragon, nothing can go wrong with her around. Maggie's in love with the new plumber, by the way, so don't expect much in the way of sense from her. Oh, and Mr Max has been asking for you.' He thrust a thick grey sweater at Bea, who donned it with a shiver. Maggie had been right. She did need something warmer to wear.

Oliver was through into the sitting room and looking around him before she could stop him. 'Is this where he was found? It doesn't smell like an old man's room, does it? Isn't there any central heating? Where shall we eat? Then I'll help you with the inventory and we can get it done so much quicker. That's why I brought the laptop. Oh, and you were right. The funeral's at Mortlake on Friday at noon. I haven't told Sylvester yet. The soup is hot, courgette and Brie, one of Maggie's best.'

Bea threw up her hands and followed him out to the kitchen. Maybe he was right and two heads were better than one on this job. Certainly the inventory would be done more quickly if she dictated the list and he took it down on his laptop.

Oliver found the central heating control on the wall by the broom cupboard. He fiddled with it, and was rewarded with a click. Soon the house would be warm enough to work in.

She took a seat at the table and reached for the shopping bag. 'Let's get one thing clear, shall we? There is no murder. Matthew committed suicide. The trouble with you, Oliver, is that you want life to be exciting, to be full of high-speed chases and beautiful spies—'

'No, that's the Thirties.'

'Real life is about making inventories and trying to see that the right people get the right jobs and are properly paid for them.'

Oliver filled a mug to the brim with steaming hot soup and handed it to her. 'Yes, of course.' He didn't sound convinced. He said, 'Actually, I thought that I could ask you something. Sometime when you're not too busy . . .'

'Mhm?' What was biting the boy now?

He wasn't looking at her, but at the sandwich in his fist. 'The sandwiches are ham and Maggie's own sweet pickle. Good, aren't they?'

'You wanted to ask me something?'

A distinct wriggle. 'It's nothing, really. Just, I was thinking of applying for a passport. A couple of mates from the gym want me to join them, skiing in Austria in January. Should be fun.'

Bea frowned. So what was the problem? Ah, of course. Young Oliver had been thrown out of the family home after he'd discovered porn on his father's laptop. Maggie had rescued the lad, rather as she might have retrieved an abandoned puppy, and Bea had recognized his talents and given him a job as a live-in assistant. Bea had also helped him retrieve his belongings from his father's house and demanded that Mr Ingram send Oliver his highly successful A level results; also his birth certificate. She had suspected at the time that brown-eyed Oliver might not be the birth child of two blue-eyed parents. His skin and hair were perhaps a fraction darker than normal for a lad of Anglo-Saxon heritage, but she'd said nothing about this. Had Oliver shared her suspicions that he'd not been Mr Ingram's son at the time? Possibly not.

She said, 'Well, if your father hasn't sent your birth certificate across, you can always get a copy.'

'Mm. I've never been sure; is it better to travel hopefully than to arrive?'

Ouch. So Oliver did share her suspicions. 'You have to decide that for yourself.'

He nodded. 'There's a chocolate brownie for each of us for afters.'

The subject was closed.

After they'd eaten Oliver said, 'Coffee?'

Bea licked up the last crumb of cake. 'Damaris took the contents of the fridge away with her, so there's no milk.' She stared at the fridge. Did suicidal people leave a fridge full of food before they killed themselves? No, they didn't. They weren't interested in eating, only in dying. So why . . .?

Oh, well. Obviously the suicide was a spur of the moment job. Obviously.

Oliver crumpled up the sandwich papers, and threw them into the bin under the sink. 'So what do we do first?'

'I must ring Sylvester and give him the details of the funeral. You can start making an inventory here, in the kitchen.'

Oliver pulled a face but opened his laptop and began work. The central heating ticked merrily away. Bea grinned to herself; how dare Damaris ask people to work on her behalf in a cold, dark house?

She used Matthew's phone to call Sylvester and give him the news. He wasn't answering his phone, so she left a message on his machine. After that, she found Gail's telephone number – engaged – and did the same for her. She hadn't got Goldie's telephone number, so had to leave that.

The rain seemed to have set in for the day so she switched on all the side lights. Oliver came in from the kitchen. 'Done that. What next?'

'I haven't got a marvellous sense of smell, Oliver. You said this didn't smell like an old man's room and it doesn't, does it? But I don't think he was that old, or incapable. He was still working, even though there was some talk of his retiring. But then, if he was getting crippled with arthritis . . . oh, I don't know.'

She beckoned him over to the big chair. 'Tell me what you smell on the arm of this chair.'

Oliver obeyed. 'Wine. A red, heavy and sweet.'

She got down on the floor. 'And on the hearth and carpet?'

'Wine and . . .' He sniffed again. 'I think . . . is it blood?'

'I've tried to clean it up, but yes, I think it's blood. What must have happened is that he knocked his wine glass over on to the arm of the chair, it fell on the tiles and smashed in pieces. He cut himself clearing up. All right?'

Oliver looked bewildered. 'When was this?'

Bea sighed. 'Wish I knew. I don't suppose it matters, though.'

Oliver stood up and inadvertently trod on the suspect floorboard. The piano string twanged and he jumped.

Bea patted his arm. 'It's all right. It's only the piano reacting to a loose floorboard. It startled me, too.'

'I thought . . .! Ridiculous!'

'I know. Let's try something else.' She led him down the stairs to the studio, turning on all the lights and ignoring the images that leaped out at her from the mirrors.

'Wow!' said Oliver. 'Will you look at this! That tape deck, the speakers, all that stuff . . . a new Apple Mac. That's a good printer, by the way. Even better than ours. This lot cost a pretty penny.'

Bea opened the first wardrobe to inspect the dresses within. Each costume had been carefully put on a padded hanger, and fitted into a zipped plastic cover. Full-length dresses, sequinned, cut high across the neckline, three-quarter sleeves. Shimmery sheaths. The grey satin outfit he'd worn for the portrait. Not much black. No red. Nothing to hint at a pantomime dame.

She pulled a full-length dusky pink sheath out at random and held it out to Oliver.

'How tall are you? You've grown a bit recently. Five nine? About that. Do me a favour, and try this on.'

Oliver gaped. 'No way!'

'Don't be absurd, Oliver. I need to test a theory, a suspicion of . . . just do it, will you? I promise not to take photographs.'

'I couldn't.'

'The colour's too bright? Let's try this blue outfit, then.'

The blue outfit had a feather boa to go with it. A fine silk jersey, with a draped bodice, slender over the hips. She held it out to him with an expression that meant, Do this or else!

He winced, stripped off his heavy sweater and put the dress on over his T-shirt and jeans.

Bea walked around him, twitching the fabric here and there. Matthew was obviously broader in the shoulder and at the hips. The hem of the skirt pooled on the floor. 'Of course, he'd be wearing high-heeled shoes.' She rummaged in the shoe closet, noting the shoes were all of the same size from a well-known theatrical costumier. No red shoes. She flourished a pair of blue ones that matched the outfit. Oliver screwed up his face as she set them on the floor before him. He shucked off his trainers, though, and stepped into the blue shoes. The skirt still dragged on the floor.

'I'm not wearing a wig!'

'That's an idea,' said Bea, opening the next cupboard along. She produced a dark, curly wig and handed it to Oliver. He gulped but put it on, checking himself in the nearest mirror to see if it were straight.

There was a long silence while Oliver looked at his image in the mirror, and Bea mused on the difference clothes could make to a man. She knew Oliver was very much a male and, from all accounts, Matthew had been, too. Yet with those clothes on, Oliver suffered a sea change. From sallow teenager, he turned into a striking woman.

Oliver said, 'That's not me. It's someone else. Someone different. The shoes aren't very comfortable, though.'

'I expect they were made for him. You can get back into your own clothes now.'

Oliver shrugged himself out of his finery. 'So what was the point of that little exercise?'

Bea shrugged. 'I'm not sure. I'm trying to get a picture of this man. He's a couple of inches taller than you, judging by the length of the skirt. He's broader than you across the shoulders and hips, but his head size is about the same as yours. That wig almost fits. In what way are the shoes uncomfortable?'

'You don't want me to take up cross-dressing, do you? The shoes are a trifle big for me, but they pinch across the top. I've got a higher instep, I think. How can women wear high heels?'

'With practice.' Bea helped Oliver to stow away the finery. 'So why didn't his red shoes fit? And where's the red dress he had on top of him when he died?'

'Perhaps his computer will provide some answers?'

'You do worry so. Everything's just fine!' The harsher voice of the two.

A whining reply. 'From your point of view, maybe. But what about me? I've got to be out of this house in a week's time.'

'I told you, we'll split everything from Matthew's house down the middle.'

'It'll take months before anything comes in. You have to wait for probate, and then put the house on the market and . . . who knows how long that's going to take? In the meantime, I've got to live. Suppose you're in a car accident or something? Where would I be then? Your husband would get the house and I'd be in real trouble.'

'I don't see what we can do about it.'

'Suppose you got sick, would your husband pay me my half?'

'You can hardly expect me to tell him what we've done.'

'What I think is that you should make out a will so that I get the house if you pop your clogs. If nothing goes wrong, we divvy up as suggested. Your husband won't need to know anything about it, and you can make a new will when everything's settled. That way I'm covered for all eventualities.'

'I don't like it. Suppose . . . no, that won't do. I agree nobody else must know. Very well, then. I'll make an appointment for us to see the solicitor.'

'I've got a will form here. I'll make it out for you, shall I? Everything of which you die possessed to your family in the usual way, except for Matthew's house which comes to me. We can take it to the solicitor this afternoon after you finish work, to get it checked over and signed. All right?'

'I suppose so. It shouldn't be for long.'

Seven

Monday afternoon

Oliver homed in on the computer. Bea followed, more slowly. Wasn't accessing a dead man's computer a trifle tacky?

Oliver turned it on. Frowned. Swivelled round in his chair. 'Someone who didn't know much about computers has been playing about with it. All his files have been deleted. Now why should that be?'

'You're the whizz-kid with computers. Didn't you say there's always stuff left on the hard drive?'

Oliver grinned. 'You want me to do a little exploring?'

Bea hesitated. 'I know your friend's father taught you all sorts of tricks to do with computers, but—'

'He's on the side of the angels, professionally, if that's what you mean. Look, you know and I know that something very odd is going on here. You don't really think Matthew Kent committed suicide, do you?'

'I really don't know what . . . no, I suppose I don't.'

'His nearest and dearest has provided us with a perfect opportunity to find out what's really been going on here. So I'm just going to press a couple of keys and see what happens. All right?'

Bea was uneasy about Oliver's use or misuse of his talents, but he was right in thinking there was something wrong with the situation. She braced herself. She started turning out drawers, looking for files, bills, general correspondence.

There weren't any. She was sure there had been some when she looked before, when she'd come across his business cards. She still had one in her handbag.

So why had they been removed? There weren't any professional photos of Matthew, either. She could see where files had been stacked in a cupboard by the side of the computer, but now . . . nothing but space. She started on the drawers below, looking for memory sticks, floppy discs, anything on which Matthew might have stored the daily details of his life.

What about his engagement book, for instance? He must have had a diary. And an address book. Yes, of course. Florrie had mentioned that she'd underlined Damaris's address in his book, and left it for Bea to find. Up the stairs went Bea to look for it. She was not terribly surprised to see that it was no longer where it had been. Damaris – or someone – had been thorough.

But, perhaps, not thorough enough. Bea had already found a leaflet from St Mary Abbots church tucked into the bookcase at the side of the big armchair. A convenient place to stash something which Matthew might need to refer to later.

She began tipping up the books, two by two, to see what other treasures might come to light. Nothing on the top shelf. Nothing on the second shelf. The third disclosed a reminder to pay a subscription to some actors' charity, plus another leaflet, dated a fortnight before, from the church. The bottom shelf yielded a leaflet about a forthcoming watercolour exhibition, a National Trust flyer, a couple of shopping lists in a rounded hand, every item crossed through.

She sat back on her heels. The lead to the church had turned up twice. Did that mean something or nothing?

Oliver came up the stairs, looking smug. 'Everything was still in the computer, in the recycle bin. It all seems pretty harmless. Appointments, business correspondence, friends and family, a file for charities, material for his monologues, notes for sketches and a play he's writing. What you'd expect, really.'

'Then why delete them in the first place?'

Oliver shrugged. 'Dunno. I copied everything on to a memory stick for you, in case you want to look at it later. Which reminds me, did you walk off with a letter from a client the other day? Someone's been ringing, saying they've asked for an appointment, but I can't find anything in the files.'

She pulled a face, remembering that she'd noted down Matthew's address on a letter when Florrie rang to report that she'd found a body. 'Sorry, yes. It must still be in my bag. I'll give it you when we get back.' She got to her feet and shook out her skirt.

Matthew's phone rang. She and Oliver stood still while the

caller left a message. Someone checking that Matthew had returned a costume that had been hired for a performance of *The Gondoliers*. Please to ring soonest.

The phone clicked off.

Bea said, 'We can't ring back. Really, it's up to Damaris to let people know what's happened.' Only, she doesn't seem keen to do so.

'I wonder what part he's playing,' said Oliver. He went to the piano and checked the sheet music resting in a pile on the top of it. 'Here it is, the full score of *The Gondoliers*. Was Matthew a bass?'

Bea clicked her fingers. 'Got it! He was playing the Duchess, and that's why he had that outrageous dress. It really is a stage costume, rented for the production. He must have brought it home for some reason – probably needed to put some extra padding around the bra area. That's why it doesn't fit the image we've been getting from the clothes in the studio.'

'Is the Duchess usually played by a man?'

'No, but if you had someone like Matthew around, wouldn't you want to make use of him? How sad that he won't be making the performance.' She brushed one hand off against the other. Well, that settled it. Everything had been neatly accounted for, more or less. Her uneasiness was not justified and they'd better get on with the job they'd been paid to do.

'The inventory, Oliver. Let's start at the top of the house. It won't take long.'

Working together, they were soon down to the first floor. Bea opened a cupboard on the landing. 'Nothing but linen in here. I suppose we ought to count the number of sheets and towels.'

'Nothing like being thorough.'

'Will you do this, and then help me in the bathroom?' Bea was of the opinion that you could tell a lot about a man from the contents of his bathroom cabinet. He'd left a rim round the bath, but it wasn't too bad. A nice big medicine cabinet, stocked with everything a man might need if he relied on his voice for a living. A full box of painkillers. An almost empty box of high blood pressure tablets. Good soap. A pack of antibiotics, almost empty. No toothbrush or toothpaste. Damaris must have removed those when she took away some of his clothes.

Her mobile phone rang. She'd left it downstairs. Who . . .?

Oh, bother. 'Oliver, I'd better answer it.' Down she went to take the call.

It was her son, Max. 'Mother, we seem to keep missing one another, and it's rather urgent that we talk.'

'We're on different time scales. You're at the House of Commons when I finish work for the day.' He was right, of course. She had been avoiding him, sort of. She had a feeling she wasn't going to like what he wanted to say. 'Actually, I'm working now.' She turned back to the stairs, taking the phone with her.

'So am I. The business of the House doesn't stop just because my marriage has broken down.'

'No, of course not.' She began to pull out bottles from the medicine cabinet, to see what lay behind them. 'Have you been able to talk to Nicole yet?'

'No, I . . .' He half-covered the phone to speak to someone nearby, 'You can leave that for the moment . . .' Then back to speak to Bea. 'The fact is that I can't work in my office at the House for the moment. You do understand why, don't you?'

'I assume you have someone with you and can't talk freely?'

'Yes, that's it. I knew you wouldn't mind. It is the best solution, after all. Though I must say that the workmen are making a hell of a racket. It's extremely inconvenient, having them in at this juncture. Can't you get them to work more quietly?'

'What?' Bea sat down on the bathroom stool in a hurry. 'Max, tell me it's not true! You aren't working from my house, are you?'

'Of course I am.' A soft puff of a laugh. 'My dear old secretary isn't used to quite such straightened quarters, but as she says, "We must soldier on, mustn't we?"'

'But Max—'

'There's just one little thing I'd like you to do for me, but we can talk about that when you get back. We'll go out somewhere for supper, shall we?'

'No – I mean, Maggie's cooking supper—'

'Till tonight, then. Half six, say?' He cut off the phone.

Bea stared at her own phone, before calling up Maggie on it. 'Maggie dear, I've just had a phone call from my son.'

'Oh, Mrs Abbot, is it all right? I didn't know what to say when he started lugging in all those files and setting up his computer and telling me to look after his secretary. I mean, you might have warned me.'

Bea bit back the words 'I didn't know'. 'Sorry, dear. I hope it isn't too inconvenient.'

'Well, it is rather, because the dragon has co-opted the dining table and the landline and glares at Mr Max's little lady, who's totally sweet but not up to her weight, if you know what I mean.'

For 'dragon', read Miss Brook, their old bookkeeper. Bea pictured the scene and grimaced. 'Listen, Maggie. This is an emergency, just for a couple of days. Can you keep the peace?'

'Peace? You must be joking. You can probably hear the workmen from here! Mr Max went down and asked if they could work more quietly. That worked a treat, as you can imagine. They turned up their radio as soon as his back was turned!'

'I'll try to sort something out with my son when I get back. He said something about taking me out for supper.'

'Oh, bother. Oh, never mind. It'll do for tomorrow, instead. When will you be back?'

'When we're finished here,' said Bea, glad to be out of the arena for the time being.

Oliver put his head around the door. 'That's done. What shall we do next? The bathroom, was it?'

Bea looked around her, distractedly. 'Oliver, I'm missing something, but I can't think what. Yes, let's do the bathroom and then take a break.'

Back to everyday life. Making inventories, checking facts, slotting people into the right jobs at the right price. There was no murder. There never had been a murder. If Damaris hadn't been such an unpleasant person, Bea would never have started to wonder about this and that.

Oliver was looking puzzled. 'Why didn't Damaris bring in a professional valuer, because some of the furniture and one or two watercolours look as if they might fetch a bob or two? . . . No deodorants, no shaver. Do you think Damaris has taken them for her husband?'

'Dunno,' said Bea, thirsty and depressed. 'Is she so short of money that she'd want second-hand toiletries? I agree some of the furniture ought to go to a good auction house. Perhaps she didn't want to spend the money on an expert? Or perhaps she thinks her mother will try to remove something before the valuer can get here?'

They took a break. Oliver went out to buy tea bags and milk, while Bea phoned home to see if there were any problems which their old bookkeeper couldn't solve. There weren't, of course. Miss Brook might be well over sixty – best not ask how many years over – but she had more than her rightful share of marbles, and liked the odd day's work even under present-day conditions.

'Though mind you, Mrs A, things are not quite comfortable here at the moment, if you get my meaning. Mr Max has been giving your phone number out to all and sundry, though I protested in the strongest terms against his doing so.'

'I'm very sorry, Miss Brook. I'm having supper with him this evening and will try to sort something out.' Bea put the phone down, and pressed her hands to her temples. She could feel a headache coming on.

They went upstairs after tea to start on the master bedroom. Oliver was fascinated by the king-size bed. 'I've seen beds like this before, in museums. French, isn't it? All that carving on the headboard – must have cost a fortune. You found the body here?'

Bea shuddered. 'Let's get on with it, shall we?'

Matthew had had a huge wardrobe-cum-cupboard full of good men's clothes in his bedroom, with a rack of handmade shoes at the side. He had used a lot of hair preparations supposed to prevent baldness, and had taken good care of his skin. 'You can see where some of his clothes used to be. Damaris said she'd taken some away already, but there's still loads here which we're supposed to bag up and dispose of. I think we'll leave that little job till we've done the inventory and seen the colour of her money.'

'You think she won't pay for work done?'

'I may have to eat my words but . . . yes, that's exactly what I do think. There's no red dress here. If I hadn't seen it with my own eyes . . . Kasia saw it, too. And Florrie. We can't all have been seeing things.'

'Damaris took the dress away, because . . . well, she didn't like his cross-dressing and wanted to protect his memory.' He ran his hands over the mahogany. 'If you lived in such a house with all this unusual furniture, it would influence the way you thought about the rest of the world, don't you think? Make you think yourself something separate, different. I wouldn't mind something like this when I get older.'

Bea sneezed. 'Kasia couldn't have cleaned so well up here. Dust!'

'Not dust.' Oliver sniffed the air. 'Aftershave?' He bent to sniff the counterpane. 'It's on this.' He sniffed again. His foot kicked against something under the bed. He disappeared from sight, to retrieve a large cardboard box with the name of a theatrical costumier on it. 'All together now . . . bingo!'

He took off the lid, to reveal the voluminous scarlet and gold dress Bea had seen lying over the body. Presumably Damaris had put it away to be returned to the hire company.

Bea stared at it, and then at Oliver.

'Oh no you don't!' said Oliver, backing away. 'I am not going to lie down on that bed, not for a hundred pounds.'

Bea grinned. 'Bite the bullet. Turn the pillow over, remove the counterpane, and do it. Oh, and take your shoes off first.'

Grumbling, Oliver did as he was told. Bea shook out the dress, trying not to show how much it repelled her to touch its slippery surface, and floated it down over Oliver's body.

When the dress was up to his neck, his toes just about peeped out of the bottom of the skirt.

Oliver yelped, and sat upright, breathing fast. 'Look, I can't . . .'

'No, it's all right. I know you can't.' She caught the dress up, folded it as it had been before, and took the lid off the box. Under a piece of tissue paper, she caught a glimpse of something else red. She twitched the paper aside to reveal a pair of red, sequinned shoes. Somewhere at the back of her head a little voice said, 'It was a mistake, leaving them out for everyone to see.'

Nonsense! She laid the dress carefully into the box, and replaced the lid.

Oliver put his own shoes on again. 'So what did that prove?'

Bea rubbed her forehead. 'Nothing, I suppose, except that I'm a sadist, and you're a star. I thought I had an idea, and I suppose . . . no, I must have been mistaken. Let's get on with the inventory, shall we?'

Another half-hour, and they had finished upstairs and were about to pack up for the day when they heard the front doorbell peal. Oliver looked out of the window, and started to laugh.

'You remember I was wondering why Damaris wanted the inventory done, rather than call in a valuer? Well, there's a drive-it-yourself van down below, and I imagine that must be the famous Gladys-cum-Goldie leaning on the doorbell. Come to collect some more trophies from her marriage?'

Bea joined him at the window. The rain had stopped but the road still gleamed wet. 'We don't need to answer the bell.'

'She'll see there's someone in. We've left all the lights on downstairs. She wouldn't still have a key, would she?'

'I hope not. I'd better alert Damaris.'

'Where's your phone? You left it downstairs after tea, didn't you? She'll see you as you cross the hall. Uh-oh, she's got her mobile out. Who's she phoning? Hang about, there's a big bloke down there with her. The sort of no-neck bruiser who you see on the door at nightclubs.'

'What do you know about nightclubs?'

'One of my friends took me once. Don't look like that! I am nearly nineteen, you know.'

'I know.' They watched, fascinated, as Goldie gesticulated her way through a phone call. She put the phone away, looking up at the façade of the house. Oliver and Bea ducked.

'This is ridiculous,' said Bea. 'We've every right to be here, and she hasn't. I'm going down to talk to her.'

'Put the chain on the door first. I'm not up to the weight of her companion.'

'I'll phone Damaris before I speak to her.' Bea sailed down the stairs and across the hall, ignoring the thumps and bell peals. She found her mobile and rang Damaris's number.

A young voice answered the phone; a teenage boy? He said his mum was at work. Bea said it was important, and might she have his mum's number at work, please. Young voice said he wasn't allowed to do that. His tone indicated that he couldn't care less.

'Listen to me, young man,' said Bea, 'your mother asked me to make an inventory at her stepfather's house, and one of his ex-wives has appeared with a drive-it-yourself van and wants to come in. Shall I call the police, or will you give me your mother's mobile phone number?'

'Wow! Really?' He was faintly amused. 'All right, then. Got a pencil?'

She hadn't. She set her teeth. Why hadn't she got a pencil?

She saw that Oliver was poised with a pen to take down the number. She repeated it aloud, as it was given to her. Said, 'Thanks!' and rang off. By which time Oliver was punching numbers into the landline phone. He got through and handed the phone to Bea.

A face appeared at the window. Goldie, furious!

'Mrs Frasier?' Bea turned away from the window. 'Bea Abbot here. A crisis.' She explained what was happening, and was relieved when Damaris said she'd get permission to leave and come straight around.

'That's it, then,' said Bea, setting the phone down. 'She's on her way. Cavalry to the rescue. But if that man doesn't stop pounding on the door, he'll break it down. I think I'll go and threaten him with instant death if he doesn't stop, or we'll have the neighbours round, complaining.'

'Don't forget to put the chain on.'

She didn't need to be told. She put the chain on, and opened the door a crack.

'Yes?'

Goldie tried to push the door open, and failed. 'You . . . you let me in, now!'

'Mrs Frasier asked me to hold the fort till she gets here, which won't be long.'

Goldie's blood pressure was climbing. 'You know who I am! Now, take the chain off, this minute!'

'Sorry. My instructions—'

'I don't give a—'

'Let me give the door a shove!'

Bea stiffened her back. Muttering to Oliver that he should close the door behind her, she said, 'Hold on a minute,' took the chain off, stepped outside, and pulled the door to behind her. 'If you don't stop this right now, my assistant will call the police!'

'What?'

Ten seconds, while nothing was heard but a lot of heavy breathing.

An elderly man with a stick had been walking an equally ancient dog on the other side of the road. Spotting trouble, he came to a halt. 'Want some help, missus?'

'Thank you, no,' said Bea, trying to smile at him and almost succeeding. One push from the heavyweight and the elderly man would end up in hospital. 'These people are just leaving. Apologies for the noise. It won't happen again.'

The elderly man had a face like a bloodhound, all droops and sags. But he didn't lack for courage. 'Is Matthew all right? Haven't seen him around for a couple of days.'

'I'm afraid he passed away,' said Bea, wondering if this were the right thing to say or not. 'This lady is one of his ex-wives. I'm doing an inventory for his stepdaughter, who's inherited everything, and my instructions are not to let anyone else in.'

Elderly man shuffled across the road towards them. 'What was it? A stroke? I never thought he'd go before me. The name's Douglas, at number five. Used to make up a four at bridge, now and then. Just wait till I tell the wife.' He eyed Goldie's short, tight skirt, and the heavyweight's look of bafflement. Neither seemed to appeal, for instead of making off, he looped his stick and the pug's lead around his wrist, leaned against the wall of the house, and took out a tin of tobacco. His hands shook – Parkinson's? – but his intentions were clear. He was not moving.

The heavyweight swung back to Goldie, looking for instructions.

Goldie flapped eyelashes, turning herself from Amazon into Goldilocks. Well, that was the intention, anyway. Breathily, innocence shining out of blue, blue orbs, Goldie said, 'I only came to fetch what's mine. A few little trinkets . . .'

'In that big van?' Bea was not impressed.

'A dear little table with fluted edges, a couple of matching chairs with tapestry seats and backs. Sentimental value, only. Oh, and a watercolour that I bought my dear husband when we were on honeymoon in Scotland. That's all. And of course the silver salver that matches my sweet little silver jug. I know I ought to have mentioned it before, but I was in shock. You understand, don't you?'

A piecrust table, a couple of Jacobean chairs, a Victorian watercolour by a named artist and a solid silver salver. *Humph*, thought Bea. *Does she think I'm a moron? That lot must be worth ten thousand if a penny.* Bea put on a sunny smile. 'I'm sure Mrs Frasier will be delighted to hear from you, and if you can prove what you say, I'm sure she'll be willing to let you have the things you asked for. But I'm afraid I have no authority to let you take anything away from the house.'

'Hear, hear!' said the elderly but courageous Mr Douglas from number five.

The heavyweight rolled his shoulders. 'You want I bust the door in?'

'No, no,' said Goldie, maintaining her smile with an effort. 'I'm sure this, um, woman, is right, and my stepdaughter will let me have my little bits and pieces. Another day.'

'Hear, hear!' Mr Douglas had at last succeeded in rolling himself a cigarette. He stuck it between his lips and sought in his pockets for a match. Or a lighter. His pug was resigned to the wait, apparently, for he was now sitting on his master's foot.

'What we do now?' asked the heavyweight.

'You go home,' said Bea, still smiling sweetly. 'And wait to hear from Mrs Frasier. I shall certainly give her your message, as soon as she arrives.'

Goldie's eyes brimmed with tears. 'I shan't forget how horrid you've been to me. As if I wasn't suffering enough from the death of my dear Matthew! Now this! It would have been such a consolation to have something of his to remember him by.'

'Bravo!' Mr Douglas clapped his hands together, slowly. 'Been on the boards, have we?'

'Oh, you . . . drop dead, you!' Goldie swung herself up into the cab of the van, motioning her heavyweight to follow suit. With a grinding of gears, the van moved slowly down the street and away.

'Hah!' said the elderly gent, cigarette alight, flourishing his stick. 'That's given me quite an appetite for my tea. Wait till I tell the wife. Any time you want help repelling boarders, Mrs Abbot, you let me know, right?'

'You know me?'

'You found us a housekeeper when my wife wasn't able to get about so much. Dudley Douglas. Remember?'

'Of course!' His wife had been confined to a wheelchair and he'd been her sole carer. He'd been an upright, soldierly figure then. Four years ago? More? He was mere skin and bones now, but still a force to be reckoned with. 'I'm very grateful, Mr Douglas. Believe me.'

'Hah! The wife will have my guts for garters if I'm late for tea. Have a good day, as they say . . .' He went off, muttering to himself, the pug waddling after him. 'Silly thing to say, "Have a good day" . . .'

Oliver opened the door to let Bea back into the house. 'That was nasty. Are you all right?'

No, she wasn't all right. How could she be? She was shaking. 'Yes, of course. What people will do . . .! I suppose we'd better ring Mrs Frasier and tell her the danger's past. I suggest that after that we pack up for the day. I don't know about you, but I've had enough.'

'Plus Maggie's doing us a big dish of lasagne for supper.'

'I'm out for supper with Max. We'll have to see what else Maggie can rustle up for you.' She rang Mrs Frasier, who was halfway along Kensington High Street by that time, and not at all pleased to have been called away from work on a false alarm.

'And thank you, too,' said Bea, as the call terminated. 'Time to go home, Oliver. Is everything off, lights, central heating, back door locked? This house is beginning to give me the willies. The sooner we're out of here now, the better.'

Oliver followed her outside.

'That woman at the agency is rubbish! Wish I'd gone somewhere else.'

'Is she very expensive? The bills . . .!'

'No, I beat her down to a reasonable fee. She called me out on a false alarm. Step number two had turned up with a van to take her pick of the valuables, and the Abbot woman didn't know how to cope. Honestly!'

Alarm in her voice. 'Did she get away with much?'

'Well, no. Changed her mind and went off without any trouble. Only, I had to wait for the manageress to come back and practically go on my knees to get the rest of the afternoon off . . . and then the agency woman rang back to say it was all right. Made me look such a fool.'

'That's a bit of a worry. I mean, if Goldie came back and insisted, she could clear the house. Has the agency woman still got keys? Can she be trusted not to let anyone else in?'

Silence. 'You've got a point, there. She said she'd let me have the inventory tomorrow or the day after. I'll get her to drop the keys in at the same time.'

'Or, I could pick them up from her at the house. I'll need a copy of the inventory, anyway.'

'Why? I said we'd split everything down the middle, and so we will.'

'I'd rather be safe than sorry. How much more is there for her to do?'

'Ground floor and basement. The costumes might take some time. She thinks they're worth something, and we can't afford to overlook any source of income.'

'That's true. Look, I'm not happy about her having the keys. Also, I think we ought to have checked over his sheet music and tapes. Suppose I get there early tomorrow before the agency woman, see if there's anything we've missed? Then I can pick up the keys from her when she's finished. It would save you time and trouble.'

'People don't realize, it's getting to be the busiest time of the year.'

'It's lucky I've time then, isn't it?'

Eight

Monday evening

Bea opened the front door of her house, only to come up against the arm of the settee which usually resided in her office downstairs. On top of the settee sat the two big chairs in which clients usually sat. Behind them, precariously leaning against the wall, were the glass windows from her bookcase. Question: where was the bookcase? She hadn't expected to have to clear her office completely, so what was going on?

As she stepped into the hall, she realized that she was going to have to negotiate her way over the length of her office carpet, which had been rolled up and jammed between the settee and the hall table on the floor. She wasn't sure the settee looked safe to lean on, so put out a hand to the table to keep her balance as she made her way along.

Maggie erupted from the kitchen, mobile to her ear as usual, to pantomime a dance of frustration, pulling faces and gesturing towards the sitting room. Maggie also had the radio on in the kitchen. Maggie didn't seem able to function without a lot of background noise.

From the basement came the merry shouts and well-timed thuds and crashes of men at work. From the living room came the mellow tones of Max, either dictating to his secretary or on the phone.

Oliver bumped into Bea from behind as he, too, made his way along the obstacle course.

Maggie switched off her mobile and said, 'I know! I'm sorry. I couldn't stop him. The workmen needed to attack the plaster and I couldn't put the furniture out in the garden because it's been raining.'

Ouch. More disruption, more expense. Bea helped Oliver, who was burdened with his laptop, to make it safely across the carpet on to the tiled floor beyond. 'I hardly dare ask. My desk?'

'In pieces on the landing upstairs. The dragon – I mean Miss Brook – has been taking calls and dealing with agency business as best she can on the dining table, but she's asked me to tell you that this is no way to run a business, and of course I agree. She's gone for the day now, but Mr Max . . .'

Bea nodded, pushed open the door to the sitting room and gasped.

'Told him so,' said Maggie, at her shoulder. 'I said you wouldn't like it.'

Bea blinked. Chaos! At the dining-table end of the room, there was a comparatively orderly area where a typing chair, computer and printer had been in use. Presumably this was where Miss Brook had been working.

Max was seated at her patience table in the window overlooking the garden, with his laptop open in front of him, and her landline phone to his ear.

Max's secretary, a fawning dormouse of a woman with wispy greying hair and a blouse and skirt to match, was seated on the settee, trying to type on a keyboard attached to an ancient computer, both of which were perched insecurely on the coffee table. In between, covering the floor and chairs in every direction, were piles and piles of files. The scene reminded Bea of nothing so much as a cross-section of a hypocaust in a Roman villa, with the files taking the place of the pillars of bricks in the cellar which supported the floor above and allowed for underfloor heating.

She felt a surge of rage. She wanted to kick and shout and demolish Little Miss Something-or-Other, and tear into Max and shove him out of the window, over the stairs and into the garden. She wanted to scream. Well, why shouldn't she?

Control yourself, Bea Abbot. If you did let fly, you'd only have to pick up the pieces afterwards.

It would be worth it, though.

No, it wouldn't. Think what Hamilton would have done.

He wouldn't have put up with this, now would he?

No, he wouldn't. But he'd have asked 'Why the mess?' first.

Miss Something-or-Other was on her feet, dithering, almost wringing her hands. She'd interpreted Bea's expression well. Max ended his phone call and got to his feet, ducking his head, looking at her with pleading, puppy-dog eyes. Her grown-up, Member of Parliament son, reduced to small boy status, knowing he'd done the wrong thing, but hoping against hope that she wasn't going to punish him for it.

Her throat was dry. She managed to say, 'Yes?' She was pleased with herself that she hadn't lost her temper.

Miss Something – Townend? Some name like that – was ducking her head, her half glasses glinting. 'I'm so sorry, Mrs Abbot, I couldn't think, I do realize that it's a bit of an imposition . . .'

Max cleared his throat. 'A word with you, Mother?'

'Indeed,' said Bea, controlling herself beautifully. Full marks, Bea. 'We're going out for a meal, I gather? I do hope you apologized to Maggie.'

'Er, I did mean . . . sorry, Maggie.'

Maggie said 'Humph!' and stalked off to clash pans in the kitchen. Oliver muttered something about taking Maggie out for a meal and disappeared after her.

Miss Townend said, 'Well, I suppose . . . for the day . . . if that's all right, Mr Abbot?' She found a coat, hat, umbrella, gloves and handbag, and made for the hallway, where they heard her squeaking her way over the carpet to reach the front door.

Bea continued to control herself. 'I've been working hard all day, Max. So I'll wash and change before we go out, which will give you time to work out where you'll be moving to, first thing tomorrow.'

He said, 'Oh, but—'

The phone rang and he picked it up, to say in a smooth voice, 'Max Abbot speaking. How can I help you?'

Bea turned on her heel and walked up the stairs, negotiated her way around her desk on the landing, and closed the door of her bedroom very, very carefully and soundlessly behind her.

She wondered what she could throw, or smash, or destroy, but concluded that she liked everything in her bedroom too much to get rid of it. Then started to laugh, which was absurd, and absolutely no help at all. Except that it did stop her being angry.

She showered, and found a good caramel-coloured silk evening blouse and matching skirt to wear. Cream coloured pumps with a medium heel. She spent some time making up her face and brushing her hair to lie flat and shining. A silk wrap, similar to the one worn by the second Mrs Kent. She eyed her reflection fore and aft, put her reading glasses in her evening bag, and was ready.

Max was still on the phone when she went down so she waited, looking at her watch, till he finished the conversation and was ready to go.

'My favourite restaurant,' he said, hailing a taxi. 'You'll like it.' A corner restaurant, exclusive. Small. Enormous menus, real linen, a quartet of wine glasses to each table setting. It soothed Max to be greeted by name and shown to a corner table. Bea could see him aiming for his normal self-confidence, his feeling of slight superiority over lesser mortals who were not Members of Parliament. A man in control of himself and the affairs of the nation. And all that malarkey.

She reflected that he was a fine figure of a man and better looking than his father had ever been. She had often been – just slightly – disappointed that Max hadn't inherited Piers' charm and ability to talk himself into and out of situations. Hamilton had been the kindest and most helpful of stepfathers and Max had learned much from him, and perhaps even more from being sent to good schools. But there was no doubt about it, he was very much her son; in perseverance and hard work, in his belief that he was there to work for the good of his party and his constituents, in his attention to detail. And in the collapse of his marriage?

She checked out the menu and sighed inwardly. Max was trying a little too hard to impress, wasn't he? Perhaps that was something else he'd inherited from her?

She laid the menu down. Max might still need the trappings of success, but she'd grown out of that habit of insecurity. She'd grown through working all those years with Hamilton, being treated as an equal, being loved thoroughly and satisfyingly . . . and learning to love back. To trust. To grieve.

She'd learned to be herself. She'd learned, more or less, what her limits were. She wasn't sure that Max had outgrown his childhood insecurities, with an absent father who couldn't be relied on for five minutes, a mother working all hours to feed and clothe him, a poor quality primary school. Yet he'd blossomed later, a reasonable academic record at a good school, captain of cricket, man about town, prospective parliamentary candidate here and there and finally – bingo! – Member of Parliament with an eye on the Cabinet.

She could scold him for moving his office into her house. Of course she could. He deserved it. She wanted to, oh, so badly. But she didn't think it would do his self-confidence any good at all. She was pretty sure that if she lifted up the heavy tablecloth, she'd see his toes pointing inwards, as they'd done when he'd come to her to confess something he'd done as a small boy.

She also remembered, with a grimace, that he'd once written an essay about her which said that if he ever got into trouble, his mother would get him out of it.

'In a draught?' he asked.

She shook her head. 'You order. You know the kind of thing I like.'

'Wine?'

She shook her head again. 'I'm working tomorrow.'

So was he. He didn't like the thought of it.

'So,' she said, spreading out her enormous and very stiff napkin, 'how are things?'

'Oh, so-so.' He leaned back in his seat to order. 'Two soups, and then the duck. And a bottle of something good. I leave it to you to choose.'

She opened her mouth to say that she preferred a light meal in the evenings and that he was going to be given the most expensive wine on the list if he left it to the waiter to choose. She closed her mouth again; she'd asked him to order and it wouldn't do to contradict him.

He fiddled with his fork, eyes on her face, and then eyes down. Nervous.

'The thing is,' he said, 'well, I know it's a bit inconvenient, but I couldn't work at the House because Lettice is there. So I asked Miss Townend to get a taxi and bring her things over to your place. I didn't realize . . . let me start again. Miss Townend was with my predecessor, knows everything about the constituency, the voters, who does what. Her files date back for years. She's invaluable.'

Bea wanted to sniff, but managed a small smile, instead. 'I understand. Miss Townend doesn't care for Nicole's sister?'

He reddened. Bread rolls came and he took one, tearing it apart, shoving some in his mouth.

Manners! thought Bea. And then, I wish Hamilton were here. He knew exactly how to handle Max, how to help without criticizing him. Oh, how I miss him, my dear one. But I suppose I could always ask someone else for help. I'm not sure He could be bothered, but . . . well, what do I have to lose? *Dear Lord, could you spare a minute? This silly boy has got himself into a mess, and I haven't a clue how to help him. That's it. Oh, the magic word . . . please.*

Max was presented with a bottle, sipped, said it was all right, watched while some was poured into his glass, took a gulp. Bea covered her own glass with her hand, asked for water. The waiter was not impressed. Well, she wasn't that impressed by the waiter, so that made two of them.

Max cleared his throat. The wine was relaxing him. 'The thing is that Nicole is refusing to talk to me. It's not that I haven't tried. I have.'

Possibly twice? 'You've been round there, taken flowers, champagne?'

'Eh? What? Well. Not exactly, no. You see, the thing is . . .'

Bea sighed. 'Nicole caught you in bed with her younger sister.'

'No, certainly not!' He appeared shocked at the suggestion.

'You were caught kissing her?'

'No! We–ell . . . no, not really. She was kissing me, when Nicole walked in and . . . honestly, you never heard such a fuss.'

'Lettice was kissing you? You'd encouraged her. Given her to think you'd like to flirt with her.'

'No! Well, no. Of course not. You don't understand. Nicole's always been jealous of her little sister, who is . . . well, sort of kittenish, always laughing, joking, you know? Not meaning anything by it, but . . . well, she does wear very short skirts . . . not that that means anything, nowadays, of course.'

'You mean that Lettice came on to you?'

He was grateful for her understanding. 'That's exactly it. I don't suppose she meant anything by it, and I certainly didn't mean . . . like an elder brother . . . just joshing around, little sister, up for any lark, but . . . it wasn't serious in any way. You do believe me, don't you?'

'Nicole didn't?'

Their soup came. She attempted hers with little sips. He drank his, greedily. He probably hadn't had any lunch. She found hers too highly seasoned, but said nothing. She wished she were back home, having lasagne with Maggie and Oliver, talking over the day's events. No stress, an easy companionship. A different sort of family gathering. Well, she wasn't at home, and she'd better get on with the job in hand. 'You are fond of Lettice?'

'Fond?' It was an alien concept. 'She's . . . no, not really.'

'But you'd like to bed her?'

He reddened again, pushing his empty plate away. 'Certainly not.'

Oh yes, you would. But you aren't going to admit it. 'Lettice likes you, though?'

'Likes me? I suppose so. She thinks Nicole will divorce me and then I'll marry her. She says she'll be a better MP's wife than Nicole, which isn't true. Lettice is . . . has . . . I don't know. Sometimes I think she'd like to be an MP herself, only she's a bit lazy – at least, that's what Nicole says – and so she latches on to me . . . oh, I don't know! I can't figure her out. All I can do is shout that I'm not in love with Lettice, but neither she nor Nicole are listening.'

'Well, you've run away from her. What does she think about that?'

'Run away? Nonsense. My secretary couldn't work in the same office as her, that's all.'

'And all those files . . .?'

'It never occurred to me that Miss Townend would want to bring all her famous files. When she arrived, I couldn't believe . . .! Honestly, Mother, if I'd known . . . and you with the builders in. Then I thought maybe the agency could use the kitchen, which would free up the dining table?'

'No.'

'That's what Maggie said, too.' He gulped wine, refilled.

Bea pushed her own soup plate away. She'd done quite well, she thought. Only a spoonful or two left. The waiter looked down his nose at her as he removed the plates. 'Some water, please?' Holding his eye, letting him read her opinion of him. She thought about what Max had said, and had not said. 'You're fond of Nicole, aren't you?'

'It's not getting me very far, is it?'

'But you are fond of her?'

'Yes, of course. I mean, I married her. She's a little softie, really, under all that super-sophisticate look. Like me. Makes a good impression. Most people wouldn't know, but she's suffered all her life because Lettice is the favourite, always has been. Nicole's the most wonderful wife, you know—'

'But not a jolly little short-skirted cutie, like Lettice?'

'No, of course not. She's not like that at all.' His voice took on a worshipful note. 'She's so beautiful, I can hardly believe sometimes that she's mine. And so terrific in the constituency, you can't imagine. They all love her, and she knows them all; all the wives, who can be helpful, who can't, who knows who . . . all that sort of thing. I don't know what I'm going to do without her.' He reached for the bottle to refill his glass.

Their main course came. At a glance, Bea saw that her portion of duck was dried up under a complicated-looking sauce. Ah, well. Indigestion, here I come. She tasted the vegetables. Underdone. She tried the duck. Passable, but tough.

'Which of them do you want, Max? Be honest with me, now. Lettice for fun and youthfulness, with the money from her parents. Or Nicole.'

He didn't have to think about it. 'Nicole, even if it means her parents drop their support. Only, she doesn't want me any more, and I suppose I don't blame her.'

'One thing at a time. You've left Lettice in possession of the field at the House. Is there any way you can get rid of her?'

'I can't think how, except . . .' He thought about it, absent-mindedly pouring himself another glass of wine. 'I suppose I could have a word with . . . suggest that she's a bit of a loose cannon . . . they don't like that sort of thing. I wondered, you see, if she were left alone at the House, whether she might sort of look around for someone else.'

'That's a brilliant idea, Max. You are clever.'

For a moment, he glowed. And then sighed. 'Doesn't help me with Nicole, though. You really think she might soften if I took round some roses or something?'

'Worth a try. She must be feeling . . . well, I can't imagine.'

'Betrayed.' Tears came to his eyes. 'She must feel really awful. She's had this problem all her life, Lettice stealing her boyfriends, her clothes . . . even a job she had once.'

'I don't remember Lettice at your wedding.'

'She was in New York, over there on some temporary post, not sure exactly what. It didn't work out, so she came back this last summer, and that's when her father suggested she'd be an asset to me as my research assistant in the House. Naturally, I thought it was a good idea and when Nicole wasn't happy about it, I overruled her, because Lettice seemed so demure, so right at first.'

'Probably modelling herself on Nicole, who is the real thing.'

'You're right, Mother! Nicole is the real thing. Pure gold. I look at her and everything I've prepared to say just flies out of the window. She must think I'm a moron.' He fiddled with his glass. 'You wouldn't think of, maybe, having a chat with Nicole for me? Would you?'

Bea thought it was the last thing on earth that she wanted to do. 'Do you really think it would help?'

'Oh, I do.'

'Then I suppose I must.'

'Good on you. I say, this duck tastes good. Aren't you going to finish yours? Let's have a sweet, shall we? I like their tiramisu. And coffee with a brandy for afters?'

Bea resigned herself to another hour at the table. She thought she'd handled that well enough. Max had managed to bring up all the right ideas, with only the tiniest bit of prompting. He was relaxed now, eating well. He was going to have to start going to a gym or thinking about a diet soon, if he weren't careful. He'd lost his early, keen-edged high-flyer look and was beginning to take on the extra poundage of the successful businessman. She wouldn't mention that tonight. She relaxed. What was an hour's indigestion compared to helping Max get back on track?

Then she went and spoiled it all. 'Isn't it about time that Miss Townend retired?'

She'd forgotten that Max had inherited another trait from her; that of loyalty. What, sack someone as faithful as Miss Townend? Didn't Bea realize that the poor woman's whole life was bound up with her work at the House? She'd been there all her working life, looking after the member for his constituency – whoever they happened to be – all this time. And Bea thought Max could turn her out into the cold, just like that? Why, she'd refused to go home to look after her ancient mother, who really needed her, just to keep Max going. He'd never forgive himself if . . .

Bea stifled a sigh. 'How difficult for you. And for her. I expect she's finding it hard to keep up with the latest technology. I mean, it's such a business having to update one's computer all the time. Perhaps we could get Oliver to show her how to put all her files on to a memory stick?'

'Not another word, Mother. You simply don't know what you're talking about.'

Oh well. She'd tried.

She feared she was in for another white night. There was too much to think about, too many unsolved problems clattering around in her head, and too much indigestible food in her stomach.

Max, having put her in her place, rambled on about plans for Christmas. Nicole's parents had booked them two weeks in the Bahamas, but now . . .? The inconvenience of breaking up with Nicole made him pause for a moment. Then he went smoothly on to tell her the latest piece of gossip circulating in the Lobby, and to wonder whether or not he should change to a hybrid car, watching out for the carbon footprint . . .

She stopped listening. All he needed now was someone appropriately dressed to sit with him, to smile and nod now and then. She could do that. Her thoughts flew back to Goldie's angry face and the menacing looks of the driver of her van. If she herself were going to be tied up visiting Nicole tomorrow, then would it be safe to let Oliver go back up to the house again by himself? Someone must help him complete that inventory . . . those dresses . . . would Oliver have the necessary know-how to itemize them? Would he know a sequin from a silver button? Silk from satin? Er, no. Would it be a good idea to send Maggie with him?

Ye–es. And no. Maggie had her hands full already with project-managing the revamp of the flat down the road, and keeping the house going. And chivvying the builders.

Who did they have on their books who might be available to do the job? Miss Brook, the dragon lady? Bea half-smiled. Yes. Miss Brook would grumble at being asked to do it, but she'd make the most of the outing, she'd know how to describe the dresses, and she certainly wouldn't let anyone invade her territory.

If Oliver and Miss Brook were out of the office, then Max could work undisturbed in the sitting room. So long as he realized this was a temporary measure, she supposed there was no great harm in it.

'. . . don't you agree?' Max was saying. She hadn't a clue about what, but she smiled and asked if he had to go to the House tonight. Apparently he wasn't needed, so she said that if they got back early enough, she knew he'd want to ring Nicole.

She hoped.

Late Monday evening

'Did you arrange everything for tomorrow?'

'Her phone was engaged for ages, but yes, I got through eventually. I left a message with some half-witted creature who said she'd tell Mrs Abbot when she got back. I wish I could afford to take some more time off. It was one long slog all day, and then I had to cook when I got back home.'

'Yes, yes. But they do know I'm going to be there early tomorrow?'

A sigh. 'If she remembers to pick up her messages.'

'I shall need your keys to get in.'

'I'd forgotten that. If I put them in the post to you . . . no, you wouldn't get them in time. Are you going in on the Tube? I could meet you at Ealing Broadway station, if you like? I usually take the Central Line in to Notting Hill Gate and walk down from there. What time?'

'Half eight on the dot, can you make that?'

'If I leave them their breakfasts.'

'Just one thing. We don't want to be observed. Suppose we do the handing over on one of the quieter platforms, not the ones for the Tube because they get so crowded? One of the suburban lines? How about the first westbound platform over the bridge, where the suburban lines go out to Slough, and the through trains go to the West Country? Perhaps directly under the stairs, where it's darkish? Then we can go back over the bridge and take the Central Line train in together.'

'We're both going in on the Tube. Why not hand over then?'

'It's so busy, we might easily get into different carriages and miss one another.'

'That's true. All right. Half eight, under the bridge, westbound trains. See you there.'

Nine

Tuesday morning

Bea couldn't sleep. At one o'clock she was still staring into the darkness, turning first this way and then that, worrying about Max and Oliver, and how soon the workmen would finish. Every now and again, she'd get a flashback to the scarlet slippers and the voluminous red costume . . . and have to shut her mental eyes and send up an arrow prayer for help.

At half past one she got up, taking care not to make any noise in case it wakened Max next door. Then she thought, Bother Max! I didn't invite him to stay, though of course it was only right and proper that he felt he could come back home when his little world fell apart . . . but . . . oh well. If I can't walk around at night in my own home, then who can?

She put on the lights and went downstairs to make herself a cuppa. Sometimes it helped. The kitchen was as neat and tidy as always under Maggie's control. Bea fiddled with the central heating switch, and the boiler puffed into life. If she couldn't have warmth and light in her own home . . . she sighed. Why was she being so defensive?

What was that? Oh dear, someone was coming down the stairs. Bea didn't feel like talking to anyone, least of all to Max.

It wasn't Max. It was Maggie, tousle-headed, yawning, bright-eyed, wearing great big bunny-rabbit bedroom slippers and a baby doll nightdress which left little to the imagination. 'Can't you sleep, either, Mrs Abbot?'

Maggie automatically reached for the button on the radio and Bea gritted her teeth. Whether Maggie actually got the message or not, she let her hand drop away without turning the sound on. She reached into the cupboard. 'Hot chocolate? Cocoa? Herbal?'

Bea wanted to make a declaration of independence and snap

that she'd make what she liked in her own kitchen, but didn't. 'Peppermint tea. Indigestion. So what's keeping you awake, Maggie? Is it having a guest in the house?'

'N–no. I mean, he has every right, more right than we have, Oliver and I, if you think about it. He is your son and we're just live-in helpers. No, I woke up and remembered that I hadn't left you any messages about the things you asked me to do.'

Bea exercised patience. 'Mm? A phone call for me? Perhaps Mr Piers?' Why had she thought her ex-husband might want to contact her? He was out of town painting a client, wasn't he? She certainly didn't need his help with anything at the moment. He'd never taken that much interest in Max, and she couldn't imagine that he'd know what to say about his son's present dilemma.

Maggie slapped her forehead. 'Right. I knew that I knew. Couldn't make out what she was on about at first, but it was the woman up the road with the man that died, the one that Oliver's been on about. He said he was going to have nightmares about it but of course he's sleeping like a baby with the light on and hooked up to his iPod. I said he'll get himself electrocuted one day, but I don't suppose he will.'

'Probably not. So Mrs Frasier rang and left a message for me?'

'Said to tell you that a friend of hers, a Ms Cunningham – if I've got the name right – is going to go to the house early tomorrow, before you get there, to check on something, she didn't say what. She's going to stay there while you finish the inventory and then you're to give her your keys. You can ring Mrs Frasier back if there's a query.'

Bea sipped herbal tea. 'Problem. I have to see my son's wife tomorrow morning, if I can. I thought perhaps Miss Brook could finish off up the road with Oliver. There's not much to do now. The costumes will take the most time, I suppose.'

Maggie was wistful. 'I'd have liked to have seen the costumes. Oliver says they're something else.' Maggie, all five foot ten of her, would dress in nothing but spangly Lurex from choice.

'Yes, but . . .'

'I know. I've got enough on my plate already.' Maggie yawned widely. 'Back to beddy-byes.'

Bea thought of asking Maggie about her new boyfriend,

the plumber, but desisted. Maggie didn't have a good track record where men were concerned.

The girl took her cuppa and shuffled out of the room on those impossible bunny-rabbit bedroom slippers. Did she take them off to mount the stairs?

Bea found herself smiling. She was now relaxed enough to go to sleep, too. Two o'clock. If she could get in six hours' sleep, she'd be all right.

Even with nearly six hours' sleep behind her, Bea didn't really feel up to talking to Nicole. She stood outside the door of her daughter-in-law's flat, and took deep breaths. She wished she liked the girl. It would make it so much easier to talk to her. Bea had always thought her an ambitious, selfish, anorexic, fake blonde. Hamilton had guessed that her marriage to Max would only last if he managed to get promoted to office. Hamilton hadn't liked her, either. Hamilton had been an excellent judge of character.

So why bother trying to save the marriage?

Well, because Max seemed to have some genuine feeling for the girl. He'd admitted he'd felt some physical attraction to the younger, livelier sister, but he said he'd resisted the attraction. Maybe he had, maybe he hadn't. But he'd chosen Nicole over Lettice even though he knew it might mean the withdrawal of their parents' backing. Also, he seemed to have some insight into Nicole's character, an insight which Bea certainly didn't have. Nor Hamilton.

Was the girl really as shallow as she appeared to be? Or were there hidden depths, tra la?

Bea rang the bell, and tried to think kind, warm, fuzzy thoughts about Nicole, who didn't, incidentally, seem all that keen to see Bea. She had some appointment somewhere – pedicure, waxing of the bikini line? Only with reluctance did she agree to give Bea a few minutes.

'Nicole, my dear.'

The door was held open, but there was no pretence at warmth or welcome. Nicole's little dog Hamish rushed at Bea with excitement. Bea picked him up and cuddled him. He licked her hands and face, his tail going nineteen to the dozen. At least there was one person glad to see her.

'Oh, Hamish. Do give over,' said Nicole, but didn't bother

to remove him from Bea's arms. Bea held on to her smile, and stepped inside. She'd never liked this rented flat much; it faced the wrong way so it didn't get any sun, and was furnished in minimalist fashion with stripped floors and a lot of overhead lighting which was not helpful to ageing eyesight.

Nicole tapped her way on high heels ahead of Bea into the reception room. She was wearing a short skirt revealing long, tanned legs; her hairdo was perfect, ditto her manicure; designer wear for shirt and waistcoat. Lots of gold chains and a few too many rings on her fingers.

'Coffee? A drink?' A tray was laid out for both on a low table.

At eleven in the morning? Bea put Hamish down and accepted a cup of coffee. It was cold, but she wasn't going to complain. She seated herself, unasked, and said how nice Nicole had made the flat look.

Nicole shrugged. She picked up a mobile phone, looked at the display, put it down again. 'I suppose it will have to be given up, like everything else.' She turned a hostile face to Bea. 'I'm expecting a call from an old friend. He's taking me out for the day.'

'I sympathize. I did the same thing when my husband walked out on me. But he was a serial womanizer, and Max isn't that.'

'Isn't he?' Nicole leaned back in her chair, playing with one of her gold chains, twisting it round her fingers. Soon it would cut into her neck . . .

'You know what he's like. Small boy, worried to death, toes turned in, big puppy eyes . . . worse than Hamish when he's been a little bit naughty, isn't he, my pet?'

Hamish said, 'Wuff!' Boot button eyes fixed on Bea. He liked Bea.

'Little boy, my foot! I caught him halfway down my sister's throat. What do you call that?'

'He didn't think fast enough, did he? She latched on to him, knowing he was a soft touch. She heard you coming I suppose, and got him into a clinch before he could work out what was happening.'

'Tcha! If you believe that . . .'

'I believe he loves you, rather than your sister. He says she's always wanted what was yours. Is that right?'

Nicole stared into the distance, seeing . . . what? A series of tussles which had always led to her defeat? She shrugged.

Bea wondered if she dared invent a selfish sister for herself, and decided she couldn't. It would be so easy to get caught out. She could, of course, ask for help . . . perhaps? No, no. She'd been overdoing that line lately. Well, if not that, she could ask for some hint as to how she should proceed? *How about a little help here, Lord?*

Nicole picked up her mobile phone again, and again discarded it.

Bea said, 'What do you think about getting Miss Townend to retire?'

Nicole showed some animation. 'About time, too.'

'The thing is, he's so loyal, he doesn't want to hurt her. Sometimes women can see exactly what ought to be done, but men are so blinded by the old school tie, or whatever . . .'

'Exactly my point! Max's predecessor in the constituency begged him to take her over when he retired, but as a secretary, she's about as much use as a . . . a feather duster. She's out of the Ark. Those files . . .!'

'They're all over my sitting room floor. I can't move! I'm sure the whole lot could go on one memory stick.'

'And he ought to have a new laptop and printer—'

'And that Wi-Fi thingy, what's it called?'

'But will he listen to me? No way!'

Bea sighed. Hamish had settled down to sleep on her foot, but she reached across to pat Nicole's arm. 'You and me both. We can see through the big, successful Member of Parliament, to the stubborn little boy within . . . a little boy with turned-in toes, crying for his beautiful wife.'

Nicole was shaken. 'Then why hasn't he called me, or come round?'

Bea took a risk. 'He has tried. Have you been out a lot?'

Nicole nodded. 'He could have written, or left a message on the answerphone.'

'Too ashamed, I suppose. Too scared.'

'Silly boy.'

'I know. You might be amused to hear that he's run away from Lettice, by moving out of his office so that she can't get at him. I think he hopes your sister will find some other person to target.'

'Some hope.'

'Can you think of another way to handle her?'

Nicole stared at Bea, and through Bea, and didn't reply. The phone on the table rang, and Nicole picked it up, eyes down, excluding Bea from the conversation.

Little flirt, thought Bea, trying not to listen to the ensuing chat. Nicole wriggled and giggled, examining her fingernails. Shot Bea a look, and giggled again. Trying the age-old make-him-jealous lark.

It might succeed with some people, but probably not with Max, who at bottom lacked self-confidence. Ouch.

Bea bent forward to put her coffee cup on the table. As she leaned back, so Hamish jumped on to her lap and snuggled into the crook of her arm. Bright eyes looked up at her through his 'fringe', begging her not to throw him out into the cold again. She liked the feel of his warm, wriggling body against her. She and Piers had only ever had the one child, and Hamilton hadn't been able to . . . ah well.

Nicole shut off her phone call. 'Sorry, but I've got to throw you out. A lunch date out in the country.'

Bea was persuaded to her feet. 'Anyone I know?'

'I wouldn't think so. Did you have an umbrella? It's raining again.'

'I'll manage. But about Max . . .?'

'Oh, tell him . . . I don't know. Tell him to do his own dirty work.'

Bea thought Nicole had a point there. Out on the landing, Bea realized she was still cuddling Hamish, so had to press the doorbell again, in order to transfer him back to Nicole. Hamish gave a sharp 'yip' of disappointment, which made Bea hasten her footsteps on the way to the lift.

Back at the ranch . . .

Bea opened the front door to hear her telephone ringing. Knowing that Oliver and Miss Brook were up at the Kent house, and Maggie out on another job, Bea negotiated the obstacle course of furniture and carpet, and arrived in the sitting room only to hear Max's ancient secretary answer the phone. 'Mr Abbot's office . . . no, this is not a domestic agency. This is the private phone for Max Abbot—'

Bea snatched the phone from Miss Townend's hand, disregarding her indignant squawk. 'The Abbot Agency here. How may I help you?'

The phone quacked at her. Confused dot com. Umbrage was taken in large doses. Over and out. The caller rang off.

Bea replaced the receiver, trying to exercise patience. There was no sign of Max. There was dust everywhere. Eeeek! The phone had felt gritty. She dusted off her fingers, noting that the chairs and settees needed a good vacuuming before she could sit on them again. Those builders . . .!

'How dare you!' Little Miss Townend was so angry she almost spat at Bea. 'This line is exclusively for the use of Mr Abbot. If you wish to use the telephone for agency purposes, then you must go downstairs and do it there.'

Bea had an impulse to seize the woman by her bony wrist and force her to walk downstairs to view the chaos there. Crumps and bashes from the efforts of the workmen below shook the house. Couldn't Miss Townend hear them? Or hadn't Max briefed her properly?

The phone rang again. Presumably the caller thought he or she might have misdialled the first time, and was trying again.

Bea got to the phone first. 'The Abbot Agency. How may I help you?'

'Well, thank goodness for that. I just got through to some idiot, a crossed line, I suppose.' The caller was the social secretary of one of their oldest clients, who wanted a butler, and wanted one straight away. Someone had let them down . . . a large party expected that weekend . . . the agency had always been so helpful in the past . . . could they help? Bea cast her eyes around the room, but of course Oliver and his laptop were elsewhere, the office computers were sitting on the dining room table, but hadn't been booted up that day, and she couldn't access their records quickly.

'Give me your number, and I'll ring back in ten minutes, see what I can find for you.'

She put the receiver down but kept her hand on it. Miss Townend glared, making darting movements towards the phone and back again. Bea's steady gaze kept Max's secretary from actually wrestling Bea for it. Bea rang Oliver's mobile, and within seconds he was giving her some numbers to try. She wrote them down, with care, recognizing a couple of the names and giving them a starred rating. This client deserved the best.

'Before you ring off . . . how are you and Miss Brook getting on? Are you nearly through? Did Ms Cunningham turn up? Don't forget to give her the keys before you leave.'

'Nearly finished. Should be back within . . . oh, half an hour. Will report then.'

Report? He made it sound ominous.

She depressed the receiver, and started to find her client a first-rate butler for the weekend. Little Miss Townend retired to the fireplace, arms crossed across thin, bony chest, indignation in every line of her.

Tough! thought Bea.

The second man she tried was able to do it and, luckily for all concerned, had presided at a successful event for the client on a previous occasion. She gave him the details, rang the client's secretary to confirm, and put the phone down.

It rang again. Miss Townend started forward, but Bea was quicker. 'The Abbot Agency. How may I help you?'

'Tcha!' said Miss Townend. With little jerks of her head, she put on her coat, hat and gloves, collected her handbag and said, 'I really cannot be expected to put up with this. Please tell Mr Abbot that I will return when conditions are back to normal. He knows where to find me.' She left in high dudgeon.

Bea thought, Good! The phone kept ringing, and she took notes, trusting that Oliver would be back when he said he would be, and could then take over. Halfway through one phone call, she heard the front door slam, but it wasn't Oliver. It was Max.

'Hello, where's Miss Townend?' was his greeting, cutting through Bea's explanation to a new client of what they might or might not be able to do to help them.

'Gone home,' said Bea, putting the phone down and making yet another note for Oliver. 'She was cross because I had to use the phone.'

'You didn't upset her, did you?'

'Probably.' The phone rang again, and Bea answered it. A tearful young nanny, who'd been pawed by the client's husband and wanted out. Bea clicked her tongue against her teeth. Properly trained nannies knew how to deal with that sort of thing. The girl sounded a trifle on the young side to have been exposed to that sort of pressure. If Bea could have got at their records, she could have checked exactly how young the girl was. 'You'd better come in to the office straight away. I shall need you to make a formal complaint . . .'

A hurricane of tears and cries of, 'Oh, no, I couldn't! You can't ask me to do that!'

Ahha, thought Bea. Was it six of one, and half a dozen of the other?

Max towered over her, mouthing, 'Get off the phone!'

She smiled up at him, mouthing back, 'In a minute.'

The front door opened and closed again. This time it was indeed Oliver, with Miss Brook in tow. The tearful girl said, 'I can't talk now,' and rang off.

Max said, 'What I want to know is . . .'

Oliver appeared in the doorway and jerked his head at Bea. 'A minute?' Oliver didn't pull rank without reason, so this was serious.

Bea said, 'In the kitchen, in five.'

Miss Brook moved into the room, as if she were on wheels. She was probably as old as Miss Townend, but unlike that poor lady, Miss Brook was still firing on all four cylinders. She had the calm demeanour of someone who never let trivialities disturb her. She was a monument to a proper secretarial training, and ancestors who had been suffragettes and manned telephones at secret intelligence hideouts during the Second World War. She terrified weak-kneed clients but Hamilton had thought highly of her and she could be trusted never to betray a client's confidence, no matter how high profile they might be.

'Good morning, Mrs Abbot,' she said, removing the cover of the computer on the dining table. 'Good morning, Mr Max.' Of course she'd known him since he was a small boy.

He muttered, 'Good morning,' back.

Miss Brook ran her finger along the table, and pinched in her lips. 'Dust is very bad for computers.'

The phone rang again, and Bea said, 'Good morning, Miss Brook. I'm delighted to see you. I'm sorry about the dust. Maggie will deal with it when she gets back. Can you take over for a bit? I've got a list of people here, queries . . . can you access our records from there? You can? Oh, bless you. If you can sort some of this out, I'd be eternally grateful. Max; a word in your ear.'

He was huffing and puffing, going red. Max wasn't getting the attention he felt he deserved as a Member of Parliament and head of the family. Max needed a kick in the pants and Bea felt she was just the person to give it to him. She took his arm and led him over to the window overlooking the garden. Her patience game had long since disappeared, of course. She hoped Max had bothered to put the cards away properly, because if he hadn't and had lost one she was going to make him go to Harrods and buy another double pack. So there!

'Now what?' Arms akimbo.

Bea raised her eyebrows. 'So how are you today, Mother? Thank you, Max. I'm not too bad, even if I did spend half the night worrying about you, and the morning with Nicole, trying to make out that you aren't quite as stupid as you've made yourself out to be. Nicole would like you to do your own dirty work. Her words, not mine. She might be disposed to listen to you if you talk to her yourself, but flowers, tickets to the theatre, whatever, would probably be helpful.'

'Yes, but—'

'And get yourself a new secretary. No, better still, ask Nicole to get you a new secretary. I can provide you with the names of various secretarial agencies. Nicole should vet your staff in future. Miss Townend has, I'm sure, been a wonder in the past, but that's it. She is the past. You must take the poor woman, out for a meal, butter her up with compliments, make sure she has whatever she is due by way of pension, and send her home to look after her dear mama. It's time for you to move on.'

'Mother, my understanding, when I moved in here, was that—'

'I don't know what you imagined you'd get here, apart from a bed for a couple of nights while you sorted things out with Nicole. You cannot run your office from this room. That phone is mine, and cannot be co-opted for your use. Understood?'

He'd gone purple in the face. Oh dear. Had she gone too far? No. It had to be said. If she relented now, he'd take full advantage of her weakness and she'd be back to square one.

She put her hand on his arm, and went on tiptoe to kiss his cheek. 'There's a good boy. Now, you go out and get the biggest bunch of flowers you can, and a huge box of chocolates—'

'Nicole doesn't eat chocolates.'

She shook his arm. 'No, but I do, silly. The flowers are for Nicole, and the chocolates are for me. Right?'

Was he going to cry?

Big boys don't cry. Or, they'd better not. She was running out of patience.

'Now, I'd better get back to work. Oliver's got a problem to discuss with me.'

He put his hand over hers, on his arm. 'Mother, where did I go wrong?'

When you married Nicole, was the right answer. But not the right answer for him. 'These things happen, dear. Chin up. We just have to muddle through as best we can.'

Lily Cunningham gulped down the whisky and shuddered. The events of the morning had taken more out of her than she'd expected.

Well, it was done and the future looked a lot brighter than it had when she got up this morning.

She stood in the centre of the living room, looking around her. How many memories this room held for her! She couldn't have been more than two years old when Uncle Matthew first sat her on his knee in the big chair, and sang her a nursery rhyme. How well she remembered playing him her first piano pieces; aged five.

Damaris used to try to scare her by jumping out at her from behind the coat rack in the hall. Well, Damaris hadn't lived in this house all that long, had she? A couple of years at most. Whereas she, Lily, had been coming here all her life.

One of the photographs on the mantelpiece was missing. That was alarming. Where had that gone?

Also the little shepherdess. And the silver jug.

She could guess who'd taken them. How dare she!

They belonged to the house and must be returned, straight away. The agency had been responsible for everything in the house, so the agency must get them back.

She glanced at the clock on the mantelpiece but it had stopped. The house lay quietly around her. Accepting her as the new and rightful owner.

Lily Cunningham ran her fingertips across the dusty lid of the piano, and grimaced. Houses needed to be looked after.

Now it was hers, she'd have to see to it. What was that Polish cleaner's number? She must look it up in Uncle Matthew's address book.

Ten

Tuesday noon

Bea went to find Oliver in the kitchen, but stopped short in the doorway. Three very large men were sitting around the table, eating sandwiches and drinking from her teapot. Also, her biscuit tin had been opened and the contents depleted.

'Hope you don't mind, missus,' said the largest and baldest one. 'Maggie said to help ourselves.'

'Care to join us?' asked a curly-headed young man, whom Bea guessed was Maggie's latest heart-throb.

Bea looked at her watch. Maggie had hoped to be back by lunchtime, but had obviously been delayed. 'How are you getting on? Is there anyone down there at the moment? I thought I'd better see what's happening.'

The large man lumbered to his feet and escorted her down the stairs. The sheet which had been hung over the staircase in an attempt to keep the dust from rising all over the house, had been hitched to one side and secured that way with a manky floorboard. No wonder the house was dusty. Bea twitched the sheet free so that it hung over the stairwell again.

'Sorry about that. The lads are up and down the stairs all the time, carrying stuff, and the sheet gets in the way.'

The chaos downstairs was unbelievable. Floorboards were up, plaster was down, wiring hung in bunches from bare brick walls. In what had been her own office, two of the panes in the French windows had been broken.

'Looks worse than it is,' said the large man, with a cheerfulness that Bea found appalling. A technical disquisition followed, which Bea only half understood. What she did understand was that old buildings needed to be watched all the time, or they'd disintegrate and make work for bricklayers, plumbers, electricians, glaziers and decorators. Stunned by science, she agreed to everything he was suggesting, and retreated to the kitchen in need of a restorative . . . and of Maggie, who might not be much cop on a computer keyboard, but understood the large man's terminology. And what was that about replacing the carpet? Her dear husband Hamilton had chosen that carpet, and she'd always liked it.

In the kitchen she found Oliver doing something about lunch. From being completely helpless in that area, Oliver was now, amazingly, beginning to learn basic catering. He lifted a couple of mugs out of the microwave. 'Cup of soup do you, Mrs Abbot? I thought we might have taken it into the garden, but it's raining again.'

'Let's try my bedroom,' said Bea, gratefully clutching her mug.

Oliver followed her up the stairs and took a seat on her dressing-table stool while she perched on a small armchair in the window. She rather wished he hadn't chosen tomato soup, because if it spilled it would stain everything in sight. She told herself to be grateful for whatever it was he'd given her.

The soup was hot. Good. 'How did it go this morning?'

He was looking down into his soup, up at the ceiling, out at the sodden garden. Why wasn't he meeting her eye? 'All right, I suppose. Miss Brook is out of this world. She'd brought a digital camera with her, and a dictation machine. It was her idea to photograph everything. She seems to know by osmosis whether a piece of furniture is worth something or nothing. When we reached the basement I got each costume out and photographed it while she dictated a description. It didn't take us that long.'

'You did a good job. Then you gave the keys to Mrs Frasier's friend and came away?'

He examined the few drops of soup left in his mug. 'She wasn't there when we arrived. She didn't come till we were nearly through. She let herself in with her own set of keys and then . . . you've told me enough times that we don't have to like our clients, but that we can pick and choose whether to take them on.' A long pause. 'I don't think – no, I'm pretty sure that you wouldn't have taken Ms Cunningham on as a client.'

'Really? Why not?'

He fidgeted. Put the empty mug down on the dressing table,

where it nearly toppled off. Rescued it. Put it back more securely. 'She's nothing to look at. I know that isn't what counts and of course it isn't. You could see she knew the house well. She knew about the loose board making the piano sing. She knew how to switch the central heating on, and she was out on the patio in two ticks, dead-heading the geraniums. She thought Miss Brook was you and she said, right out loud, that Miss Brook wasn't what she'd expected.'

Bea was amused. 'Because I dressed down when I saw her friend, I suppose.'

Oliver was still not meeting her eye. 'She acted as if she owned the place, touching things, shifting ornaments. I know she was all shaken up, but she, ugh! She *tittered*. That sounds awful. I know it's no excuse, but she forgot to ask me for the keys and I did mean to give them to her, but when I got halfway back down the hill, I put my hand into my pocket and realized I'd still got them. I'm sorry.' He took the keys out of his pocket and laid them on the dressing table.

'Oh. Well, no great harm done.'

Oliver was trying to justify himself. 'Something as important as keys to an empty house, Mrs Frasier ought to have put it in writing. It might have been anyone at all who rang up asking for us to hand the keys over to a third person. It might even have been Ms Cunningham herself.'

'That's true.' Bea reflected that if she hadn't been distracted by Max and the builders, she'd have taken the phone call herself. To put it bluntly, the agency was not functioning as it should. Ought she to close it down till they could get back to normal, or try to struggle on? 'I'll let Mrs Frasier know that we've still got them. You can deliver them with the inventory and the photographs tomorrow. All right?'

He tried to laugh. 'Blame it on me. My head's like a sieve.'

Ah, yes. He was still waiting for a copy of his birth certificate, wasn't he? Would it prove that Mrs Ingram, who'd brought him up, really was his mother? Bea was pretty sure that nasty, viewing-porn-on-his-laptop Mr Ingram had not been his father. But she wouldn't raise the matter if Oliver didn't. 'No problem. The Kent house is a bit creepy. I felt it myself.'

'Miss Brook didn't like Ms Cunningham, either. You know how her nostrils twitch when something annoys her? As if they'd registered a nasty smell? She was doing that all the time Ms Cunningham was in the room with us.'

'Really?'

Oliver shrugged. 'I'll dump the mugs back in the kitchen, shall I? Then get back to work.'

Bea said, 'Would you ask Miss Brook to come up for a moment? I'm worried about the computers and the dust downstairs. Perhaps she could work up here for a while, if I cleared my dressing table.' She had another idea. 'How would it be if you took over the guest bedroom for your office, just for the time being?'

A slow grin was the answer. Oliver hadn't liked Max taking over downstairs, either. 'Will do. I'll check what she'll need in here. May have to bring up a typing chair for her.'

He took both mugs and went out, while Bea went to stand by the window overlooking the garden, pushing back the floor-length curtain, leaning against it. Yes, it was still raining. Drip, drip, thud, thud. That 'thud, thud' meant that the guttering above wasn't coping too well with the downpour, and that water was pouring over the top of it. More expense. Getting at the guttering would mean putting up scaffolding.

The sycamore at the bottom of the garden was losing its leaves, the 'keys' swirling round and round in the air, the leaves following. The spire of the church had retreated into the distance, the curtain of rain sheeting down between.

Miss Brook tapped on the door, and came in. Bea wondered if Miss Brook would say, 'You rang, madam?' but of course she didn't. Miss Brook didn't believe in what she called 'feudal' ceremonies.

Bea gestured Miss Brook to the comfortable chair. 'I appreciate your helping us out, Miss Brook, and I do take your point about the dust downstairs. I've asked Oliver if he'd like to work in the guest bedroom next door for the time being, and I wondered if you'd like to take over in here?'

A comprehensive survey of the room. A nod. 'Young Oliver will have to bring up a proper typing chair for me. And the printer, of course. Is there a phone here?'

'An extension beside the bed.'

'Not a perfect arrangement, but under the circumstances, I can probably manage.'

'Miss Brook, about this morning. I'd not put Oliver down as an imaginative boy, but . . .'

Yes, definitely Miss Brook's nose was signalling displeasure. 'I cannot say that I was impressed, either, but I suppose we must make allowances as Ms Cunningham had been greatly distressed by an incident on the Tube which made her late. Being a Londoner, you'd think she'd be used to it by now.'

Bea sank on to the bed. 'By incident, you mean . . .?'

'It usually means someone's jumped in front of the train. She was all of a dither. I offered to make her a cup of tea, but she refused. I suspect she'd be at the sherry the moment our backs were turned.' Seeing that Bea looked blank, Miss Brook added, 'In the cupboard next to the piano.'

'I didn't get that far.'

Miss Brook's nose twitched. 'She looked straight at it, the moment she came in, and I guessed why. She's that type.'

'Secretive? Underhanded?'

A pause while Miss Brook considered her answer. 'Under the circumstances, having experienced a shock, you or I would have gone straight to the cupboard and poured ourselves a drink. She wanted to. She kept looking in that direction, but she made herself wait till our backs were turned. Did she think her friend Mrs Frasier would have refused her a drink in the circumstances? *Sneaky* is not perhaps the word that comes to mind, but she has not an open personality.'

'Oliver didn't like her, either.'

'Beggars can't be choosers. We had a job to do, we did it, and we came away. Young Oliver did well, all things considered. Are you going to keep him on at the agency?'

'If he'd like to stay, yes.'

A nod. Miss Brook got to her feet. 'I'd better get on. I may need a desk lamp. It looks as if it's going to get dark early.'

Bea started as the room filled with a livid light. Thunder rolled. She waited for the lightning to strike and counted a slow 'two'. The storm was almost overhead. She drew the curtains closed, shivering. She'd always been afraid of violent storms.

She picked up the bunch of keys and popped them in the top right-hand drawer of her dressing table. She must see that they got returned the following day. She cleared her dressing table, which was big enough to serve as a desk for Miss Brook with a computer and a printer. Dust, dust. It was even up here.

The builders were thudding away downstairs. Bea went into the guest room, and tidied Max's overnight things away. There was a desk already there, next to a power point. The bedside table would do for the printer. Oliver would certainly be able to work there, and if the door were kept closed the room would be comparatively dust free. She could hear Oliver thumping up the stairs with a typing chair for Miss Brook.

Where was Maggie, who might have been able to keep the dust at bay? Bea sat down on her bed, rang Maggie's mobile.

'Mrs Abbot? Are you OK? I know I said I'd be back by now, but the plumbing suppliers have delivered the wrong shower cabinets for the en suites, and I'm not letting them get away with it. Would you believe, I had to get on to their head office before they agreed to change them? What a waste of time. I can't leave, either, because the plumbers have arrived to install the shower cabinets so while they're here, I'm having them look at the shower trays which have not been fitted properly. Not that they want to do anything about it. Refurbishing this flat is three steps forward and two back.'

'But you're the very person to see it's done right, Maggie. You'll be back for supper?'

'There's the chicken pie.'

'Bless you, yes. I'll see to it as soon as the builders are out for the day.'

'Did they drop that sheet over the stairs to the basement? They had it hitched up this morning and the dust was coming through something chronic, but they promised me—'

Bea laughed. 'What did you expect, Maggie? I could carve my name, let alone write it, in the dust. See you soon.'

Miss Brook appeared in the doorway, carrying the big printer without any sign of stress. 'In my mother's day, we covered the furniture with dust sheets when the builders were in. I don't suppose any of the younger generation know what a dust sheet is.'

Bea stared at her. Of course they didn't, but decorators usually provided their own. She didn't have any, she knew that. Oliver helped Miss Brook to set out her typing chair and computer.

Bea felt that she was in the way. What could she do to be

useful? Miss Brook and Oliver were perfectly capable of the day-to-day running of the agency, and Maggie was more than earning her keep at the client's place. As if to underline her decision, the phone rang and Miss Brook answered it.

Bea went downstairs, noting with resignation that the sheet over the stairs had been hitched to one side again. She pulled it down, but guessed it would be lifted up again soon. There was a bunch of flowers in a vase on a chest in the hall which was so powdered with dust that you couldn't tell what colour they were supposed to be.

She got out the hoover and started work. She knew the cleaning would all have to be done over again tomorrow, and the next day, but she had nothing better to do. At least . . . she had got something better to do, hadn't she? She'd promised herself another chat with Kasia, and she had Kasia's home address now. She thought about it, as she hoovered dust off the upholstery. Should she use one of her linen sheets to cover the settee when she'd got the dust off today? And if she put the upright chairs together, and stacked them to one side? A king-size sheet might cover them nicely. She went upstairs to see what sheets she could spare to cover furniture, and found several.

There really was no need for her to speak to Kasia again, was there? The inventory had been taken, and would be delivered tomorrow or the next day. The circumstances surrounding Matthew Kent's death were odd but not inexplicable. It had been an unusual case, certainly. But it was all over.

Sometime or other, when Piers returned, she might chat to him about it, tell him when the funeral was to be. Laugh with him about the oddities of life.

She worked her way through the room, cleaning and covering up pieces of furniture as she went. She took down the clock on the mantelpiece and the pictures, wiped them clean and stacked them neatly to one side. There was no point in trying to spend time in this room till the dust had settled. She unplugged the television, wiped it down, and covered it over.

She came to her husband's portrait on the wall, and took that down, too. She decided to hang it in her bedroom for the time being. He seemed to be looking at her almost sorrowfully.

Why was that? What had she done wrong?

The wrong feet . . . something's wrong . . . the bedroom door was open . . .

'Nonsense!' Bea set the portrait down on the floor, where it continued to look at her, so she turned it to face the wall.

The dress was too big for the man on the bed.

'It was a theatrical costume! He'd taken it home to make it fit better.'

There was blood on the fender.

'There was a perfectly good explanation for that,' snapped Bea, vigorously setting the hoover going again. The floor looked beige instead of cream. The hoover cut swathes through the dust. She hadn't enough spare sheets to cover the carpet.

Taking the hoover out to empty the bag, she noted that the builders had hoicked the dust sheet up again over the stairs. She didn't even bother to remonstrate with them, but set her teeth and went on into the kitchen. If Maggie's kitchen were not in pristine condition when she returned, there'd be all hell to pay, and no supper to eat.

The phone rang and this time Miss Brook leaned over the banisters to call for Bea. 'It's for you. A foreign name which I didn't quite catch.'

Bea hadn't realized there was anything Miss Brook couldn't deal with. 'Is it Kasia?'

'Yes, Casher.'

Bea took the call in the kitchen. 'Yes, Kasia?'

The Polish woman sounded hesitant. 'You said . . . if I have problem . . .?'

'I did, and I meant it.'

'I am at work, finish soon. I come to see you, please?'

Bea cast a frantic eye around. 'We're in a mess, builders in, but—'

'Is a problem, not to worry. Another day, maybe.'

'No, no. Do come. As soon as you like.'

The woman hesitated, then shut off the call.

A cheerful voice boomed through the hall. 'We're finished for the day now, missus. Short of . . .' something unintelligible. 'Back tomorrow, after we been to the tiling warehouse, right?'

'Right,' she said, and went out to replace the sheet over the stairs. Closing the barn door after the horses have fled. From upstairs came the merry ring of the phone being answered, and the printer going swoosh, swoosh. At least some parts of the agency were still functioning properly. At least Max had kept out of the way, and Miss Townend, too. Bea felt sorry for little Miss Townend. Well, a little bit sorry. Bea told herself that she ought to have handled her son's secretary better.

She went back into the kitchen to continue wiping surfaces down but had only just decided that she'd better put everything that had been left out on exposed shelves into the dishwasher, when the front doorbell rang.

Kasia, looking wary. 'Oh!' When she saw the mess in the hall.

'Come on into the kitchen,' said Bea. 'I think the stools are clean enough to sit on, but I won't offer you a cup of tea till I've washed out a mug or two.'

Kasia seemed to grow two inches. She reached capable hands for the mugs the builders had been using, and put them in the sink. 'This my job. You sit, right?'

'You wash, and I wipe.' Bea seized a tea towel. 'And now, you tell me what the problem is.'

'This afternoon I get phone call from lady who say I am to work for her at Mr Kent's. And I feel . . . huff . . . huff . . . cannot breathe!'

'What?'

Kasia nodded. 'Lady say I must work there again, but is not Mrs Frasier, who is Mr Kent's daughter. Is another name. I think I go crazy!'

'But . . .!'

'She say, house is dirty, is my fault, all my fault, because I ran away last week instead of cleaning. She say, "You work and you get paid. You not work, you not get paid."'

Bea gaped.

Kasia nodded, swiftly emptying the sink of dirty water, and tackling the work surfaces. 'She say, "Come on Thursday, one hour only, nine o'clock, and I let you in." She say, "You not to be trusted with keys now." She say, "I check on you, see you not steal any more . . .!"'

'What!'

Kasia scrubbed down the central work table, nodding. 'She say, "You bring back the things you steal from me, or I call the cops!" She mad, I think.'

Bea put a hand to her head. 'I don't understand any of this . . . Ah. Hang about. Miss Brook and Oliver – two of my agency staff – they were working at the house this morning and a woman came in who had Mrs Frasier's keys. Her name was . . .' She clicked her fingers. 'Cunningham. Would that be the same person?'

Kasia shuddered, her whole body trembling. 'I have bad dream every night about that house. I no thief! And I not go again. No!'

'Don't blame you. I wouldn't particularly wish to go back there again myself.'

'But she say, she call the cops. I try call Mrs Green. No answer.'

'She's gone away for a bit.'

'Then I call my mother in Poland, and tell her. She say, "Come back home"! But, I go home, no work. I need job. I earn good money here. I send back money for my mother and my little house that is not finished. What for I should go back now? I not steal. No! But . . . what to do? So I think what you said, and I call you.' She sprinkled water on the floor to stop the dust floating up again and attacked it with a soft broom. The dust rolled into clumps, which Kasia dealt with before using a mop.

Bea got some potatoes out of the vegetable drawer and sat on a stool to peel them for supper, lifting her feet from the floor so that Kasia could clean around her. 'Ms Cunningham sounds a nasty piece of work.' Bea remembered that neither Oliver nor Miss Brook had liked the woman. 'I signed a piece of paper for Mrs Frasier, taking responsibility for what was in the house. What is it that's missing?'

'A silver jug, a china lady. A photograph.'

'I know who took those. Mrs Frasier was there when the jug and the shepherdess went, and she didn't object to their going. The photograph was taken by Mrs Frasier's mother. None of those things were stolen.'

As Kasia moved through the kitchen, order and cleanliness was restored. There was still a fine mist of dust in the air, and tomorrow it would all need doing again, but for now, the kitchen was usable.

Kasia said, 'You tell this woman "No cops"?'

'I can tell her that, certainly. I don't think we have her phone number, but I think I know how to get it. I don't understand why she should be taking over from Mrs Frasier, but I'm sure I can sort that out for you.'

'You say to her, I not go back to that house. She find other cleaner.'

'Who won't be half as good as you, Kasia,' said Bea. 'Do you want to work for me instead of Mr Kent in future? My assistant usually cleans the house, but she's getting more and more other work to do, and I need someone like you to keep us straight.'

'I have to sign papers, pay registration fee, national stamp? All outgoings, no incomings.'

Bea gestured widely. 'We're a domestic agency. We work according to the laws of the land.'

'I like better to work cash in hand. You understand?'

'Yes, but . . . look, we'll discuss this properly some other time. You've cleaned the kitchen up for me beautifully, and I owe you for that.'

Kasia put up her hand. 'No cops, no pay. I have more work already, always people say, "Who is your cleaner? Give me her number". I no need Mrs Green or her jobs any more. I am full up. And no cops.'

Bea heard Miss Brook calling out from the hall that she was leaving for the day, but would be back tomorrow if needed.

Bea sang out, 'Thank you, yes, Miss Brook. Definitely, we need you.' Turning back to Kasia, she switched on the kettle, offering her a cup of tea. 'I understand what you're saying. Tell me a bit about yourself.'

Kasia seized another cloth and started wiping down the glass fronts of the kitchen cupboards. 'I came here with my husband five years now. He is very good builder, has much work. We rent nice house with a friend and his wife, and we send money back to look after his mother and my mother. Then we start to build a house back at home, for ourselves later on, you understand? Then he becomes sick. They say it is cancer, and we go back home to Poland.' Kasia stared into the distance.

Bea passed her a mug of tea. 'My husband, too. Also cancer. Last year, far from home.'

'It took many, many months.'

'Mine, too.'

Kasia said, 'You know how it is? No work, no money. My mother help, his mother help, but they are old and can find little work, too.'

'That is hard.' At least Bea hadn't had to worry about money, for Hamilton had provided well for her, and business was booming.

'When he die, I not know what to do. There is no work for me in Poland. Our house there is not finished, no water, no power. My mother, his mother, both need money. Here I have cousin and friends, but I alone cannot pay for the house we rented before. So I come back here, start again. I have a room in the house where my cousin is, and I look for work. It is good to be busy.'

'I understand. I am sorry.'

'No good to be sorry. No good to cry. Always look forward. Only, sometimes . . . not possible.'

Bea bowed her head. Very true.

Kasia stood up straight. 'So, you sort this for me, right?'

'I'll do my best. Will you keep in touch?'

Kasia shook her head. 'Please, not to ring me again. And you tell that woman I not work for her and no cops. Right?'

She picked up her bag and negotiated her way over the furniture to the front door and out.

The phone rang, but this time no one picked it up. Oliver either hadn't heard it, or was too engrossed in something to respond. Bea got to it just before the answerphone clicked in.

'The Abbot Agency. How may I help you?'

A woman. A voice Bea did not recognize. 'This is Ms Cunningham, the new owner of Mr Kent's house. I find that several valuable items have been removed without permission. At first I considered that my uncle's cleaner might have taken them. I was afraid I would never see them again, cleaners being a notoriously light-fingered breed. But then I remembered that your agency signed a note saying you would be responsible for the contents until an inventory had been prepared and agreed, so I am holding you responsible. If you cannot find and return the items within twenty-four hours, I shall go to the police. You may contact me on this number when you are ready to replace them.' She reeled off a string of numbers which Bea hurriedly wrote down.

'Would you repeat . . .?'

The caller rang off.

Bea had been prepared to apologize to Mrs Frasier for Oliver not having left the bunch of keys, but this wasn't Mrs Frasier, was it? Thinking hard, Bea checked over the numbers she'd written down. Who was this Cunningham woman? Why did she say that she was the new owner of the Kent house?

Bea went to look for the papers given her by Mrs Frasier, and found them on Miss Brook's temporary desk upstairs. Oliver was still tapping away next door; hopefully he'd be able to print off the inventory and send it on . . . but where to?

Bea rang the landline telephone number Mrs Frasier had given her. An outer London number; inner London used the 0207 series and outer London was 0208.

The phone rang and rang.

At last someone with a gruff voice answered. An adolescent boy?

Bea said, 'Is it possible to speak to Mrs Frasier? It's the Abbot Agency here.'

'Who . . .? No, I'm afraid . . .' There was a babble of sound in the distance and someone took over the phone. A man, with doom in his voice. 'You can't speak to my wife. She's dead!'

Eleven

Tuesday evening

Bea looked at the phone in her hand. Had she heard correctly? No, it wasn't possible. Damaris Frasier, dead? She'd been so full of life the other day . . . was it only yesterday? At her stepfather's house?

Bea put the receiver back on the phone and sat down. What a terrible thing. But oh, dear! A nasty thought. Where did this leave the agency? Damaris Frasier had asked them to prepare an inventory, and they had done so. Who was going to pay for that? Would the agency have to write the cost off?

Bea told herself that she ought not to be thinking of the loss to the agency when a client had died so suddenly. Only, too many bad debts and the agency would soon be in trouble.

She remembered Ms Cunningham and her very odd behaviour. What had that woman meant by saying she now owned the Kent house? It wasn't possible, was it? No, no. Of course not.

Bea tried to rationalize the situation. Damaris Frasier had been looking after her stepfather in recent years, he had made a will in her favour. He had died and she had inherited. Bea had just been speaking to Damaris Frasier's husband, and presumably her estate – including the Kent house – would now pass to him. There would be inheritance tax to pay, no doubt, but he must now be the rightful owner of the keys currently residing in Bea's dressing-table drawer.

She drew the phone towards her, with the intention of ringing him back. Then desisted. No, she couldn't intrude on his grief at such a moment, and for such a reason. Every feeling revolted.

On the other hand, there was someone else who would be very interested to hear the latest news. She tried to get through to Sylvester, but he seemed to be permanently on the phone. She couldn't hang around waiting for him for ever, so left a message for him to ring her, urgently.

The next problem was how to deal with Ms Cunningham, who seemed to expect Bea to produce items taken by Goldie and Gail. Presumably Ms Cunningham didn't yet know about Damaris's death?

Bea clutched her head. Wait a minute. How could Ms Cunningham now be the legal owner of the house unless she knew that Damaris was dead?

Bea's mind zigzagged from point to point. Had Damaris legally turned the house over to her friend Ms Cunningham, and if so, why? It must be worth a pretty penny. Damaris had shown no sign of wanting to be rid of the house when she'd engaged the agency; indeed, no.

Damaris had taken a phone call from someone when she'd been at the house. She'd spoken as if to an old friend who knew all about the arrangements for the funeral and the link to Sylvester. There'd also been something about shredding papers. Could that phone call have been from Ms Cunningham?

Too many questions, too few answers. And the only answers that did occur, failed to satisfy. Yet she couldn't leave it alone. Bea looked at the clock. Maggie hadn't yet returned, but it was time to put the supper on.

She had to clean the jets on the oven before they'd light. Dust, everywhere. She felt as if there were dust in her head, too. *Dear Lord, this is me bothering you again. Sorry and all that, but if you could spare a moment, I could do with some words of advice.*

No one answered, of course. She laughed at herself for thinking they would. She took Maggie's chicken pie out of the fridge and put it in the oven. Put the potatoes on. One thing was for sure; she was not going to hand those keys over to Ms Cunningham till she'd proof that the woman had a right to them.

Think straight, girl! Mrs Frasier engaged you to prepare an inventory and you signed a paper to that effect. So the agency was due to hand over said inventory to Mrs Frasier – or her heirs – and the family were now liable to cover the agency fee. Mrs Frasier had handed over a bunch of keys and Mrs Frasier – or her heirs – must have them back.

Ms Cunningham – whoever she might be – had not engaged Bea to do anything, had not given her anything in writing and was not responsible for paying the agency fee. The agency had no agreement with Ms Cunningham and therefore could not in all conscience hand over the inventory or the keys to her.

Bea congratulated herself on a piece of clear thinking. She was glad that Oliver hadn't handed the keys over because – now she'd thought it through – she realized she ought never to have told him to do so.

In fact, she would go upstairs now, this minute, while the supper was cooking, and if she could find a computer which was connected, she'd run off a letter to Mr Frasier to apologize for troubling him at this difficult time, to explain that his wife had asked the agency to do this and that they had done the inventory and would be happy to deliver the keys at his convenience.

She was halfway up the stairs when she heard the front door open and slam. A tearful Maggie wobbled over the carpet and ran up the stairs in high heels.

'What?' said Bea, standing back to let the girl go past on her way up to the top floor where she and Oliver lived.

Oliver came out of the guest room, looking bemused. 'Mrs Abbot, just the person. I'm getting phone calls about Matthew Kent's car. The callers seems to think we're responsible for selling it, but . . . what's the matter with Maggie?' They followed Maggie's progress upwards until she slammed her bedroom door on the world.

Bea looked a question at Oliver, who said, 'The plumber?'

'But I thought . . . not the one here?' Bea gestured down the stairs to the basement.

'Nah. It's another one. Putting in walk-in showers for the flat down the road where Maggie's been working. Polish. Probably got a wife and three kids back home.'

Bea started for the upper stairs, but Oliver put his hand on her arm. 'Let me. She doesn't have to explain anything to me. I'll just switch off my computer first.'

Maggie turned on her radio, full blast. Bea winced. When Maggie was happy, she liked to live with a lot of background noise. When Maggie was miserable, the noise increased to deafening proportions. The house began to throb.

Was that the front door banging shut? Bea couldn't be sure. The telephone rang. Let it. The answerphone could take a message. She watched Oliver climb the stairs to the top floor and hung over the banister to see if anyone had come in downstairs. They had.

Max was climbing over the carpet, while trying at the same time to fend off an assailant. He was flailing at her with his briefcase while holding a huge bunch of flowers aloft in his other hand. His tie was at half mast, his shirt pulling out of his trousers, his hair all messed up.

He was shouting something which Bea couldn't understand for all the racket from above. Then the sound above reduced to reasonable proportions and Bea could hear Max yelling, 'Gerrof!'

Dear Lord, have mercy, thought Bea, walking down the stairs and taking her time about it. *Suppose I turn tail, go into my bedroom and shut the door? But if he really needs my help . . .?*

Max's assailant was a luscious blonde who was laughing and clinging on to his trousers even while he, red-faced, was trying to beat her away. Bea thought, He's not trying hard enough, but I suppose he doesn't want to hurt her.

The blonde was giggling. 'Is he trying to run away from his little lovey-dovey, then?'

Max swung into the living room, with the girl still hanging on to him. He pulled up sharply, and she cannoned into his back. 'Oh!'

Bea didn't know whether to laugh or scream. Evidently Max hadn't expected dust-sheet covered furniture. She called out, 'Hello, is that Max? Supper's almost ready.' She reached the hall and turned in to the kitchen. The vegetables were boiling over. Time to adjust the gas.

'Is it?' Max appeared in the doorway. 'Oh.' He handed her the flowers.

She bit back the words 'Did you give the chocolates to Nicole?'

The luscious blonde sashayed forward, holding out her hand. 'I'm Lettice, and you're the famous Mrs A? Delighted to meet you at last.'

Bea ignored the outstretched hand to reach for the oven gloves. 'Ah, yes. Nicole's younger sister. Nice to meet you. I was only talking to my daughter-in-law about you this morning.' The vegetables were almost done, the pie crust browning nicely. 'I'm not sure there's enough food for everyone. Max, dear, were you intending to stay for supper?'

'Me, no.' He was righting his tie, tucking his shirt in. 'Got to go back to the House, three line whip, you know. I just came back to . . . I didn't realize Lettice was trying to reach me . . .'

'I followed him all the way from the House. Wasn't that clever of me?' Lettice perched herself on a stool, all wide blue eyes and peach-bloom skin. Her clothes were almost modest, but not quite, with a trifle too much skin exposed, top and bottom. She was a more rounded, lovelier version of Nicole, and if you put the two of them side by side in a beauty contest, Nicole would undoubtedly come off second best.

But, Max was signalling by his body language that Lettice made him feel uncomfortable. He was trying to edge away from her. He was afraid of her. Oh, dear.

Bea went to the door and yelled upstairs that supper was almost ready. When she turned around, it was to see Lettice stroking Max's sleeve, whispering in his ear . . . and Max trying to push her away.

Lettice turned a wonderfully white array of teeth to Bea. 'Silly Max; he thinks you might disapprove of my falling in love with him, but there it is; the deed is done. The parents will be delighted; they always thought I'd marry into politics.'

Max squawked out some sort of protest. 'Lettice, don't. This is all wrong.'

'My darling, your mother is not so old that she doesn't recognize true love when she sees it. Of course she'll be happy for you to follow your heart.'

'Nicole—'

'Is a loser. Always has been. Don't worry about her. The parents certainly won't.'

Max tugged at his collar, reddening. 'Must go. Mustn't be late. Talk later, Mother.'

He disappeared, letting the front door bang to behind him, leaving Lettice to pout and dig in her enormous handbag for a mobile phone. Two sets of feet pounded down the stairs.

Oliver appeared in the doorway, looking preoccupied. 'All right if I take Maggie out for a meal? She's feeling a bit under the weather.'

'Of course,' said Bea, taking the pie out of the oven. Who was going to eat it now?

Not Lettice. That luscious lady grimaced a smile at Bea, waved a hand and followed the youngsters out of the door, talking to someone she called 'darling' on her mobile. Bea dished up the vegetables. She supposed they could all go into a soup sometime. The front door slammed, opened and banged again.

Someone padded softly into the kitchen and dropped car keys on the table. 'Some dolly bird let me in. Not a new temp, is she?'

Bea blinked. 'I thought you were up north somewhere.'

'So I was,' said Piers. 'The client was taken off by the police for questioning into some financial irregularity or other and I couldn't get Matthew's death out of my mind. Also, I was worried about you . . . can't think why. I never worried about you when we were married. You've always been able to look after yourself, haven't you? Anyway, you kept turning up in my head, so I thought I'd drop in, see if there was any food going.'

'Help yourself.' Bea whizzed plates, knives and forks on to the table, and pulled up a stool for herself. Piers divided the pie into two, taking the larger portion for himself. The phone rang again. Piers raised an eyebrow, but she said, 'Let it go. I've had enough for today.' She heard the caller asking about a car, and shrugged. Oliver could deal with it some time.

'Isn't this nice. Just like Darby and Joan.' He reached a long arm for some fruit juice from the fridge.

Bea glowered. 'We'd never have made Darby and Joan. I'm amazed I haven't spent the last twenty years in prison for murdering you.'

'Manslaughter, surely. With me not able to keep my hands to myself and enough women on the jury, you'd probably have got off with a slap on your wrist. What's with the dolly bird?'

'Her name is Lettice. She's Nicole's younger sister, and she's under the impression that she's only got to get Max in bed with her, and he'll switch partners. Max says her parents think Lettice is perfect and will happily back her choice. Nicole threw Max out because she found them kissing. He says Lettice came on to him, and that he prefers Nicole. He's abandoned hearth and home to avoid Lettice and has taken refuge here, but we're all topsy-turvy because of the builders and I haven't a clue how to mend the marriage.'

He took a knife to scrape the last of the pastry off the dish. 'It's up to Max, surely? She's younger and prettier than Nicole. If her parents continue to support Max, why bother to do anything?'

Bea tried not to feel scandalized. Of course Piers would think that, being the tomcat he was. She supposed a lot of people would think that way. She could see his point of view, but . . . 'If it were as straightforward as that I might not approve but I could probably live with it. Only, Max really seems to care for Nicole. He just doesn't know how to convince her that he does.'

'Especially if he's bedded the blonde bombshell already.'

'Oh, no. He wouldn't.'

Piers snorted. 'Be your age. He's my son, isn't he? Of course he's had her. Only, since he's your son too, he's now conscience-stricken and doesn't know what to do next. Is there anything to eat for afters?'

'Cake in that tin over there, if the builders haven't had it. I don't believe you, about Max.' But she did, really. With reluctance. 'Well, even if you're right, he still wants to stick with Nicole. He ran away from Lettice tonight even though she was practically tearing the clothes off his back. I can see him ending up without a wife and without a constituency if this goes on. You're his father; can't you think of anything that would help?'

Piers took the last remaining lump of chocolate cake out of the tin. He didn't offer any to Bea, but bit into it with an expression of bliss. With his mouth full, he offered some words of advice, which Bea interpreted with an effort.

She couldn't help laughing. 'What? Get Nicole to tell him she's pregnant? I can't do that. No, that's . . . Piers, you're incorrigible!'

'Am I not?' he said, with pride, clearing his mouth. 'It always worked for me when I wanted to end an affair. I'd tell the girl that my other girlfriend thought she was pregnant and with great sadness, I felt I must stand by her, et cetera. Even when there wasn't another girl in the offing. I got the idea from you.'

Bea felt herself go pale. 'Piers, you didn't decide to stay with me just because Max was on the way, did you? I mean . . . no, that's despicable!'

'Sort of, yes. I knew I wouldn't be able to keep it up, but I did think that I ought to play the good husband for a while. I haven't much of a conscience, I know, but it does twitch now and then.'

'Well, you were no help at all when I had Max and he was nearly five when I finally threw you out. Do you mean that you stayed all that time because you were sorry for me? I . . . I'd like to do you an injury!'

'Sure. I can understand that. I felt like hitting me, often. But the flesh was weak. In a way I was relieved when you threw me out. I was also sorry. You deserved better.'

'Would you have stayed if I'd been a different kind of woman, more . . . I don't know . . . up for it?'

He sighed. 'It wasn't that. I really did love you, you know. As much as I could. It's the way I'm made. I could never bear to do the same thing two days running, and there was a whole world out there to explore. At times I missed you terribly, but there was a certain sense of relief, too.'

She digested this in silence. Did this make her feel better, or worse?

'Any coffee on the go? And, while it's brewing, suppose you tell me what you've got the builders in for. And have you any idea when Matthew's funeral's going to be?'

Wednesday morning

By nine o'clock in the morning, the agency answerphone was full, and had stopped taking any more messages.

Oliver appealed to Bea. 'What do we do? They're all enquiring about Matthew's car.'

Bea gulped hot coffee. Piers had taken one look at the sheeted living room last night and taken her off to a pub where they'd talked about Matthew and listened to some rather good jazz till closing time. She didn't feel like work this morning. Still less did she feel like confronting builders with the instructions Piers had left with her for them. Fortunately Piers had said he'd drop in that morning and have words with the foreman himself. The men hadn't arrived yet, so the house was comparatively quiet, if dusty. Max had come in late, and hadn't surfaced yet. Just as well. She really didn't feel like coping with his melodramas.

'Where's Maggie?'

'Still in bed, I think. The plumber stood her up and she got all weepy last night, so I took her for a long walk . . .' He shrugged. 'She said she was going to take the morning off and I didn't argue.'

Bea nodded. This was only her first cup of coffee; after the second she'd be able to think straight. She hoped. 'First things first. Clear the answerphone tape. Put a message on it to say that if anyone is ringing about the car, it's been withdrawn from sale. Mrs Frasier did say we were to take messages about the car, but I have no instructions about how much to ask, where it is, and who has got the keys.'

Oliver pulled the morning papers towards him. 'I suppose she put an advert in one of these?' He began to check. 'If she gave them our telephone number, we should at least be able to work out what make of car it is and how much she wants for it.'

Bea refilled her cup. 'If you've finished running off the inventory and the photos, I suppose I could take them round to Mr Frasier with the keys. Normally I'd put the stuff in the post – well, not the keys – but under the circumstances I think I'd better deliver them by hand. I'll be glad to get shot of this business.'

'Two-year-old Jaguar, warranty, etc. Garaged, it says. I wonder where? Hm. A bargain. She could have asked more. Give me ten minutes and I'll have everything ready for you to take. You don't suppose they'd let me buy it, do you? I'm taking my test next week.'

Bea raised an eyebrow. 'Are you so sure you'll pass?'

He raised an eyebrow in return. Of course he'd pass first time.

She said, 'All right, being you, you probably will, but . . . first things first.'

'Clear the answerphone. Right.'

It was still raining. Bea set the dishwasher running and cleaned down the surfaces. How long would it take for the dust to subside for good?

Oliver returned in record time. 'Tape cleared. New message inserted. Here's the address for Mr Frasier. This envelope has two copies of the inventory in it, plus the photos, and our bill. There's also a release form for the keys, which are . . . where?'

'I've got them. Mr Piers is coming round this morning to deal with the builders for us, so you can let him in. Miss Brook will be back today, too. Can you cope if I leave you in charge?'

He looked pleased and said of course he could. Well, it was nice that someone was feeling pleased with themselves that morning.

Bea rang Damaris's home number, introduced herself and said she knew it might be a difficult time for Mr Frasier, but if he could spare a moment or two that morning to clarify his wife's instructions regarding her stepfather's house?

'Getting the house is the one bright spot on the horizon,' said a depressed male voice. 'Come when you like. I'll be in all morning.'

Bea checked the Frasiers' address with the *A to Z*. At least she'd be travelling against the morning flow of traffic coming into London.

The Frasiers' house was a 1930s semi-D in a quiet street lined with flowering trees. The house had been less well-maintained than its neighbours. The front garden wall had been removed to allow an elderly Escort to park off-street in what had once been a garden and was now an area of shingle ringed by unkempt bushes. The car had been in the wars, to judge by scratches on the doors and a dented wing.

Bea began to wonder if the Frasiers were living on the breadline and might not be able to meet her fee. Oh dear.

A long-haired black cat sat on the doorstep, waiting to be let in. When he saw Bea, he lifted one paw to her in supplication, blinking enormous golden eyes.

'Charm gets you nowhere with me,' said Bea. She rang the doorbell. There was a recycling box in the porch, empty apart from last week's local free paper, which had been turned to the job section. A downpipe hung at an angle by the porch, allowing rain water to stain the pebble-dash and setting up perfect conditions for dry rot. The paintwork was shabby, to put it politely, and there were a couple of tiles missing off the roof.

The door opened. A middle-aged man with a weight problem stood there. He had thinning, improbably dark hair, drooping shoulders and wore an air of defeat which must tell against him every time he went for a job.

'Mr Frasier? I'm Bea Abbot, of the Abbot Agency. I rang earlier.'

'Come in, come in. All at sixes and sevens. Such a shock.' He put out a foot to stop the cat entering the house. 'Mind the cat. It's hers. Was hers. Don't know what we're going to do with him now. I can't be bothered, that's for sure. I suppose he'd better go down the vet's this afternoon.'

He ushered her into a sitting room dominated by a huge flat-screen television set, brand new, tuned to a sports programme. The packaging for the television set had been left sprawling over the carpet. Would Damaris have left it there? Probably not. Apart from the discarded packaging, the room seemed to be clean and tidy.

A teenager with straggly hair over his eyes lounged in a bean bag which had seen better days. He was playing with some electronic game or other and didn't look up when Bea was shown to a chair and offered a drink. The packaging for the game was on the window sill, next to a vase of chrysanthemums. The water in the vase could have done with being topped up, but Bea guessed that wasn't going to happen now.

'Would you like a drink? Whisky, gin? Or tea, if you prefer. I think there's some milk, isn't there, Tom?'

Tom shrugged, intent on his game. Mr Frasier made no move to turn off the television and when Bea gestured towards it, he said, 'Got to have something to keep the old brainwaves ticking over, haven't we? You into sport?'

Bea shook her head. 'We were so sorry to hear about your wife.'

'Me too. I don't know how we're going to cope, I really don't. Tell the truth, neither of us is used to shopping, or cooking and cleaning.' He sounded more annoyed than upset.

'What happened?'

'She must have lost her balance, fell in front of an express train. Nothing anyone could do. The police said we wouldn't want to see her. I said I thought I could cope, but not Tom here, who has a delicate stomach. We're both on medication, you know. In the end, I met her mother up there, and we did it together. Weird woman. Didn't cry at all. I did. So did Tom.'

Tom didn't look particularly grief-stricken to Bea. She told herself; what did she know about it? 'That's terrible. What a shock.'

'It was. When they rang at first, I told them they'd made a mistake, but they said they'd found her handbag and it was her. And of course it was. No suicide note, thankfully. I don't know what I'd have done if they'd found a suicide note. No, it was an accident, pure and simple.'

'Why did they think . . .?'

'Her stepdad killing himself like that. They said it often happens, one set of miseries triggers another. I said Damaris wasn't at all upset by her stepfather's death, but they didn't like that, either. I suppose she was upset in a way. A terrible thing. Platform crowded with people all waiting for the local stopping train, express comes along, everyone warned to stand back, everyone does except for Damaris, who falls straight into its path. They shouldn't let the express trains run through the same platforms as the stopping trains. I'm surprised it doesn't happen more often.'

Bea shook her head in sympathy. 'Dreadful for you. So sad.'

Tom abandoned his game and stood up. He must have been well over six foot, and thin with it. A slight odour emanated from him. Not too keen on washing? An immature face. Age twelve or thirteen? He ignored Bea to demand attention from his father. 'Are we going down to get me those new trainers or not?'

Mr Frasier huffed. 'Not today, Tom. There's so much running around I've got to do. Registering the death, seeing the solicitor, getting rid of the cat, all that sort of thing. That's if I can get the car started. The battery's flat.'

'Hire one. We got money now, haven't we?' Tom had very light-blue eyes with a hard expression; just like his mother.

Bea said, 'Which reminds me. Mrs Frasier asked the agency to take enquiries for Mr Kent's Jaguar, and we've been fielding telephone enquiries for it since yesterday afternoon. Only, she didn't give us the details or the keys, so we weren't able to take the matter any further. In fact we're not sure we should.'

'We can't touch it yet,' said Mr Frasier, his tone warning his son to be careful what he let slip. 'You know what Trixie said yesterday.' To Bea, 'My sister, she works in a solicitor's office, knows the law, told me yesterday that we can't touch anything till it's cleared for probate.'

'Aunt Trixie said we could get some money quickly by—' He realized what his father meant, shot a sideways look at Bea and mumbled, 'But maybe I've got it wrong.'

'Yes, you have,' said his father. Meaning, 'Shut up, you fool!'

Bea hid a smile. Had they intended to sell the car for cash to cover their immediate needs? Also the costumes? The Frasier house could certainly do with an injection of funds. The carpet was threadbare, the three-piece suite had seen better days, and the room hadn't been decorated in years. The only new things in it were the television and Tom's electronic game.

Bea got down to business. 'Your wife asked us to prepare an inventory for the contents of Mr Kent's house, to include the theatrical costumes. We have done this for her, with photographs. I hope this is satisfactory.' She handed over the package.

'I'm sure it is,' said Mr Frasier, shuffling paper. 'Any idea how much this stuff will fetch yet?'

Tom abandoned his sulk to look over his father's shoulder. 'I thought we could move into the house. I mean, that would be a bit of all right. Better than living in this dump.'

'Maybe so,' said his father. 'It will take about six weeks to get probate, Trixie said.'

Bea held out her invoice. 'Well, I'm sure your solicitor will be able to give you some definitive advice. Meanwhile, here is the invoice to settle our account.'

Twelve

Wednesday morning

Father and son looked at Bea with open mouths and calculation in their eyes. It was clear to her that neither had a penny to bless themselves with. Damaris Frasier had had a job. Presumably it was she who had paid the mortgage and run the house. Without her, what did they have? He would have a disability pension, perhaps? And Tom? Child benefit, presumably? Why wasn't he at school today? He wasn't showing any sign of shock or sorrow at his mother's death.

Mr Frasier held the inventory and photos to his expansive stomach, gripping them as if he'd never let go. 'You'll have to wait till probate, when everything's settled, right?'

Bea had been afraid this might happen. She was sorry for the Frasiers, sort of. 'There are various grants you may be entitled to and back pay from Mrs Frasier's job. Have you any insurances? No? Well, I'm sure your solicitor will be able to help you. In the meantime, can you tell me anything about a Ms Cunningham? She contacted us last night claiming to be the new owner of the Kent house.'

'What!' Father and son looked shocked. Mr Frasier said, 'Cunningham? That . . . no, I can't believe it, not even of her!'

'Dad! You know Mum promised I could have Uncle Matthew's recording equipment and—'

'Shut up!' Mr Frasier snarled at his son.

Bea waited for clarification, which wasn't forthcoming. 'You know the woman?'

'She's . . .' Mr Frasier huffed and wheezed, reaching for an inhaler. Asthma? He puffed, got his breathing back under control. 'She's an old friend of my wife's, a music peri . . . that is, she goes into schools to teach keyboard a couple of days a week. She gives piano lessons in their front room, too. She's no relation to Matthew. I can't think why she should say—'

'Dad! That's my stuff that—'

Mr Frasier turned on his son. 'Shut up!' He swung back to Bea to say, 'The Cunningham woman's a poor sort of creature, always hanging on my wife's coat-tails, wanting a lift here or a favour there. It's preposterous for her to claim she's inherited the house. We have! Or rather, Damaris did, and of course she's left everything to me.'

Bea said, 'The problem is that Ms Cunningham now has a set of keys. to the house. Your wife phoned and left me a message to say Ms Cunningham would be there early yesterday to check over one or two things, and that we should hand over our own bunch of keys when we'd finished taking the inventory. Ms Cunningham arrived rather later than we expected, and let herself in with her own keys.'

'She's got keys? But . . . how could she . . .? You think my wife gave her some keys?'

'That's stupid,' said the boy, scrabbling around under the settee, and producing a once-expensive but now slightly scuffed leather bag. 'This is Mum's handbag. They gave it back to us last night. The keys to Uncle Matthew's house must be here.' He pulled out a wallet, a coin purse, tissues, make-up bag. He emptied the lot out on to the carpet. 'These are her house keys.' He held up a bunch with a small teddy bear hanging from it. 'And her shop keys.' These had a twinkly star attached. There were no other keys at all.

The Frasiers looked at one another in consternation. 'Why would Mum give Uncle Matthew's keys to that old bat?'

Derek Frasier rounded on Bea. 'Well, if you had a set to do the inventory, then you don't need them any longer, do you? You'd better let me have them, right?'

Bea wasn't so sure about handing them over to this precious pair. They might use the opportunity to clean the house out, and if they weren't going to inherit . . . no, she couldn't let them have the keys. Then she remembered where she'd left them, upstairs in her dressing-table drawer. 'I have a set back at the office. I'll be happy to hand them over to you when you've paid my bill and I'm clear in my mind as to who now owns the house.'

'What? Hand them over, now!' Tom was getting aggressive.

Bea spread her hands. 'I'm sorry. They're at the office.'

'But if we don't have the keys . . .'

If they didn't have the keys, they couldn't lay their hands on anything to bring in some much-needed cash. Consternation!

Bea gathered her things together and stood up. 'You know where to find me, when you've taken advice from your solicitor.'

Neither man moved to show her out, so she stepped ahead of them to the door. She felt, rather than saw something swish past her shoulder, and turned in shock to see the older man helping his son to his feet. Mr Frasier was wheezing again.

'Sorry,' he huffed. 'My son slipped. Can you see yourself out?'

Tom had slipped all right. He'd aimed a blow at Bea, but had been pushed aside by his father. The look Tom sent Bea was enough to convince her that she'd better wear chain mail next time she was in his vicinity.

She walked with unsteady steps to the front door, and let herself out. The fresh air revived her a little. She leaned against the front door, recovering. The cat sat up and blinked – or winked? – enormous yellow eyes at her. A tiny slip of pink tongue appeared and disappeared. The cat said, 'Yow?'

In other words, Are you going to feed me now she's gone?

Bea said, 'You'd better find someone else to look after you, or you're for the chop.'

Still shaken, she found her car keys, used the remote to unlock the doors and started the engine. There was a chill wind blowing, so she put the heater on. Two black ears and two large eyes appeared over the window. The cat was taking her at her word.

'Get in, then,' said Bea, opening the door. The cat obliged, curling up in the foot well on the passenger side.

I suppose, if we never get any money for the work we've done, we can console ourselves with the cat.

The engine was playing up. Bother. More expense. When she stopped at the traffic lights, the noise of the engine grew louder. Whatever was wrong with it?

She laughed. It wasn't the engine. It was the cat, purring.

As she stepped over the carpet into the hall proper, Bea wondered why she'd always thought of hell as freezing cold and quiet. Hell wasn't like that, she thought. Hell was people shouting, drills grinding, hammers banging and a tranny blasting out the latest rap. Hell was dust and disaster.

She very nearly backed out of the house, got into her car, and drove away. Only, she couldn't do that for the cat had swayed over the carpet and disappeared into the kitchen. How did he know where the kitchen was?

Ah, Maggie had been cooking. Apart from the delicious smell of bacon, Bea could tell that Maggie was in because the radio was on in the kitchen, and the sound was at odds with the music – to call it by a polite name – which was coming up from the basement.

'Hey, there, missus!' The foreman that she'd spoken to yesterday hove into sight, red in the face from anger or exertion. 'Can I have a word?'

She followed him down the stairs, noting that the dust sheet was once again hitched up and not doing its job. Piers was nowhere to be seen, but he'd apparently been in earlier and upset the whole workforce, who were now determined to go on strike or botch it or something, because . . . at this point the plumber and the carpenter joined in, all speaking at once.

Apparently the foreman objected to Piers saying that something or other had been done with the wrong gauge of pipe. And the electrician said . . . and the plumber disagreed, and they were both going to walk off the job and not return till they'd been paid something on account. And, and, and.

Bea closed her eyes, mentally, to the mess around her, and calmed them all down, one by one. She knew little enough about gauges of piping and where the electrics ought to run, but she knew someone who did. She promised to send Maggie down to sort it all out, and went upstairs to look for her assistant.

The cat was ahead of her, sitting on the kitchen table between two large workmen . . . a different set from the ones she'd just dealt with down below, and different again from the ones she'd seen the previous day. The cat was turning his head from one man to the other, blinking enormous yellow eyes. Maggie was pouring out mugs of tea for the men, while talking on her mobile phone.

'Maggie, you're needed downstairs,' said Bea.

'One minute.' Maggie said, 'Ta-ra,' to whoever she was on

the phone to, and switched it off. 'Who's the little stranger, then, and how did it get in? Take it off the table, someone. Food preparation and cats don't mix.'

The cat raised one paw in tentative fashion, and the larger of the two workmen teased out a piece of bacon from his butty, and handed it over. The cat took it, delicately, and it disappeared. He lifted his paw, indicating he would like some more. He was charm incarnate. Bea's heart sank. Did she really want to take on a cat? No, and no. What's more, she agreed with Maggie that animals should never be allowed on work surfaces.

The larger of the two men turned a moon face to Bea. 'Is he yours, missus? What's his name?'

'I don't know. He's been thrown out of house and home, so I'll have to find someone to take him in.'

The large man picked the cat up and ran capable hands through the long fur till he located a name tag on a tatty, chewed up collar. 'Winston. Neutered. He's a bit of all right, isn't he? Hey, Winston? How're you doing? Like it here, do you?'

The cat licked the man's fingers. He laughed, set the animal down on the table, and said, 'Well, back to work. We got the tiles, missus. Did you see them? All right by you?' Maggie picked the cat up and put it down on the floor, clearing the work surface with one efficient movement. 'I'll be down in a sec, right?'

The two men disappeared, well fed and watered. Maggie wrung out her cloth. 'I don't mind cats, but not on the table. Oh, the tiles are not the ones you picked but they're OK, I think you'll like them. I'm going to have to make the plumber replace that bit of piping, Mr Piers was quite right, it's the wrong gauge, and the electrician's mate cut his hand quite badly this morning and has had to go to hospital, but I don't think there's much else. Mr Piers said he'd be back later if he could, but not to count on it.'

'The job you're doing down the road . . .?'

'I popped in there this morning, checked it out, no problems today, and I don't have to go back till tomorrow afternoon. Just as well; this lot need someone to hold their hands even to go to the lavvy.' Maggie had been crying recently, and even now was turning away so that Bea shouldn't see her face properly.

'Maggie, if something's bothering you—'

'Nothing's bothering me.' She was lying, but what could Bea do about it?

Maggie whisked herself away, and Bea heard her arguing with the foreman downstairs. Bea switched off the radio. It reduced the noise level, somewhat.

Where could she go for a bit of a think? The sitting room was under another film of dust, but luckily the sheets seemed to be keeping the furniture reasonably clean. No Max. Goodie.

Miss Brook was working in Bea's bedroom, of course. She was on the phone, dealing with a query in her usual efficient manner. Bea ascertained in sign language that Miss Brook did not need her to sort out any queries for the time being.

Oliver was beavering away in the guest room. There was no sign of Max, and his things had been neatly put in piles on the bed. Presumably Maggie had been in there, too, since Oliver – despite chivvying from Maggie – still didn't understand the principle of putting once-worn clothes away.

'All right?' Bea enquired of the back of Oliver's head. He nodded, without turning his eyes from his screen.

Bea felt a sudden chill sweep across her shoulders. It wasn't that the window had been pushed up an inch or so. She didn't know what it was. Ah, was it that Oliver usually turned to speak to her when she intruded on his territory, and this time he hadn't done so? Something had upset Oliver?

'No problems,' he said, still not turning round. 'The morning post's in with Miss Brook. Nothing we can't handle between us. Maggie's on about having the floorboards stripped and polished. I think maybe she's right. It's a bit dark down there and lighter floors would make sense. Anyway, there's been no more calls about the car, and everything in the garden's lovely.'

He didn't sound as if he thought it were lovely. He sounded . . . she hesitated . . . angry?

He said, 'I can cope.'

Now what did he mean by that? Something had upset him, but he could cope with whatever it was? A communication from his estranged father, perhaps? A copy of his birth certificate which proved he was – or was not – his adopted mother's child?

The back of his neck insisted that he wanted to be left alone, so Bea left, closing the door behind her.

What next? If she went up to the top floor, there would be nowhere she could sit and think, since that was where Oliver and Maggie had their rooms.

It wasn't fine enough to sit out in the garden.

Well, she could go to visit the second Mrs Kent, Damaris's mother. Perhaps she would like to take the cat?

Bea got the phone number from her paperwork, and rang. Yes, Gail was at home and would give her a few minutes. Bea thought of taking the cat with her, but Winston was nowhere to be seen.

How could he have vanished? The doors from the kitchen and living room were firmly shut and locked at the moment. Perhaps the cat had sneaked out when one of the workmen had gone out to fetch a tool or the tiles or whatever from their van? Bea shrugged. The noise was giving her a headache. There was nothing for her to do that Oliver and Miss Brook and Maggie couldn't do better, so she might just as well make herself scarce.

Gail lived in a flat in a quiet road running parallel to a busy High Street in West London. Everything about the place said that this was a well-maintained block for residents who were decorously behaved and of sufficient means. The landscaping was harmonious, the paintwork fresh, the entrance hall attractively furnished and sparklingly clean.

Altogether a far cry from the depressed looking Frasier residence.

Bea announced herself on the speakerphone and was let in. The lift was in working order, and purred as it took its occupant to the top floor. Gail was waiting for her there, and ushered her into a light and airy sitting room.

Bea saw that Mr Frasier's comment about Gail had been wrong; the woman had suffered, was suffering from her daughter's death. She was becomingly dressed in a fine wool fawn trouser suit, her hair and make-up had been carefully done, but she looked haggard. The grey marks under her eyes were more pronounced, and she seemed to have lost weight. At least her hands were not trembling today.

Bea had forgotten that the last time she had met Gail, Bea had been dressed 'down' to play a part. Today Bea was wearing a sage-green skirt and paler-green silk shirt, with a tan leather jacket over all. Her hair was in its usual smooth style, with the fringe brushed sideways across her forehead, and her make-up – though discreet – made the most of her fine eyes and good skin. She'd even struggled into her best tan boots. Today Bea looked what she was; a successful business woman.

Gail narrowed her eyes. 'I'm sorry, but who are you, exactly?'

Bea gave her one of the agency cards. 'I must apologize. Mrs Frasier made certain assumptions and perhaps foolishly, I went along with what she expected to see . . .' Bea explained how she'd been drawn into the business. 'Mrs Frasier told us she wanted the agency to prepare an inventory of the house and to take care of any phone calls there might be about selling Mr Kent's car. We finished the inventory but needed more instructions from her when we heard . . . I am so sorry. Coming so soon after the other . . .'

Gail cut Bea off with a wave of her hand. 'My daughter and I were not that close.'

'A horrible thing to happen, though.'

Gail inclined her head. She started to speak, then stopped herself. 'You wanted to see me?'

'You asked if I could find out when and where Matthew's funeral would take place. I left a message on the phone for you. Did you get it?'

Gail inclined her head again. 'Thank you. It appears I have to arrange for my daughter's funeral as well. My son-in-law is not . . . not well able to . . .'

'Understood. I visited him this morning. I don't want to add to your problems, but have you any idea what ought to be done about the cat, Winston? Mr Frasier said he would have him put down, but I wondered if you . . .' She looked around at the impeccable modern furniture, and guessed what the answer would be.

'I'm sorry, no. I'm on the top floor here, as you see, and I've never particularly cared for cats. Matthew gave him to Damaris as a kitten. I think she loved that cat far more than she ever loved me.' Gail closed her eyes for a moment. She was very pale under the make-up. 'What an epitaph for a daughter! I think I must still be in shock.'

Bea looked around. 'Would you like me to make you a cup of tea?'

Gail sighed, and let herself down on to a modernistic chair

which for all its angles, seemed comfortable enough. 'Do take a seat. No, I don't want any tea. I didn't sleep much last night. I had to confirm that it was Damaris at the . . .' She put the back of her hand to her forehead. 'Stupid of me.' She started to laugh, and stopped herself. 'No hysterics. No regrets. No looking back.'

Bea said, 'It's the "might have been" that does it. You think, if only . . .'

'Yes. If only. Not that it would have made any difference to my relationship with Damaris. She was always a cold fish. Rejected me from the word go. I did love her, you know. Or rather, I loved her as much as she would let me. She loved Matthew more than she loved me, and I think she loved that cat more than she loved either of us.' She stopped, putting the back of her hand to her mouth, and biting on it.

'Matthew was another "might have been"?'

A shrug. 'There have been other men in my life. I might have married again, if I'd wanted to, but Matthew was different. If only I hadn't been so set on climbing the career ladder. If only he'd been able to cut down his work load. But there . . . crying over spilt milk . . . stupid, stupid! I did love him, you know.'

Bea nodded. She'd worked that out already.

Gail got up, jerkily. 'Care for a drink?'

Bea shook her head. 'I'm driving. Forgive me, but when did you last eat?'

Gail began to laugh and this time didn't stop. She leaned over the back of an immaculate white leather settee, until her hair touched its cushions. She retched, and laughed, and coughed. And eventually stopped. She stood upright and smoothed back her hair. Tears smudged her mascara. 'Eat something? I've been throwing up ever since I heard.'

'If you can't eat anything, you must drink. Water? Tea?'

Gail reached for her handbag. 'I suppose I should try. I fancy I could keep down a basic spaghetti, and perhaps a glass of red wine. There's an Italian restaurant nearby. Come with me? My treat. Take my mind off things.'

The restaurant was small but not too noisy. The food was plentiful and what Piers would have termed 'rustic'. Basic, properly cooked, no frills. The wine was plonk but Bea had a glass, as did Gail.

Bea was hungry and did justice to her cannelloni, but Gail picked at her plate. They ate in silence, but over the coffee Bea asked if Gail had anyone who could stay with her for a while.

Gail shook back her hair. 'I don't have anyone really close since my best friend died of cancer last year. I don't know you from Adam, but I need to talk to someone and it might as well be you. And then I'll shut up for good. I've never seen the point of whining about the bad choices we make in life.'

'Agreed,' said Bea, who had made a bad choice when she married Piers, all those years ago. A bad choice at eighteen can affect your whole life.

'You think I'm a hard case, grieving more for the might-have-been with Matthew than for my daughter, but you see, she took after her father, who was a cold-eyed, manipulative bastard. I was twenty when I married him, stars in my eyes. My parents wanted me to wait, said I was too young, still doing my teacher training. I didn't listen, we had a big wedding, and then on the honeymoon . . .'

She looked down at her hands, adjusted the gold band she wore on the ring finger of her right hand. 'I got pregnant. He was horrified. It was too soon, he was too young, he wanted me to have an abortion. I refused so he beat me up. Oh, he promised never to do it again. We agreed to put the "incident" behind us, but I realized he wasn't what I'd thought him, that I'd made a terrible mistake. But I'd made my vows in church. I stayed.

'He expected me to produce a son, of course, so Damaris was a disappointment. He said that next time I'd surely be able to do the job properly and give him a son, but I never conceived again. He started to hit me again when Damaris was five. Not much. Not often. Damaris adored him, and each time he promised . . . but of course he didn't keep his promises. Only, when Damaris was seven, she ruined his favourite jacket with some indelible ink. It was an accident, but he backhanded her across the room.

'When he went off to work next morning I packed a rucksack with Damaris's toys and one suitcase, and went to a women's refuge. I was too afraid of him to stand my ground and tell him to get out. He divorced me for desertion, I rented a one bedroom flat, started all over again. Damaris hated me for taking her from her nice room and lovely toys and making her live in a flat over a shop. She'd heard him say often enough that everything was always my fault, that I wasn't a lovable person and she believed it.'

'You got maintenance?'

'A little for Damaris. I was only too happy to make a clean break, though I'd have preferred it if he'd kept in touch with Damaris. He chose not to. She wasn't an easy child. Just like her father, she'd work herself into a temper and lash out at anyone who got in her way. I loved teaching and was good at it. Things gradually improved and we'd moved into a housing association flat when I met Matthew and . . . pause for laughter . . . we fell in love, just like teenagers. Damaris was twelve and prickly, but he paid for her to go to a private school. She really liked that.'

'What went wrong?'

Gail looked into space. 'For a while it was wonderful. I'd never known anyone like Matthew, and Damaris loved having a daddy again. She's a mercenary little being, you know. *Was* a mercenary little being. She loved Matthew's house, his money, everything that he could provide for her. And he? He didn't have a mean bone in his body. He offered her unconditional love. He'd not had any children by his first wife and Damaris was a plus factor for him in our marriage.

'He adopted her formally, took out an insurance policy for her. She'd cuddle up to him on his big chair, giggle at his jokes, and coax him to give her . . . whatever it was she'd set her heart on. He spoilt her. She took advantage of his good nature, of course. She wasn't an academic; no patience. "So what?" he'd say. "Haven't I enough for the three of us?" I think perhaps I was jealous of the way she could get round him. She said I was, anyway. She said . . .' Gail bit her lip and looked away.

'She said Matthew had really only married me because he wanted a daughter. She said no one could really love me, because I wasn't lovable. Perhaps I wasn't . . . do you think we could have a brandy or something?'

'Not on top of the wine,' said Bea. 'Go on.'

'She told him I kept comparing him to my first husband who'd been so handsome and had such a brilliant job and came from a good family. Matthew's family weren't top drawer.

He wasn't particularly handsome and he was beginning to lose his hair, but he was really nice to look at and he was such a kind man. Women value kindness more than good looks, don't they?'

'Yes, they do,' said Bea, who had married twice and placed an equally high value on kindness.

'I stopped going to see him perform because . . . I had a dozen excuses; I was working hard, wanted to relax when I came home, which was when he was due to go out himself. Then he'd be away for a week or so at a time, working the clubs up in the north of England. He did a cruise once, and was asked to go again but said he preferred a home base. Damaris told him I was ashamed of what he did for a living, and perhaps he was right, perhaps I was a bit of a snob. When he taxed me with it, I shouted at him . . . stupid, stupid!

'The crunch came when Damaris told me she'd caught him cuddling that silly creature Goldie. He said he'd been comforting her over some family drama or other, but I wouldn't listen. I knew Goldie fancied him, and of course they had a lot in common. I lost the plot completely and stormed out.

'I didn't listen to Matthew when he begged me to return. He bought me this flat when we divorced. I didn't want maintenance. I was deputy head of my school by then and within a couple of years, I made head. Damaris imagined she could stay on with him after I left, but I could have told her that Goldie wouldn't hear of it, and of course she didn't. So Damaris had to move into this flat with me, hating me even more for . . . everything. Matthew continued to see her at frequent intervals; she got him to pay for her to go to college; a media studies course, would you believe. She was the little daughter he'd never had, remember? She's never been able to keep a job for long. Her temper always gets the better of her and she'll say something, do something, shout and throw things . . . it's tragic, really.

'When she fell pregnant with that all-time loser, Derek Frasier, Matthew paid for the wedding, gave her away, helped them out with the deposit on the house. As a matter of fact, I doubt if my beloved son-in-law would have gone through with it and married Damaris if he hadn't thought she was Matthew's real daughter and therefore due to inherit . . . oh, what does it matter now!'

'It matters,' said Bea, 'because Damaris seems to have willed Matthew's house away to a friend of hers. Someone called Cunningham.'

Gail clutched at the table with both hands and froze, her eyes blank. Then she made a dash for the toilet.

'Is that Marsh and Parsons, the estate agents? I've inherited a house just up the road from you and need to put it on the market straight away. A very desirable property, consisting of studio-cum-basement, large living room and spacious kitchen with a patio off it. On the first floor there are two bedrooms and a bathroom, and above that another bedroom and shower room with access to a roof garden. When can you meet me to value the property? I am not free tomorrow, unfortunately, but you may obtain a set of keys at any time from the Abbot Agency. Let me give you the address.'

Thirteen

Wednesday p.m.

Bea helped Gail out of the restaurant. 'You're ill. What's your doctor's telephone number?'

Gail leaned against the window of a newsagent's. 'It's a Wednesday, isn't it? The surgery's closed on Wednesday afternoons.'

'You'll get dehydrated if you go on like this. Suppose I take you to the Accident and Emergency department at the hospital?'

'I've been like this before. It wears off eventually. I've just thought of something that will help.' She went into the newsagent's, came out with a plastic bag which seemed to weigh heavily. She was wobbling a bit, but set off for the flats with Bea in tow. In the lift she leaned against the side, but managed to get her key into the door of her flat at the second attempt.

Bea hovered, not knowing what best to do.

Gail went into the kitchen with her purchase and came out pouring a can of Coca-Cola into a glass. It fizzed. Gail said, 'Works wonders on an upset stomach. Add a few more grains of sugar to kill off the bubbles. Goes down a treat, and stays down. Electrolytes? Something like that.' When the drink had stopped fizzing, she drank a few mouthfuls.

'I'm worried about you,' said Bea. 'Don't you have any family you can call?'

'No family, except son-in-law and grandson. Can you see either of them looking after me?'

'Friends? Someone to keep an eye on you for a bit?'

'Loads of acquaintances, people I play bridge with, people in the Flower Arranging Club, the other volunteers at the Homeless Families Centre. I'm the strong one they take all their troubles to. The people in the flat opposite are away. I don't know anyone else. I'll be all right.'

Bea shed her coat. 'Then I'd better stay for a bit, till I can be sure you're not going to be sick again. Because if you are, I'm taking you straight down to the hospital, understand?'

'Promises, promises.' But Gail managed half a smile. She sipped her drink, dropped into a chair, put her head back and closed her eyes. 'You said something about the Cunningham girl.' She gasped, sat upright, struggled with the urge to vomit, subdued it. Sank back again. 'Sorry. Useless.'

'Rest,' said Bea. 'Go to bed for a bit?'

'Can't sleep. Keep thinking.'

'Suppose I find you a nurse through the agency, someone to move in here, look after you for a couple of days? Otherwise you'll be featuring in a small paragraph in the local paper next week; retired teacher found dead in her flat.'

Gail spurted into a laugh. 'I'm not dying yet. I've got to change my will first. I left everything to Damaris, some idea of making it up to her because after all her high hopes, she ended up with such a miserable life.'

'What's wrong with her husband? Asthma, but what else?'

'Chronic self-indulgence. Betting on anything that moves. Oh, and bad cheques. That's what finally turned Matthew off them. The dear boy was stupid enough to forge Matthew's signature on a couple of cheques. Matthew honoured the cheques – which were for a sizeable amount – but said that in future he'd be giving Damaris only small presents in kind, and that if it happened again, he'd prosecute. Next birthday he gave her the kitten, and no cash.'

'Derek doesn't work, I take it. What sort of job did Damaris have?'

'Most recently she's been working in a shop in Kensington selling expensive trivia for people who have everything. It wouldn't have lasted. She's already had one row with the manageress, and no doubt she'll be asked to leave soon. I mean . . . would have been asked to . . . She took home the lolly and her menfolk spent it.'

Bea remembered the brand new television and the game that Tom had been playing with. Had they the money to pay for them? Probably not. And if they weren't going to get Matthew's house and they'd lost the breadwinner of the family, they were in real trouble.

Gail lay back with her eyes closed. 'I have a guest bedroom

always made up. Sometimes out-of-town friends stay over. Would you stay tonight? You, yourself? Not someone I don't know. I can't face anyone I don't know. I'd feel safe with you. I can pay.'

Bea grimaced, thinking of the chaos ruling back at home; the builders, the noise, the dust, the rubble . . . Maggie and her love troubles, Oliver and his birth certificate . . . Max and his two women. She ought to be back there, sorting everyone out, but Gail's need of her was greater, wasn't it?

She'd have to ring the office and let them know what was happening, ask Miss Brook to stay on at least one more day, leave messages for Max and for Piers. Then Maggie would have to bring some things over for her. 'Yes,' she said. 'I'll stay.'

Wednesday night

Gail managed not to be sick again. She even ate a piece of dry toast at supper time and kept it down. Bea microwaved herself something from Gail's freezer, and thought wistfully of Maggie's cooking.

Speaking to Oliver on the phone, Bea learned that the plumber had finished and the electrician only had a bit more to do. The floorboards were being laid back down, though some had needed to be replaced. The plasterer had done the reception room and would do the kitchen the next day. The tiler had finished.

Maggie was going out with a girl friend that evening, Max hadn't been seen or heard of all day, and Miss Brook had delivered an ultimatum – either the dust was banished from the house, or she would give in her notice.

'She doesn't mean that,' explained Oliver. 'She's enjoying being in charge, but it's true that the dust has got everywhere upstairs. Even in our bathroom up at the top. Maggie says she's going to get the Green Girls in to give us the once over every day till the dust's gone.'

'I'd forgotten. Is Florrie back yet? How are they coping without her to manage the team?'

'Florrie's still missing, but they're managing pretty well. There's a niece helping them out. There's nothing much in the post that Miss Brook or I can't cope with, and the builders have put a cat flap into the kitchen door so that Winston can get down into the garden when he wants to. He's a charmer, that one; the way he puts up one paw and blinks at you! Works a treat every time. Slept on my bed last night.'

Bea had forgotten about the cat. 'That's good.' It was good that Oliver had some comfort in his life. She feared that the information on the birth certificate had not been what he'd wanted to see, but she wouldn't raise the subject unless he did.

'Will you put Maggie on for a moment? I need her to bring one or two things over for me before she goes out for the evening. Tell her to take a taxi. I'll pay. I'll be back tomorrow morning. Ring me on the mobile if you need me.'

It was Gail who needed her in the night. The flat was quiet, being so high up and on a side road. The windows were double-glazed and central heating kept the rooms at a reasonable temperature. Gail said she didn't want to talk about anything disturbing that night, and would Bea care to play Scrabble, or watch television? They did both. Maggie delivered Bea's overnight bag before going out for the evening. Gail's guest bedroom was prettily furnished, and had an en suite shower room and toilet.

The two women went to bed early. Bea drifted off to sleep quickly enough, though it irritated her that she hadn't thought to ask Maggie to bring her bible over. She'd grown accustomed to reading a chapter every night, and without it she felt restless, almost guilty. But she did sleep, lightly. Once or twice she woke and found herself listening for the sound of Gail moving around, but there was nothing . . . till at three she shot upright in bed, only half awake. Had the flush of the toilet woken her? Was Gail all right?

No, of course Gail wasn't. Bea blinked. Was that a streak of light she could see under her bedroom door? Yes. Gail must have left her bedroom and moved into the living room.

Bea was feeling tired, draggingly tired. The last thing she wanted was to get out of bed, pull on her jacket – Maggie had forgotten her dressing gown but anyway it was probably covered with dust by now – and bedroom slippers, and try to comfort a grieving widow. Because that was how she'd come to think of Gail. Not as an ex-wife, but as a widow. *Dear Lord, do I have to?*

Yes, you do. You know you do. You'll be all right. Give her my love.

That made Bea giggle. If she went out there and said to Gail, 'God sends his love,' whatever would Gail think?

Bea stumbled out of bed, found her slippers and jacket, and went out to join her hostess. Only one small side lamp had been switched on. Gail had drawn back the curtains and was standing at the window looking out on to the night sky. The moon was up. Some stars. Not many. Light pollution rules in London town.

'Are you all right?'

'I haven't been sick again, if that's what you mean.' Gail sipped something from a mug she was holding in both hands. 'Hot lemon and honey. Want some? No? My brain is sluggish and I can't concentrate. Perhaps that's just as well because I keep getting such weird ideas. I know I'm not thinking straight. I tell myself I'll make sense of it all in the morning. People are always doing stupid things; things out of character, I mean. Life isn't neat. We can't always understand why things happen the way they do.'

She put the empty mug down. 'I'd like to talk it all through with you tomorrow, if I may. Then perhaps I can draw a line under it.'

Bea put her arm around Gail's shoulders. 'God sends his love.'

Gail's shoulders went rigid. She turned her head to Bea, her mouth working. 'He loved that church, so why . . .?' Tears came, at long last. She wept, clinging to Bea, who hugged her close, patting her on the back, saying, 'There, there.'

When at last her tears dried up, Bea urged Gail back to bed and tucked her in, 'Sleep now. We'll talk tomorrow.'

Thursday morning

Bea didn't feel up to much next morning. Gail didn't talk at breakfast, either, but switched on a big television to hear the news while she cleared away yesterday's newspapers and topped up the water in the flower vases. Bea was standing at the big window, looking at the low clouds which foretold more rain, when a familiar word spoken by a newscaster caught her attention.

'. . . waiting for you on your return, Mr Abbot?'

What was that? Bea turned to look at the screen. Not her son, surely!

Gail exclaimed, 'Abbot? Any relation?'

Bea held up her hand to stop Gail speaking, while on the screen appeared the front door of her own house, with Max standing on the doorstep. He had a bandage rather becomingly arranged around his head, and a black eye. Max? Whatever . . .?

'. . . I was visiting my mother and I'm afraid he got me just as I was pulling out my keys to get in. Hit me from behind, so I didn't see him. The next thing I knew, I was lying on my back in the garden, my coat open, my keys, mobile and wallet gone. Also my laptop.'

'Let's get this clear? You lost your laptop with important Government information on it?'

'Everything's password protected, naturally. As a Member of Parliament, I'm always very careful about what I put on my laptop. I don't suppose he had any idea who I was. It was an opportunist burglar, waiting for anyone with a laptop to come back to his house in the dark. I shall offer a reward for its return.'

'He took your keys to get into the house. Did he steal any official paperwork from there?'

'No, no.' A grimace for a smile. 'It seems he tripped over the carpet when he got into the hall – we've got the builders in and the house is at sixes and sevens. When he fell, he dropped my keys, which was fortunate. A couple of my mother's guests were just returning from an evening out, saw what was happening, had the wits to phone the police straight away. So the man only had the chance to poke around the ground floor before the police car arrived. Unfortunately he eluded them by getting out of the back door and making his getaway across the garden wall.'

The picture switched back to the interviewer, who said something sharp about yet another laptop going missing with government secrets on it and then the picture changed to that of the newsreaders, talking about the prospects for a big sporting event that weekend.

Gail used the remote to kill the picture. 'They should have rung you.'

Bea was scrabbling in her handbag. 'He doesn't look badly hurt. I'm an idiot. I must have switched my mobile off after I'd talked to Maggie last night. They should have rung you, though. They knew where I was.' She punched her home number in, held the phone to her ear.

Gail said, 'You'll want to get back as quickly as possible.'

'Yes, but . . . are you going to be all right now?' Bea ran to the bedroom, bundling her overnight things together. Why didn't someone pick up the phone?

Gail said, 'Of course I'll be all right.'

Bea wasn't so sure. Why didn't someone pick up? She killed the call, listened to two voicemail messages, one from Oliver and the other from Max, saying there'd been an incident at the house but not to worry, Max hadn't been badly hurt. Bea tried Maggie's mobile.

Maggie answered with a cautious, 'Hello?'

'It's me. I'm on my way back. Are you all right? What did the police say?'

'Thank goodness. We were trying to reach you, but your phone must have been switched off. The police were here till ever so late but they've gone now, only there's reporters on the doorstep and they're ringing us all the time wanting to talk to Mr Max about losing government papers because there's been a couple of cases recently where they have gone missing and—'

'Yes, I know all about that. Is Max all right?'

Oliver took over the phone. 'Is that you, Mrs Abbot? Mr Max is fine. He's in the living room, giving an interview to some journalist or other. Mrs Max called to ask if he were all right, but he was on the other phone and missed her. That Lettice woman rang, too – at least, we think it was her, but he's said we're to field all his calls and so we just took her phone number and I don't know if he rang her back or not. It's a nuisance about him losing the laptop but at least he's still got all his credit cards.'

'Didn't the thief take his wallet?'

'He took the money out and abandoned it by the front door, leaving all the cards. Not a professional, one assumes. Oops, that's the doorbell again. We have to answer it in case it's the builders . . .'

His voice faded, and Maggie came back on. 'The builders are enjoying it no end, there's seven of them here today, would you believe! Falling over one another they are. Plus the Green Girls, who are rolling up the dust like nobody's business.'

'Maggie, stop! Nobody's mentioned the alarm. Wasn't it switched on?'

Silence. 'We think . . . we're not sure . . . Mr Max was still here when we went out last night. He had someone with him. Oliver did remind him about the alarm when we left, but . . . no, it wasn't ringing when we got back and found the circus in progress.'

Bea digested this in silence. So Max had left the house with the alarm off when he went out for the evening. Ouch!

Maggie was subdued. 'We didn't say anything about it to the police. Was that right?'

Bea sighed. 'Yes, of course.'

'Will you be in for lunch?'

'I'll be there as soon as I can.'

Bea switched the phone off, picked up her overnight bag and checked she hadn't left anything behind. She found Gail standing by the window, looking out into space. 'Gail, I don't like to leave you here by yourself and we haven't had our talk yet. It's chaos back at the office but I expect we can find a corner somewhere if you'd like to come back with me.'

Gail turned her head to look at Bea, her expression remote. 'You won't want to be bothered now.'

'Fantastical thoughts are catching. I've just had one and need to test it out on someone who knows what's going on. So, come with me?'

'I've never liked fantasy.' Gail picked up her handbag and collected a coat from the hallway.

As Bea had forecast, her house was in chaos.

A television van was parked outside, and a reporter was speaking into a camera in the front garden. Two other men with cameras were hanging around, waiting for someone to appear from the house? Bea slid her car into a vacant space, making sure that her residents' parking permit was properly displayed. She hoped the parking warden might be round soon, and ticket the television van . . . although the company was probably used to it and regarded parking fines as part and parcel of everyday life. Several neighbours were out on the other side of the road, clustering to ask one another what the fuss was all about. The blinds were drawn at all the windows of her house. Bea got out her front door key.

She advised Gail, 'Take a deep breath, answer no questions.' Head down, the two women charged up the path, pushing their way between the journalists . . . and slipped in at the front door.

'Mind the carpet,' said Bea, a fraction too late.

Gail picked herself up, and dusted herself down. 'A nice burglar trap.'

Oliver appeared in the door to the kitchen, with Maggie peering over his shoulder. They were both sizzling with excitement.

From the living room came Max's sonorous voice, declaiming his undying loyalty to the party and the impossibility of anyone decoding anything on his stolen laptop. From upstairs came the whine of the vacuum cleaner and the voice of Miss Brook saying 'No comment' to someone on the phone. From the depths rose the head of not one but two of the building team, not wanting to miss a trick.

Miss Townend appeared in the doorway to the living room, bearing a tray containing used coffee cups and an empty cafetière. She looked unusually flushed. Bea could imagine her turning up on the doorstep determined to 'protect Mr Max, no matter what'. Seeing Bea, she said, 'Mr Max was wondering where you were. May we have some more coffee, please?' She handed the tray to Bea and disappeared back into the living room.

The Green Girls clattered down the stairs, bringing their vacuum and dusters with them. Yvonne, their temporary leader, said, 'What a carry on, eh, Mrs Abbot? We done what we could, but it'll all be needing doing again tomorrow. Got to get a move on. Fitting this job in is taking some doing, right?'

'Right,' said Bea. 'And, many thanks, Yvonne. I don't know what we'd have done without you. No word from Florrie? Hm. But you're coping, otherwise, right?'

The foreman of the builders gave a little cough. 'Can I have a word, missus?'

Maggie took the tray off Bea and told the builder to behave himself. 'I told you, Mrs Abbot doesn't want to be bothered with your nonsense today.' And to Bea, 'He's got a young wife he thinks needs watching, but I told him, the Abbot Agency doesn't do divorce – or murder.'

'Quite right, too, Maggie,' said Bea. 'Now—'

The living-room door opened and a journalist backed out, only to fall over the carpet, landing on his back, winded. Max said, 'Let me give you a hand up,' and also ended up sprawled on the floor. The phone rang. Someone answered it. The front doorbell rang. Miss Brook called down from the landing, 'That woman's been on the phone again, Mr Max. She says you know the number. Will you kindly inform her that this phone is not for your use.'

Miss Townend appeared in the doorway. 'Oh, Mr Max, don't forget that you've got to ring the Chief Whip's office.'

Gail found a safe place to stand, leaned against the wall and began to laugh.

Max shot the journalist out, banged the door to in the face of whoever it was outside, and said, 'Really, Mother! Where have you been?'

'Attending to my own business, Max. Are you all right? Have you had that knock on the head looked at by a doctor?'

'I spent an hour in Accident and Emergency last night. They wanted to keep me in overnight, but I discharged myself. I'm all right, I tell you.'

'Is the stuff on your laptop really important?'

'Of course it's important!'

'No, but I mean, is it really important. "Important" as in affecting your career? Or just inconvenient?'

He deflated. Suddenly looked tired. His black eye wasn't helping, either. 'It's important.'

Bea gestured him to follow her into the living room. 'Max, what about the alarm? Why didn't you put it on when you left last night?'

'I forgot. I had a visitor, and things got a trifle heated.'

'Lettice?'

He gestured in surrender. 'There's no need to go on at me. I realized straight away, as soon as I came to myself. One moment's stupidity and my career's ruined.'

'Not ruined, dear. Just blighted. Let's hope it's only temporary.' She left him to it.

Gail was still in the hall, blowing her nose and wiping her eyes. Tears of amusement this time. 'Is your life always like this?'

'In spots, yes. Oliver, Maggie; before we go any further, did the intruders get upstairs?'

Oliver whistled. 'Now how did you know there were two

of them? No, they pulled out every drawer in the living room and emptied the contents on the floor. They upended Miss Townend's files, got into the kitchen and took everything off that little rack where Maggie keeps the household keys. And that's it. They didn't go upstairs.'

'Fine. Now, since the living room seems to be out of bounds, let's all go into the kitchen and bring one another up to date.'

Winston was sitting in the middle of the table. Maggie picked him up, kissed the top of his head and put him on the floor. Bea held out her hand to Gail, urging her to join them in the kitchen, but that lady hung back.

'You won't want—'

'You're in this up to your neck, Gail. Come and meet the crew. Don't let their comparative youth put you off. They're as bright as buttons, if not brighter. Oliver here is a computer whizz-kid; it was he who discovered where the funeral's going to be, and he helped me do the inventory up at Matthew's house. Maggie can keep more plates spinning in the air than Houdini . . . that is, if Houdini ever spun plates. Anyway, I suggest you hear their story before you form any judgement upon their discretion.'

'What story?' Oliver was grinning.

Maggie produced mugs, put ground coffee into a clean cafetière, and poured on boiling water. 'Start at the beginning, Oliver – and don't let that cat get back on to the table. Is everyone going to be in for lunch, by the way? Home-made soup, bread and cheese do you?' She started chopping vegetables and throwing them into a big pan.

Oliver said, 'It was like this. Maggie was a bit down so I went with her to check on the job she's project-managing down the road. And yes, we reminded Mr Max that the alarm wasn't on when we left, didn't we, Maggie? He'd come back a while before with that woman who keeps ringing him, not his wife, but the other one. They were having a right to and fro in the living room, so I popped my head around the door to tell them we were going out, and not to forget about the alarm—'

'But we think he must have,' said Maggie.

'That's about it,' said Oliver. 'After Maggie had checked on her job I took her to the gym where I introduced her to a couple of my friends and we got chatting, you know how it is, so we were a bit late getting back. About half ten. As we walked back along the road, we saw there was a light on in the living room next door, but the blinds weren't down and the curtains hadn't been drawn. We knew you were away, but we thought Mr Max might have gone in there and not bothered about the curtains—'

'Until we fell over him in the garden, at the top of the stairs to the basement,' said Maggie. 'I checked and he was still alive, which we thought at first he might not be—'

'He was lying on his back, sort of snoring. Out cold. His coat was open and it looked like he'd been mugged and robbed but we could see into the living room, and there was this man in black with a funny sort of blurred face—'

'A stocking or tights over his head, just like in the old films—'

'And he was shouting – we could hear him, faintly – and another man came to join him and they were opening drawers and throwing Miss Townend's files about. One was tall and thin, the other short and stocky. We could see them quite clearly through the window. So I got out my mobile and rang for the police and an ambulance, and we argued about what to do but I wouldn't let Maggie dash in to interrupt them in case she got hurt, too—'

'But I couldn't let them steal anything and get away with it, so I rang the front doorbell, and Oliver rang the landline phone in here. I was looking through the letterbox though Oliver told me not to, and I saw them both come out of the living room, colliding in the doorway, it was really funny to watch, and then they shouted to get out through the kitchen. Only Winston must have been sitting on the table here – I'm sorry to say he gets up on it as soon as my back's turned – and I heard one of them shriek something about "That something cat!" so I suppose Winston scratched him in passing.'

'Bully for you, Winston,' said Bea, on to whose lap Winston had climbed. 'Know your enemies, right? So you waited for the police to come before you went in, right?'

'Well, sort of.' Oliver wriggled. 'When we heard the back door slam, we let ourselves in and saw Mr Max's wallet lying on the carpet. No money, but they'd left the credit cards.'

'But no laptop or mobile,' sighed Maggie. 'Then the police came, and the ambulance. We made a statement, but we didn't say anything about the alarm because Mr Max looked totally shattered. Oliver went with Mr Max to the hospital, and brought him back in a taxi about three o'clock. The police said they'd come back again this morning, which they did, and somehow the press got hold of it, and . . . well, that's it, roughly.'

Bea sipped coffee, half closing her eyes. She knew where the laptop and mobile were. At least, she could guess. 'Do you know what they were looking for?'

Oliver shrugged. 'The police thought . . . opportunity knocks. Mr Max had his keys in one hand, laptop in the other, snatch one, look for things that might be picked up quickly.'

Maggie said, 'Casserole for supper, I thought. And I might make a couple of Victoria sandwiches for tea. What did they want with my household keys?'

'Indeed,' said Bea. 'I suspect that they were after the keys to Matthew's house, which I'd tucked into a drawer upstairs in my bedroom. Luckily you disturbed them before they got upstairs. Oh, is Miss Brook coping all right?'

'Of course. Enjoying it, in a way. But I suggest you arm yourself with a cast-iron shield before you speak to her. Miss Brook is "not in the habit of having to deal with people who are careless enough to lose their laptops on their very doorsteps". I quote.'

Maggie was wide-eyed. 'Mrs Abbot, do you mean that you know who the burglars were?'

'I can guess.' She shot a look at Gail, who was staring into space with an appalled look on her face.

Maggie crashed dishes. 'Who is it? Oughtn't we to tell the police?'

Oliver grinned. 'They weren't professionals or they'd have taken his credit cards. Not professionals, but after keys. I wonder. The only place Mrs Abbot has been recently – apart from last night – was to Mrs Frasier's. It must be her husband and son who came after the keys. Right? Can I come with you?'

Gail shot to her feet. 'Where's the . . .?'

'Out here,' said Bea, guiding her to the ground-floor cloakroom, and shutting the door behind her. She heard Gail retch, but at least she didn't actually throw up. In a few minutes she was out, looking pale, but composed. She said, 'You think the intruders came for the keys to Matthew's house, but took the laptop and mobile because they failed to win first prize?

If it was my son-in-law who burgled this place last night, then I don't mind if you do tell the police.'

'I would, if it weren't for the fact that I think Max has every right to be worried about what's on the laptop. Hold on a moment, while I ring the Frasiers.'

She found the number, and let the phone ring. Were they not going to answer? The phone rang and rang. Bea could imagine the Frasier house, with its already neglected air.

Finally, someone picked up. 'Ugh? 'Lo? Who's that?' Tom, the teenager.

'This is Mrs Abbot. I'm coming round this afternoon to pick up the laptop and mobile. Be there, right?'

'Dunno what you're talking about . . .' He sounded more awake this time.

'About three o'clock.'

'We don't have a—'

'Oh, I think you do. So don't try selling them or tampering with them in any way, or it'll be Special Branch visiting your house this evening. Do you understand?'

Silence. The phone went dead.

'Cross fingers,' said Bea. 'Although a prayer or two might help. Gail, my dear, you're looking peaky. You ought to go somewhere nice and quiet and see if you can doze for a while. I'm going to take you right up to the top of the house and you can doss down in Maggie's room till it's time for lunch. All right?'

Gail tried to smile. 'You must think me a poor sort of creature.'

'I think you're doing just fine.'

Bea settled Gail upstairs and came down again, thinking that she'd better find out what sort of reward Max was prepared to offer for the return of his possessions.

The figures didn't add up. There must be a way to get some money in, somehow. Matthew's car? No one seemed to know where it was. If only Damaris hadn't been so anxious to get an inventory done, it would have been easy to whip something out of the house to sell. As it was . . .

She'd like to do something cruel to that solicitor, telling her she couldn't touch anything for at least six weeks. He'd even asked her for her keys to the house! The nerve of the man! If only she'd thought quickly enough, she would have chosen another solicitor to prepare Damaris's will . . . only Damaris would have baulked at that.

The new owners of the house she'd always called home were agitating, wanting to move in. In a way, she'd be glad to walk away from the place, but . . . where was she to go? Sit and wait for a council flat? She'd have to move into a B&B somewhere for the time being. This was not what she'd planned, not at all.

Fourteen

Thursday afternoon

Max goggled at Bea. 'You think you know where my things are? You can't! Don't be ridiculous! How could you? Impossible!'

Bea had excluded Miss Townend from the room while she talked to Max, but now the dear woman tapped on the door. 'Mr Max? There's another journalist at the door.'

'Let them wait, Max,' said Bea. 'Now, listen. This is important. To a certain extent you've brought this on yourself by forgetting about the alarm, but I don't want that momentary lapse to ruin your career. As I said, I may be able to get your laptop and mobile back for you this afternoon. If I can, what reward are you offering?'

He gasped. 'What? You're asking me for money to—?'

Bea set her teeth. Miss Townend was tapping at the door again, raising her voice. 'Mr Max, it's urgent!'

Bea exercised patience. 'No, I would spend it on drink. Be your age, Max. I may need to recompense the burglars. So, how much?'

He called out, 'In a minute, Miss Townend.' There was a sheen of sweat on his forehead. 'Mother, this is not some childhood game. This is serious. Whatever bee you've got in your bonnet, I'm not playing, and I'm amazed that you should think I would.'

'Very well, Max. I'll give them something out of my own pocket, and get it back from you by way of rent for your room. All right?'

'No, it isn't all right! I can't believe we're having this conversation. You can't possibly know how to stop these people blackmailing me—'

'Ah. Someone has already phoned you, asking for money?'

He closed his mouth. 'No, of course not.'

She could always tell when he was lying. Oh. Dear. Someone had. It was either an outsider, a chancer who'd learned that Max had lost his laptop and was making a bid to cash in, or one of the Frasiers. Derek, probably. It was right up his street.

'Max, promise me one thing. Don't pay anybody anything till I've had a go at sorting it out myself. This afternoon I'm going to see some people who may be able to help and if so, I shall phone you with the good news about, say, four o'clock. If I fail, I'll be back before five and then obviously you must let the police deal with the burglars.'

His eyes went all round the room as he calculated the odds . . . and decided she didn't know what she was talking about. 'Mother, you are right out of your depth on this one.' He lifted his hand to prevent her saying any more and, taking her by the elbow, manoeuvred her out of the room and into the hall. 'Suppose you go and do something useful like fixing someone up with a nanny, and let me deal with this. Now, Miss Townend . . .?'

Bea seethed. Of all the idiots!

Miss Brook was hovering at the top of the stairs. 'Mrs Abbot. A word?'

Now what? Miss Brook was making it clear that she was not going to come down the stairs to Bea, so Bea had to mount the stairs to her. With an effort, Bea kept her voice calm. 'Yes, Miss Brook?'

'There's a person been on the phone from an estate agency, checking that you have the keys to a house that's just been put on the market. Apparently the agency need the keys from you, in order to show people around. I told them I would speak to you about it and get back to them . . . when and as I can get the use of the phone again!'

Bea's legs folded up under her and she sank down on her bed, hands to forehead. Ms Cunningham wasn't wasting any time, was she? Well, if she really had inherited the house, then she would need to get a valuation on it for probate purposes. But surely it was too early to put it on the market, or to show people around? The agency wouldn't know that, of course. They would have taken Lily's instructions at face value.

Bea pulled open her dressing-table drawer, and checked that Matthew's keys were still there. They were. She shut the drawer again. What to do now? Pray?

Dear Lord, here's a how-de-do. Everyone wants the keys, and I haven't a clue who they really belong to. If it's Lily, then surely it's not right that she should put the house on the market before probate is granted? Why, Matthew's funeral isn't going to be held till tomorrow, and as for Damaris's . . .? This whole thing has got way out of hand.

So, take it one step at a time.

'Miss Brook, if the agency rings again, tell them there may be a problem about the title to the house, and that I'll get back to them when and if it gets sorted out. That should make them wary of Ms Cunningham and her claim to ownership.'

Miss Brook's nostrils quivered. 'Very well, but how I am supposed to carry on the work of this agency without a telephone, I do not know. If Mr Max is proposing to move in here, we will need an extra landline. And now I have you here, would you care to cast your eye over one or two matters . . . nothing urgent . . . but I need your signature on this letter here, and on this. With your permission, young Oliver can bank the cheques which have come in.'

Bea dealt with everything, her mind distracted by different scenarios. She was pretty sure that Max had already been contacted by someone with blackmail in mind, and that he'd promised to pay whatever was demanded to get his laptop back. She guessed that he'd lied through his teeth when he'd said everything on his laptop was password-protected. She, his own mother, wouldn't have thought he'd have been technically up to it.

Max didn't believe she could sort things out for him as she'd always done when he was younger. Max was entranced by a vision of himself as an important man of affairs and Member of Parliament, and Members of Parliament didn't get their mothers to help them out when they got into trouble. Perhaps, thought Bea, parliament might be a lot better run if they did!

Max, of course, didn't know about the Frasiers and what they might really have been after when they mugged him and took his keys to get into the house. Would Max believe her if she did tell him? Well, possibly. On the other hand – a nasty thought – it might be that she'd got it all wrong, and that the Frasiers were as innocent as newborn babies. It wasn't likely, of course. But it was possible.

If only she could stop the blackmailer from contacting Max till she'd dealt with the Frasiers!

Bea had a sneaky idea. 'Miss Brook, it seems to me that you have first call on the telephone line here. I can't physically throw my son out of the house, but I might be able to get him to think about going somewhere else, if I could stop him getting incoming calls on this phone. May I suggest that you commandeer it? Use it as much as you like. I'm sure you must have a backlog of calls to make, if my son has been using it all morning. When you finish one call, why not keep the phone off the hook till you need to use it again?'

Miss Brook raised one eyebrow, considering Bea's suggestion. She took the phone off the hook and left it there. They could both hear Max quacking into it. The call ended. Max put his receiver down. Miss Brook didn't. There was a tight smile on her face. 'Of course, it's not foolproof. If he were quick enough, he might be able to take an incoming call before I could get to it.'

'I have an idea about that. So, may I leave the matter in your capable hands?'

'Certainly, Mrs Abbot.'

'Thank you, Miss Brook.'

Bea took herself down the stairs and walked into the living room, undeterred by Max's frown. Max's colour was poor. His blood pressure must be going through the roof. He ought to cut down his intake of alcohol and take more exercise. Fat chance.

Before he could object to her presence in her own living room she said, 'I have to check, see if the burglar stole anything from here last night. He turned out all the drawers, I gather?'

Miss Townend warbled, 'Oh, Mrs Abbot, there was such a mess, you wouldn't believe, but I put everything back as far as I could, and he didn't take any of your pretty little china pieces, or the silver thimbles from the cabinet.'

'Why, thank you, Miss Townend. You relieve my mind. But I must just check for myself.' Max was busily trying to get a line clear on the phone. Bea said, 'Miss Brook has been complaining about an intermittent fault on the phone. I expect it will clear soon.' She pulled out drawers to check contents. Nothing had been stolen that she could see, but nothing was in its right place, either.

Max began to pace up and down. 'I'm expecting a very important phone call. Can't you tell that woman to get off the line?'

'She has her own work to do. Did you check that the key to the grille over the window was still in place? You know where it is, don't you? No, not behind that side of the curtain, Miss Townend. Max, would you show her . . .?'

Max went to look. Bea slid the volume control on the phone down to silent, and walked over to join them. 'The key's still there? Oh, that's a relief. I was just wondering what I'd do if he came back tonight and could get in this way.'

Max pontificated. 'You should have a security light fitted over the front door.'

'So I should. What a good idea. And a different alarm system, perhaps? Well, I must leave you two to get on.'

She left the room, closing the door softly behind her. If he didn't hear the phone ring, he wouldn't be able to take the call from the blackmailer. With luck. What next? A late lunch. She looked at her watch. Did she have time to hear Gail's story before she left for the confrontation with the Frasiers? She had a feeling that it was important.

With a bowl of Maggie's freshly-made vegetable soup inside her, Gail told what she knew.

'You wanted to know about Lily Cunningham. Well, she's the daughter of Matthew's long-time accompanist, Bert. Matthew and Bert were old friends and colleagues. Bert's an odd one. Bags of charm for those who could be of use to him, coldness for those who can't. Very thin, chain-smokes, drinks too much, earns his living as a session musician, arranging other people's songs, doing some accompanying . . . that is, till karaoke came in and did accompanists out of a job.

'He was Matthew's best man first time round; that was for Gerda, his first wife, the one who was killed in a railway accident. Matthew used to put work Bert's way when he could, never heard a word against him. Bert didn't like me, of course. I wasn't his sort. He told Matthew I wouldn't last and of course he was right. Bert liked Goldie, though. Oh well . . .

'Bert never married, but he had women move in with him now and then, sometimes for months at a time, sometimes for only a few weeks. One of them presented him with a daughter, Lily, and then ran off with a much younger man, never to be heard of again. I felt sorry for Bert. A little. He was never convinced that Lily was his daughter.

'So there was Bert, bringing up Lily with the occasional help of his live-in girlfriends. Poor little scrap. I tried to help, offered to get her some maths tuition since the child was not exactly bright at school . . . though who am I to talk since Damaris wasn't exactly a good scholar, either. Bert told me to stop patronizing him and . . . well, maybe I wasn't as tactful as I might have been. Lily came around quite a lot at weekends to play with Damaris, since they were about the same age. At least I could see the child got a square meal now and then, but I haven't seen anything of her for, well, must be nearly fifteen years now. What's she doing now?'

'Have you any idea why your daughter made a will, leaving Matthew's house to Lily Cunningham?'

Gail shrugged, wide-eyed. 'I had no idea they were still in touch with one another. I don't understand anything. I mean, my daughter had enough to do to keep her own household going, so why on earth would she give Matthew's house away?'

'You said there was something else bothering you?'

Gail drew in her breath, sharply. 'You'll laugh at me when I say . . . but I don't understand why Damaris was on that particular platform at Ealing Broadway. She takes . . . took . . . the Central Line from Ealing Broadway into Notting Hill Gate every morning. Then she'd walk down Kensington Church Street to the High Street to the shop where she worked. So why was she on a mainline platform instead of a Tube? They say no one was standing anywhere near her except a Muslim woman shrouded to the eyeballs in black. She's disappeared and I can't say I blame her. Apparently Damaris just toppled in front of the train. Vertigo, maybe? Perhaps she'd taken something for a cold or . . . I'm clutching at straws, aren't I? I would have said she was the last person to commit suicide. I can't make sense of it.'

She had a point, there. Add it to the list? Bea said, 'There's a lot I don't understand, either. I tell myself there's a simple explanation for everything that's happened, but I haven't a clue what it is.'

Gail was sharp. 'I don't do fantasy. I feel as I'm being manipulated by someone, but I can't see who it is who's pulling the strings.'

'Lily Cunningham?'

Gail pulled a face. 'That poor creature? I don't think so.'

'Maybe Derek knows something we don't. I'm paying him a visit this afternoon, see if I can recover Max's laptop and mobile. Want to come?'

'Certainly. I need to see him, too, find out what I can do to help. There's the funeral to organize . . . oh, dear. No, I am not going to be sick again!'

'Of course you're not. I'm relying on you to help me put the fear of death into the Frasier boys. You can do that, can't you?'

Gail tried to smile. 'Give them detention? Threaten them with suspension from school? What other cards can we play?'

'Bluff our way in, and bluff our way out. You back me up, and we win. Right?'

Maggie took a red pencil and circled a date on her big calendar. 'Are we all going to the funeral tomorrow? It sounds as if it's going to be fun, with all the wives and everyone being grabby. Only, I've got so much on, I'm not sure I can make it.'

Oliver drove them to the Frasiers', saying he needed the practice before he took his test next week. It was a mark of how competent a driver he was, that Bea didn't find herself trying to push her foot through the floor of the car at every traffic light. Besides which, Gail needed someone to listen to her.

'I wonder how they'll manage now. Damaris did everything for them. Will he want me to help clear out her clothes . . .?' Gail shuddered, looking out of the window, not looking at Bea. 'It's a terrible thing, having a child die before you. I said we weren't close and we weren't, but I always hoped . . . silly of me. She couldn't admit that she'd made a mess of her life, married the wrong man. She was always dreaming that one day they'd get out of that house and he'd find a job which would make him a millionaire, and the boy would get into Oxford or Cambridge . . . stupid, stupid!'

'How often did you see her?'

'Every other month, just the two of us. The theatre, a good meal, an exhibition. The sort of thing she couldn't afford herself. I hardly ever went to the house. The last time I was there was on Christmas Day. I'd taken them all out for a meal, the three of them plus Derek's sister and her two. Nothing pleased them, though it cost me an arm and a leg, what with presents for all of them and . . . well . . . they gave me a couple of DVDs which didn't work. Typical. The kids whined throughout.

'After the meal we went back to their house and everyone settled down to some serious drinking and watching a violent DVD. Not my scene. Damaris asked if I'd like to go out for a walk with her. She said she was a bit desperate for money, and would I lend her a couple of thousand, and I felt dreadful but said no because I knew Derek would only take it. Sad, sad. Perhaps, if I'd given it to her . . .? But no. She's "borrowed" money from me before and never been able to pay it back.

'I felt miserable about it, but then it occurred to me that Matthew had taken out an insurance policy in her favour years ago. I suggested she enquire whether she could borrow money on that. She said she hadn't seen him in a couple of years, but maybe my mention of him made her think she should look him up.'

The Frasier house looked as depressed as before, and there was no large black cat sitting on the doorstep any more. The car had been moved and returned to a slightly different position. Bea wondered how Mr Frasier had managed to get it started. Had he called on the services of a friendly neighbour?

Bea looked at the well-kept houses on either side, and thought they would have to be extremely charitable neighbours to help Derek out. But perhaps they were being helpful, in view of the circumstances? Grieving widow, motherless child. Hm. It was a trifle difficult to see Derek and Tom in those roles.

Oliver held up his mobile phone. 'You'll signal if you can get hold of Mr Max's stuff, right? Then I'll ring Maggie and get her to tell him he can relax. But if there's the slightest hint of trouble, I'm contacting the police, understood?'

'Don't be so melodramatic, Oliver,' said Bea, ringing the doorbell. The drainpipe was still hanging at an angle. Nothing had been added to the recycling box. She could see the television was on inside the front room, so presumably the Frasiers were in.

Gail hugged herself. 'Let me do the talking, Bea. He knows he can't push me around.'

Derek Frasier opened the door, looking wary. When he saw Gail as well as Bea, he tried to smile, his eyes flickering from one woman to the other . . . and then flicking to the car outside, where Oliver was staring at him. Derek's eyes almost disappeared inside their lids as he computed what a visitation by three of them might mean.

'Gail,' he said. 'I wasn't expecting you.'

'Derek. How are you doing? My friend here offered me a lift and I thought we could have a chat about the funeral arrangements.' Gail didn't offer to kiss him, and he didn't seem to expect it, either. She stepped past him into the hall. There was a coat-stand in the hall, with a couple of women's jackets on it. Damaris's jackets. Gail took off her coat and after a moment's hesitation, draped it over the newel post at the bottom of the staircase. Bea kept hers on.

'How am I doing?' said Derek. 'Oh, you know . . .' He held open the door to the front room, so that they could go through. 'Tom's been poorly again, but my sister's coming over this evening to get us some supper.'

'That's good,' said Gail, without a flicker of sympathy for her grandson. So what could be the matter with Tom? Nothing serious, to judge by Gail's reaction.

Bea followed Gail into the front room and took an upright chair by the door. As she'd expected, the packaging from the new television and from the electronic game was still there. The flower vase was empty of water, the flowers dying.

Tom was half lying and half sitting on the settee, wearing the same clothes as on the previous day, laces undone on his trainers, a fresh stain on his T-shirt. There were three long, livid-looking scratches on his left hand and wrist. He didn't get up or move over to let the visitors sit down and appeared glued to his electronic game.

Gail hovered by the settee.

'Move over, Tom,' said Derek. 'Can't you see your grandmother needs somewhere to sit down? She's come to discuss the funeral arrangements, so we'll excuse you if you like.'

'Before you disappear, Tom,' said Gail, 'I promised my friend here that I'd collect the things you picked up by mistake last night.'

'What things? Dunno what you mean,' mumbled Tom, without looking at her. He pulled the sleeve of his sweatshirt further down, to hide his scratched wrist. 'I was in all night.'

'I can confirm that,' said Derek, with a wide smile. 'We watched the football together. Most exciting. I didn't think you were interested in sport, Gail. I'd be most interested to hear what you thought of that disputed decision in the first half.'

Gail looked at the brand new television. 'You recorded it to watch later, I suppose. I came here to discuss the funeral arrangements, but we have to get this other business out of the way first. I know you and Tom paid a visit to Mrs Abbot's last night and came away with a laptop and a mobile phone belonging to her son.'

Derek mimed shock, horror! 'What a terrible thing to say. I think your daughter's death must have turned your brain.'

Tom giggled, eyes still on his game.

'Mr Abbot is offering a small reward,' said Gail, in full head-mistress mode. 'Generally speaking, I am not in favour of rewards being offered for the recovery of stolen items, but as this particular theft has resulted in considerable inconvenience for Mr Abbot, I am prepared to act as go-between, provided we can clear the matter up straight away.'

'I am astounded,' said Derek. His colour deepened, but his smile never wavered. 'I would never have thought it of you, Gail. Lending yourself to criminal activity! Whatever would Damaris have said?'

'It's because I'm thinking of my daughter that I'm offering to help you out. She wouldn't have wanted you dragged down to the police station and charged with assault and theft before she's buried.'

'Assault and theft? My, what big words. I deny them, I absolutely do.'

Time for Bea to take a hand. She said, 'A cat's scratches can so easily turn septic. Perhaps it would be a good idea to take Tom to the doctor's, get him some antibiotics. They might save his life. The DNA we took from the cat will provide a good match, of course.'

'What . . .?' Tom looked alarmed, losing interest in his game and turning to his father for reassurance. 'They can't do that, can they?'

Bea raised her eyebrows. 'Do what, Tom? Place you at the crime scene? Yes, of course they can. You may not have your DNA on record as yet, but when we give the police your name, they'll be out here asking for a sample straight away. Your father didn't get scratched, did he?'

Derek's eyes almost disappeared into his head. 'The cat scratched Tom earlier, before you stole him from us.'

'How do you know that the cat ended up at my place,' said Bea, 'unless you came across him at my place last night?'

Silence.

Derek gave a short laugh, conceding a point but not giving up.

Bea said, 'We could call the police and let them search the house—'

'Not without a warrant, you don't. Where's your proof?'

Gail took over. 'Derek, let's talk finance. Without Damaris's wages, it's going to be hard for you to keep this house on.'

'I have my disability pension, and Tom's child benefit. Besides, my sister's planning to move in here with her two. She's in a really run-down council flat at the moment, been looking for something better for ages. She'll see us all right.'

'You also have a gambling habit. Now I know that Matthew took out a life insurance in Damaris's favour, so—'

'We cashed that in ages ago, when we got behind with the mortgage. I've been down the Social and they tell me there's some money coming in here and there, enough to pay for the funeral and that's it. In the meantime, we'll do all right.'

Bea smiled, too. Not nicely. 'Derek, do you really think you can get my son to pay a considerable amount of money for the return of his laptop and mobile? Perhaps you think he's already agreed to your terms?'

Derek grinned even more widely, and tapped the side of his nose.

Bea said, 'What you don't realize is that you've been taken for a ride. Oh yes, he took your call and agreed to your terms. But you haven't been able to get back to him this afternoon to make the final arrangements, have you?'

His grin morphed into a stare. He could sense the fist of fate was about to deliver him a knockout blow, but he couldn't see where it was coming from.

Bea leaned forward to emphasize the point she was making. 'He kept you on the phone long enough for the call to be traced but he had no intention of paying. Do you understand?'

His mouth slackened. The blow had landed.

Bea said, 'Neither Gail nor I want this silly little affair on tomorrow's front pages, so if you hand over the laptop and mobile, we'll see that the matter goes no further.'

Tom was shocked. 'You mean, Special Branch taped our call?'

'What did you expect? Assault, theft and blackmail on a Member of Parliament gets you first-class attention. Now I have the reward money here, so if you'd . . .?'

Tom scrambled out of the settee and hitched up his low-slung jeans. 'I'll get the stuff, Dad.' He shot out of the room.

Derek was blinking, trying to adjust. Bea held out an envelope to him, and he took it, slowly. Disappointment in every ample line of him. 'There's not much here.'

'One hundred pounds in tens. Better than handcuffs for you and Tom having to go into care. You'd better get that arm of his seen to, by the way. I wasn't joking when I said it looked bad.'

Derek counted the notes, slowly.

Tom returned with Max's laptop and mobile. 'We didn't do anything with them, honest.' He fidgeted with his sleeve. 'Dad . . . how's about taking me down the hospital? My arm really hurts, you know.'

Derek was not sympathetic. 'When they've gone. Shut up and sit down.'

Bea went to the window, waved to attract Oliver's attention, and held up the laptop and mobile for him to see. Oliver nodded, and started to make the call to Maggie to say all was well. Bea returned to her seat, content to let Gail take over again. Tom collapsed on to the settee, looking sullen. Gail took a notebook out of her handbag. 'Now that that's out of the way, let's get down to discussing funerals. Derek, have you and Tom got something clean and decent to wear to Matthew's funeral tomorrow? Did Damaris invite people back here for a cuppa afterwards?'

Derek shrugged. 'Damaris made all the arrangements for the funeral but she said there was no point in laying on a spread afterwards. It's going to be such a small affair. I suppose we'll have to go, even though there's nothing in it for us now Lily's crawled out of the woodwork.'

'You don't know that,' said Gail. 'Not until Matthew's will is read. So far all we've got is hearsay. Is your solicitor coming back here to read his will to you afterwards?'

'Yes, but how's that going to help us? Damaris inherited

Matthew's house and money and then handed it all over to Lily.'

'Do you know that, or is it just something that Lily has told you? I realize that normally we wouldn't be able to have the reading of Damaris's will until after she's buried . . .' And here Gail winced, but went on, 'But you could ask the solicitor – is it the same one who made both wills? – to read hers tomorrow as well.'

Derek was slumped into a chair. 'Damaris's will cuts us out of the loop altogether, though I'll never understand why she did it.'

'Neither can I,' said Gail, 'and that's why I think it would be a good idea for us to wait and see exactly what the two wills have to say. It's in my mind that you might be able to challenge her will. I mean . . . it was the most extraordinary thing to do, wasn't it? I wonder what the solicitor has to say about it. What's his name, anyway?'

'Greenberg, Greenham. I've got his card somewhere. Trixie, my sister, used to work for him, which is why Damaris mentioned his name to Matthew when he wanted to make a will. Greenham, Greenberg, whatever, he's local, a one-man band, it seemed so convenient.' Derek was beginning to look hopeful. 'So, really, it's all to play for still, isn't it? How soon do you think we can lay our hands on some real money?'

'Not till probate is granted,' said Bea.

He turned on her, speculation in his eye. 'But you could let us have the keys, couldn't you, so that we can get a feeling for how much the contents might fetch?'

'A lot of people are after those keys,' said Bea. 'I'm hanging on to them till I'm sure what the legal position may be.'

Derek became positively chummy, laying a pudgy hand on her knee. 'You could come and ask the solicitor tomorrow, couldn't you? Bring the keys, and we'll see what he has to say.'

'I'm not committing myself,' said Bea. 'But it's true we could do with a legal mind on this tangle.'

'We'll both be there,' said Gail, turning over a page in her notebook. 'Now let's move on to Damaris's funeral. Would you like me to make the arrangements? What exactly do you have in mind? Have you a list of people who need to be informed?

And would you like me to help clear out her clothes? I'm willing to do whatever you think appropriate.'

Derek waved the questions away. 'Trixie'll see to all that. She said she could maybe use some of Damaris's clothes herself, take the rest to a car boot sale . . .'

Bea saw Gail repress a shudder.

'But if you could see your way to paying for a good send-off here afterwards . . . why, we won't say no, will we, Tom?'

Tom grumbled, 'I don't see why I have to move out of my room to let the pests have it.'

His father was terse. 'Either that or you bunk in with me. Take your pick. And remember your manners. Your aunt Trixie's going to move in to help us out. So you'd better mind your Ps and Qs, for she won't stand any nonsense from you, I can tell you.'

Gail got to her feet. 'I'll set aside four hundred pounds for a party after my daughter's funeral. Let me know when it's to be. I'll go to the funeral, but you'll excuse me from the party afterwards, I'm sure.'

'Could you make it cash, now?'

Gail shook her head. 'Let me know when you need to buy the stuff. I'll go to the supermarket with you and settle the bill. I think it's time we went and left you in peace.'

Tom held out his arm. 'Dad, you've got to take me down the hospital, now!'

'Not now. Your aunt's due to arrive any minute. I have to be here to let her in, help her settle the kids.'

Gail took hold of Tom's arm. 'When did you have a bath or shower last? You need to keep clean to avoid infection. Come into the kitchen and let's see what we can do to clean these scratches up. Your mother had some antiseptic wipes in her medicine cabinet, didn't she?'

Bea got to her feet. 'I'll wait for you outside in the car, Gail, shall I?'

'I won't be long.'

Fifteen

Thursday evening

Bea and Oliver dropped Gail back at her place and struggled back through the rush-hour traffic to get home. Even on that tiring journey, Bea found she was not worrying overmuch about how well Oliver was driving. She told him so, too. She also wanted to tell him that she was more worried about how thin and strained he had been looking these last few days, but refrained. She told herself that he was growing up fast, and that if he wanted the opinion of an elderly employer, he would ask for it. She would not intrude on his private life. Well, not yet, anyway. Maybe he'd snap out of it.

Oliver lifted Max's mobile and laptop out of the car, and got out his key to let them in.

The house was uncannily silent.

There were no sounds of workmen, no cheerful banging and crashing as Bea and Oliver negotiated their way over the carpet in the hall. There was no noise of television, radio or clashing of pans in the kitchen. Maggie was not in, obviously.

Bea ran her hand over the top of the chest in the hall. There was more dust in the air and on the furniture. But no pinging of telephones, no one shouting.

Oliver said, 'Like the *Mary Celeste*, isn't it? Do you think there's been an air strike or something, and everyone's vanished off the face of the earth while we've been away? Do you think Mr Max is out, too?'

Max opened the door into the living room, and peered out. He looked haggard.

Bea said, 'Relax. We've recovered them. Here they are.'

Oliver handed over the laptop and mobile. Max took them, but his expression hardly changed. He looked punch drunk.

Bea put a hand on his arm and guided him back into the living room. There was no sign of Miss Townend.

'All's well, Max. You'd better check, but I don't think anything has been tampered with. They were a couple of incompetents who just wanted a look around on the off-chance. It only cost me a hundred to get the stuff back. You can thank me another time.'

He sank on to the settee, staring at her with wide eyes. 'You can't imagine what I've been through.'

'Maybe not,' said Bea, who considered she'd imagined it all, and pretty accurately, too. 'But it's all over now. Hadn't you better report to your Whip or something? Tell them the panic's over and you are as trustworthy and reliable as ever?'

'What? I . . . .yes, of course.' He repeated, 'You've no idea what it's been like . . . the Chief Whip said . . . and Miss Townend broke down and cried and said she was no use to man nor beast and if she hadn't gone home early and left me with Lettice . . . because of the alarm not being left on, you know.'

Bea was soothing. 'I don't suppose it would have made any difference. Oliver and Maggie interrupted the burglars before they could do any real damage.'

'I'm so afraid she's going to leave me, too. She was so upset this morning. She said she ought to have retired ages ago, but she knew I relied on her, and that it was all her fault for not staying to look after me yesterday, but she had one of her migraines coming on, so of course I said she had to go home and she did. If I'm not careful, she'll leave me in the lurch, and go off to live with her mother in Bournemouth in a retirement flat, and then where will I be?'

Bea sat down beside him. She thought this was good news, on the whole. 'Well, you'd be free to look for someone else, someone slightly more up to date.'

'But the files . . . all the information . . .'

'You will get me to find a suitable secretarial agency to copy the constituency files and put them on some memory sticks. It'll cost you, mind.'

He grimaced. 'It's all too much.' Gave a loud sob, and turned it into a guffaw. 'Lettice was all over me yesterday, trying to make me promise to marry her, trying to get me to take her there and then, on this very sofa, and . . . that's why I got so het up last night that I forgot about the alarm. I had to practically drag her out of the house and shove her into a taxi and then I stood there, totally out of it, thinking what a relief it was and dreading that she'd come back at me again . . . and then I thought I'd better eat something and went off without remembering to set the alarm.'

Bea patted his hand. Poor love. He really wasn't very good at handling his women, was he?

He took a deep breath, grimacing again. 'You know what? As soon as Lettice heard that I was in trouble this morning, she rang to say she never wanted to see me again.'

'Well, that's good news, isn't it?' said Bea, trying not to be too hopeful.

'Yes. It is. Or rather, it would be if only Nicole . . . but I've behaved so badly, I can't imagine, especially after . . . you know?'

She patted his hand again. 'I rather think Nicole's been trying to get in touch with you all day.'

'Probably to tell me to get lost.'

'You don't know that. Suppose you check your belongings, see that there's no damage, tell the Chief Whip that you've retrieved them and then buy the biggest bunch of flowers you can find and go to see Nicole?'

'She'll never want to see me again. Not after . . . you know.'

Bea gritted her teeth. 'You don't know that, do you? Now, I really must see what's going on with the rest of the team. I gather you haven't been able to use the phone here this afternoon. Has the fault cleared yet? You can always use your mobile anyway. And you can go back to your office at the House now that Lettice's taken herself off.'

'Yes, but when she finds out that I've got the stuff back . . .'

Bea held on to a smile with an effort. 'Don't tell her. Yet. See Nicole first.'

He followed her to the door like a toddler seeking reassurance. She shut the door in his face. Whatever next?

Someone heavy started to climb the stairs from the basement, and a workman's head appeared. 'Want a look before I go, missus?'

Inspection next. The tiler led the way down past the dust-sheet – which had been hitched up again – to show off what he'd been doing. The tiles were indeed not the ones which Bea had chosen but, as Maggie had said, they were perfectly acceptable. The electrician was still there, whistling through his teeth as he fitted the last of the switches. The floorboards had been replaced where necessary. Fresh wood had been inserted in the skirtings here and there. The walls which had had to be replastered were drying out nicely.

'Well done,' said Bea, and meant it.

A banging front door heralded Maggie's return, but she did not appear downstairs to check on the workmen. Instead, Bea heard her footsteps climbing up the stairs to her own room at the top of the house.

Well, Maggie had the right to take time off now and then, didn't she?

Bea made her way back up the stairs to the kitchen for a cuppa. The kitchen was quiet, the only sound the clock ticking.

Tomorrow, thought Bea. Tomorrow ought to see some progress in disentangling the mystery of the two wills, who owned what, who inherits what and, perhaps, why.

The cat Winston plopped in from the garden, looking for love and titbits. Bea obliged, kissing the top of his furry head, and putting a spoonful from a tin of cat food into his dish. Both the tin and the dish were new. Had Maggie bought them? If the cat were going to move into their household, he'd better be booked into the vet's for a check-up.

She could hear Max on his mobile in the living room. Speaking to his boss, no doubt. She wondered how soon he'd be claiming all the credit for retrieving his possessions. Tomorrow morning, perhaps?

She got out her own mobile phone and rang Nicole. Pick up, girl. Pick up! Now is the time for all good men – and women – to come to the aid of the party.

'Nicole? Bea here. You've been trying to reach Max all day, I gather . . . yes, things have been slightly tense. Yes, he's all right, got a bang on the head, but it's not serious. He's been worried sick that you'll drop him like a hot cake, just as your sister has . . . oh yes, that's exactly what she's done. She thinks it's the end of his career.'

'Well, if it is, he only has himself to blame.'

'Yes and no. There may be a way out and, if there is, would you be prepared to stand by your man?'

'He doesn't want me. He's made that very clear. She wins again.'

'Not necessarily. You'd like to see her off, wouldn't you?'

'Fat chance. She always wins. Always.'

'As I said, there might be a way in which you could win. It depends on you. Would you like to try again? He's been sitting here at my house, imagining the worst, not daring to contact you.'

'I'm not surprised, after what he's been up to with Lettice.'

'The trouble with nice men is that they are naïve when it comes to dealing with women like your sister. They've been brought up to be polite to them, and can't bring themselves to give them a black eye, or a sound thrashing, which – pardon me – is what Lettice has been asking for.'

Nicole gave a harsh laugh. 'Him and who else?'

'I know. He's a total pussy cat. You should have looked after him better.'

'You must be joking. My sister holds all the cards.'

'Oh no, she doesn't. What about the oldest trick in the book?'

'What's that?'

'Tell him you're pregnant.'

Nicole drew in her breath. 'What? I couldn't! Besides, he'd never believe me.'

'Nonsense. Of course he would. Can't you see him just swell with pride to think he's going to be a father? It will go down well with the constituency, too, undercutting Lettice's influence with your parents at one stroke.'

'But . . .! No, I . . . oh! You're right. My parents would love it . . .'

'Mm,' said Bea, considering her fingernails. Did this new colour really appeal? 'Of course, it would mean a considerable sacrifice on your part. Would you mind?'

'I . . . you mean, that I'd have to actually want to have a baby myself? Come off the pill and let him have regular sex? I thought we might have children some day but I hadn't really considered . . . and to make it work, I'd have to pretend I'd forgotten to take the pill recently and . . .' A change of tone. 'I wonder! I did run out a couple of weeks ago and I'm not sure . . . I'll have to look in the diary . . .'

A long pause.

Bea did a little praying. *Dear Lord, I know what I'm suggesting is not at all ethical, and I'm not sure how you'll look at it, but . . .*

it would keep the marriage going, wouldn't it? I mean, Nicole is not exactly my favourite person in the whole world, and I'd never have chosen her for a daughter-in-law if it had been left to me, but Max does seem to love her, and if this works out then I promise always to look for the best in her in future, amen.

Nicole said, 'I'll have to think about it.' And put the phone down.

As did Bea. She discovered that she'd been crossing her fingers so hard that it took an effort to prise them apart.

Dear Lord, forgive me if I've done the wrong thing. I'm in such a muddle about so much.

She remembered Hamilton's daily prayer, something about telling God he was going to be very busy that day but that if he forgot God, would God please not forget him. That made her giggle, if weakly. *That's it, Lord. I'm muddling through this and that, and I could do with some backup. If you can spare the time.*

And now what?

There'd been some coming and going in the background. The front door opening and shutting, people going up and down the stairs. The workmen were leaving for the day. Oliver was talking to someone in the hall. Was that Maggie's voice? No, just a couple of workmen using four-letter words as they trampled down the carpet to get to the front door.

Bea went into the living room to find Max striding up and down, talking to someone on his newly-recovered mobile. It sounded as if he were being told off, and not enjoying it. Well, who would?

When he finished the call, Bea said, 'I've been speaking to Nicole. She doesn't know you've recovered the stolen goods and she'd really like to hear from you.'

'What? After everything that's happened?'

'Oh yes,' said Bea, crossing her fingers again. She left him fingering his mobile because she could hear Miss Brook coming down the stairs.

Miss Brook was wearing her outdoor coat, and inserting herself into a pair of leather gloves. 'Mrs Abbot, a word if I may?'

'I was just coming up to speak to you. I know the circumstances are far from ideal, but would it be possible for you to help us out again tomorrow?'

'Naturally,' said Miss Brook. 'I understood there's still a great deal to do and a funeral to go to.' She exited over the carpet without holding on to anything. Mary Poppins, here we come, thought Bea.

Matthew's funeral. A depressing thought. Bea wondered how Matthew's one-time agent Sylvester had been getting on with his plans to give Matthew a better send-off than the one which had been planned by his nearest and dearest. Bea used her mobile to get through to him, half expecting to hear that he might not be up to attending the funeral himself. He was huffing and puffing as he answered the phone, and she could imagine him heaving himself forward in his big chair to stub out a cigarette as he reached for the phone.

'Sylvester, my dear friend, how are you today? Ready to run a marathon tomorrow? Did you get my message?'

He wheezed out a laugh. 'Bea, my darling girl, I'm sorry I haven't rung you before. I've been that busy, haven't had time to turn round. The old ticker was playing up yesterday, but I put the word out and there'll be a goodish turnout for Matt tomorrow. Would you believe, there isn't going to be an organist? And nobody to officiate from his church, either? Just someone the crem pays to say a few words over the coffin.

'I got on to the funeral directors, said I'd be responsible for an organist at the very least and he had the nerve to say we've only got a short slot and there won't be time for music! There isn't even going to be a proper printed order of service. What a shabby do, eh?'

'You can make up for it later with a memorial service.'

'We'll do that, arrange a proper send-off for him later on, at the church, with his own minister and an organ and soloists and readings and everything done properly. But when I get hold of the ghastly stepdaughter—'

'Hold on, Sylvester. There's something you need to know. Damaris Frasier died in an accident on Tuesday, going in to work.'

'What? What was that?'

Bea repeated her words. 'Now I've been in touch with her mother, Gail—'

'Bossy-boots with a cut-glass voice?'

'That's her. I think she must have mellowed over the years because I like her very much. She still has a lot of feeling for Matthew. She'll be there tomorrow, and after that she's got to bury her daughter.'

Sylvester's breathing became even more laboured. 'What a carry-on . . .! Then who's paying the bills tomorrow?'

'I suppose Derek Frasier, Damaris's husband. I don't think you'll find him a sympathetic soul. What's more, there's no get together been arranged for after the funeral.'

'How sad. How dreary. How unlike everything that Matthew stood for.' He shut off the phone.

'Problems?' Her ex, Piers, appeared in the doorway. 'Oliver let me in. I'm on my way somewhere but it doesn't matter if I turn up late, or not at all come to think of it. I've Matthew on my mind. What's the latest for tomorrow? Would you like a lift to the funeral, or have you arranged something already?'

'Oh, Piers. Such a muddle.' She held out both hands to him in an impulsive gesture which she regretted as soon as she'd done it.

He took her hands and pressed them before releasing her. He was wearing a good-looking black silk suit over a sage-green silk shirt, no tie. He was obviously due at some important function. 'Tell Daddy, then.'

She began to laugh, at herself and at the absurdity of the situation. Whatever had she been thinking of, to reach out to Piers like that? Luckily he'd turned the situation off into comedy. 'Have you a half-hour or so? Do you want some supper? I think something's in the oven.' She called out, 'Oliver, is Maggie around? Has she prepared anything for supper?'

Oliver appeared at the top of the stairs and made his way down. 'Maggie says she's coming and that supper's up.' He, also, was dressed for a night out. Piers led the way to the kitchen as Maggie clattered down the stairs after Oliver.

Bea thought Maggie had been crying lately, but she'd made up her eyes with bold black strokes around them and used a sparkly eye shadow, so it wasn't easy to tell. She was dressed from head to foot in black – not from Bea's wardrobe for a change – and had brushed and gelled her hair into a wild bush.

She dived into the oven to draw out a large casserole and plonk it on the table. 'Everyone hungry? Aaah! Where did that cat come from?' Winston was first to the table. Maggie scooped him up, kissed the top of his head and put him on the floor.

Piers seated himself. 'On the pull tonight, Maggie?'

She stuck out a hip, striking a pose. 'Fending them off, I am.'

Oliver said, 'It's all right. I'll look after her.'

Maggie slapped the back of his head. 'In your dreams, brother.'

Oliver said, 'Grrr!' He reached up and behind himself for a bottle of a hot sauce which only he liked.

Bea opened her eyes wide. When Maggie had first brought the bedraggled boy to the house, he'd been undersized and looked twelve years old at most. Going daily to the gym and eating Maggie's meals must have caused a growth spurt for Bea knew he couldn't have reached that shelf when he arrived. Now that she had a chance to look at him properly, she realized he now appeared older than his actual age. The lines of his face had hardened, the bones becoming more apparent. He met her eye and sent her half a smile before holding his plate up to Maggie to be filled. If Bea read his attitude correctly, he was telling her that he was finding life difficult but he was coping.

Piers murmured, 'How quickly children grow up nowadays.'

The front door banged. Max on his way out. Bea did hope he'd contact Nicole. She thought there was a fifty-fifty chance of a happy ending there.

Bea's nose twitched as she savoured the aroma from Maggie's casserole. She was going to enjoy this. 'Time for a debrief after supper, everyone? I want to make a list of all the odd things that have been happening. Each one can be explained away pretty well, but taken as a whole . . . this business stinks.'

'This is what I like about working here,' said Oliver, mounding vegetables on to his plate. 'Stretching myself. Dealing with oddities. Having to use my brains.'

Piers took almost as big a helping as Oliver. 'Is there the slightest piece of evidence to prove there's been some hanky-panky? Eccentricity, yes. Suspicious circumstances, no. You can't cry wolf to the police just because you smell rotten fish. The police take a dim view of people who waste their time that way.'

'Believe me,' said Bea, 'I am struggling hard to pretend that all is well. It's like standing on shifting sand. If I could find one bit of evidence . . . it's so frustrating . . . I know something's not right.'

'Proof, o Peg o' my heart!'

Bea pulled a face at him. 'Oliver, you copied the hard drive off Matthew's computer. We couldn't find a diary for him earlier but . . .'

Piers pointed a fork loaded with food at her. 'That's no reason to suspect someone's been breaking the law.'

'No, but . . . I could do with getting a better picture of who visited him and when. Oliver, you said he kept a note of his appointments on the computer. Would you run them off for me for, say, a couple of months before his death and the month which follows? Oh, and are there any pictures of him on his website? Preferably Matthew as Matthew and not in character. Oh, and preferably with his accompanist.'

'All the pics were of him in drag. I don't think there were any of him as Matthew Kent. No pics of anyone else that I can remember.'

'Well, let me have what you can.'

'Will do.' Oliver scraped his plate clean and eyed up the leftovers. 'Any chance of seconds?'

Friday morning

A dull day. A mountain of work came in through the mail and on email. Miss Brook, luckily, liked a challenge and though Oliver said he wanted to drive Bea to the crematorium, she left him behind to deal with their bread and butter work. Maggie had an argy-bargy with the electrician, reiterated that they would do better to get rid of her office carpet – the one now in the hall – and strip and polish the existing floorboards, before shooting off down the hill to check on the job she was project-managing.

Bea dreaded the prospect of yet more dust circulating through the house, which it would if they had the floorboards downstairs stripped and polished, but decided to let Maggie have her way. Bea told herself that Maggie probably knew better than she about how to make the refurbished offices look good. At the same time Bea sincerely hoped that after this Maggie wouldn't turn her energies to refurbishing the rest of the house; Bea liked it just as it was. Well, maybe a quick lick of paint on some of the woodwork but . . . no! She'd had enough of workmen around the place, and for the moment she was going to forget about that dicey guttering at the back of the house.

The Green Girls arrived to do a quick clean-up – no sign of Florrie yet. Bea checked with Gail to see if she were all right and wanted a lift to the crem. Gail said she'd take her own car, just in case.

Bea didn't find it easy to get ready in her bedroom while Miss Brook was using the phone, but with some give and take they managed it. Bea took the keys to Matthew's house out of the drawer and put them into the most businesslike of her handbags before checking her appearance in her full-length mirror. She was wearing dark grey today; she didn't like herself in black. Hamilton hadn't liked her in black, either. A severely-cut dark-grey suit was her compromise for funerals; she wasn't a relative or even a friend of the deceased. A soft pink scarf relieved the sobriety of the suit. She checked that she had her reading glasses, notebook, make-up bag, car keys and house keys; all present and correct.

At the last minute she took Matthew's house keys out of her handbag and dropped them back into the drawer of her dressing table. She wasn't sure why she wasn't taking them with her. She had no right to hang on to them. But there it was; something in her rebelled from handing the Frasiers an undeserved pot of honey.

She scolded herself as she drove out to the crematorium. Who was she to decide who did or did not deserve to inherit the house? It was all wrong of her. She ought to turn round and take the road back to her house to retrieve the keys.

Of course, that might make her late for the funeral, and she didn't want to do that, did she? Sylvester needed her to be there. Piers expected to meet her there. As did Gail. Each in their own way was grieving for Matthew and needed Bea's support.

Really, she was going out of curiosity. A poor excuse.

Dear Lord, if I am doing the wrong thing, then help me to keep my mouth shut, sit in the back row and not say anything to upset anybody. Let everything be peaceful and quiet. Let everything be done decently and in good order. For Matthew's sake, amen.

There were a lot of cars parked at the crematorium, but Bea found a space for herself in the end. Was the right word a 'fleet' of cars? A 'convoy'? Or, possibly, a 'hiring'? The word 'hiring' occurred to Bea because a great many of the cars were the sort which celebrities arrived in for film premieres and other public jamborees. Also among them was the Frasiers' ancient and possibly unroadworthy car. She found herself checking that his tax disc was up to date, and was irritated to find that it still had a month to run.

Bea made her way in to the chapel, half recognizing some well-known faces. The coffin was already in place; a simple affair, not to say cheap. There were no flowers on it. There were no flowers anywhere. Bea remembered Matthew's patio, brilliant with red geraniums, and Goldie's remark that he'd loved flowers. Bea had never met Matthew in life, but she sorrowed gently for him because there were none to mark his final journey.

The chapel was pretty full; a good crowd of well-dressed people, mostly men, but with one or two women as well. Piers was sitting near the front. Bea half lifted a hand to him, until she saw he was paying close attention to a youngish, well-dressed woman on his left, and had no eyes for anyone else. Tomcats didn't change their ways, did they! Bea found a seat near the back and looked around her.

She saw Sylvester puffing and panting on his way to the front, leaning on the arm of the son who now ran the agency. The Frasiers, husband and son, were in the opposite front row, next to a depressed looking man in heavy-rimmed glasses.

A woman in black was sitting next to Derek. Presumably this was the sister, Trixie, who'd worked for the solicitor who'd done Matthew's and Damaris's wills? The one who was going to move in with Derek and Tom? Judging by the way she kept bobbing her head down to the right, Trixie had brought her children with her. Not suitable, thought Bea. And then, Ah well, what is suitable for children these days?

Gail had seated herself near the back on the other side to Bea. She was wearing a good black suit, but no hat. Gail had her eyes down, making herself small and unobtrusive. She didn't make eye contact with Bea.

There was a stir in the doorway, and a woman with bright hair under a fashionable hat made an entrance, followed by the stockily-built man who'd accompanied her on her foray to try to remove furniture from Matthew's house earlier.

Goldie, Matthew's third, was all in black; skirt too short, heels too high, perfume too strong. With some difficulty she carried in an enormous sheaf of red roses, which she placed tenderly on the coffin. She stood back – a wonderfully theatrical moment – and produced a handkerchief, which she pressed carefully to the outer corner of one eye. Sylvester half rose in his seat and with an ironical bow, gestured that she and her companion should sit beside him.

Some recorded music was being played. Bach? A reasonable choice. The usual service books were available, but no order of service.

A subdued murmuring filled the chapel. Bea glanced at her watch. Wasn't it time to start?

A solitary woman appeared in the doorway and stood there, hesitating. She was in her thirties, white-faced, podgy-faced, with a sharp nose. She was wearing a black coat that reached down to her ankles, and black boots. Neither of them new. Her hair had been dyed black, parted and hung loose on either side of her face, but her eyebrows were barely existent. Was this the new heiress?

The latecomer appeared surprised to see so many people in the chapel. She turned on her heel as if to retreat but thought the better of it. She stalked down the aisle to accost the minister, who had just appeared from the vestry and was in the act of turning off the taped music.

Derek Frasier got up from his seat and joined them in a short conversation. No doubt he was as much taken aback at the numbers who'd turned up, as the newcomer. Derek returned to his seat, and the woman in black stood aside to let the minister address the congregation.

'One moment, before we start. Mr Frasier and Ms Cunningham have pointed out that this is a private service for Mr Matthew Kent. Very few people were expected. Perhaps some of you are here for the twelve thirty service for someone else? If so, would you kindly wait outside?'

Sixteen

'We're here for Matthew.' Sylvester's voice, still rich in spite of his years of smoking.

There was a general chorus of agreement. Craning her neck, Bea managed to see Goldie start to her feet, handkerchief fluttering. 'Here's to my poor dear Matthew!'

If her words were inappropriately expressed, at least they conveyed the sentiments of everyone in the chapel. Or almost everyone. Lily Cunningham looked as if she were going to cry as well, though in her case the tears would be those of rage. Bea wished she could see the faces of the Frasier family. They must be as bewildered as Lily at seeing the chapel fill up with so many mourners.

'Continue!' This was Sylvester, again.

'Well . . .' The minister glanced at his watch, realized he was going to run late if he were not careful, and proceeded to tell the congregation to turn to the service book. Lily Cunningham now needed to find a seat, but the front rows were full. It seemed the Frasiers were in no mood to make room for her, and neither was Sylvester. In fact, most rows were full. As Lily retreated back down the chapel, looking for a place, it seemed at first that no one was willing to let her in. Finally one woman shuffled along to give her a seat.

The service proceeded as had been planned; a poor, rushed sort of send-off. Bea wondered where God was in all this. It must grieve him to see what was going on. She thought of her dear Hamilton's funeral service, on a fine afternoon on the other side of the world. Tears gathered in her eyes and she wiped them away. She realized, with a jolt of pain, that she was wearing the same outfit today that she had worn for his rite of passage.

Gradually the age-old words of the service captured her attention. She bent her head to pray. The chapel was filled with a hushed silence, save for the voice of the minister, who seemed at last to enter into the right frame of mind. He even appeared to be slightly apologetic as he read out a curt, two-line eulogy of the deceased and pressed the button for the coffin to slide out of sight. No one moved as their eyes followed the disappearance of the coffin. Even after it had gone, a very real sense of loss kept the congregation still. The minister pronounced a blessing and disappeared into the vestry.

Before anyone else could move, Sylvester heaved himself on to his feet, wobbled, but made it upright. Turning to the mourners, he said, 'This is not the last we'll hear of our friend. The life of our very good friend Matthew, merry monarch of comedy, will be celebrated in a memorial service at his own church in due course. Meanwhile, if anyone would like to meet back at my place, I've got in a couple of cases of champagne, and some eats. You are all very welcome.'

The spell was broken. People began to move out of the chapel, talking in a subdued fashion to one another. Some used handkerchiefs, some sniffed. A lot of air-kissing, hugging and hand-shaking went on. Bea hung back, watching people's reactions.

She was shocked to see how ill Sylvester looked, and how loud his breathing was as he made his way slowly outside, surrounded by a crowd of friends and acquaintances. She caught snatches of conversation.

'Where's the daughter? What's her name?'

'Damaris. Dead too, Sylvester says. It must be catching.'

'Who's the death's head? I don't recognize her.'

'Bert's daughter, I think. Although he always denied she was his. A shame he couldn't make it.'

Knots of people formed in the aisle, only to be moved on by deferential officials, worrying about getting the next cremation going on time.

Goldie moved down the aisle, graciously accepting condolences, her companion one step to the rear.

Sylvester offered her his arm. 'Doing the old boy proud with those roses. Come and sink a glass or two in his memory?'

She fluttered eyelashes. 'I have to be at the reading of the will.'

Sylvester bent his head and whispered in her ear. She looked shocked. 'What? Damaris is dead, too? But . . . surely . . .' She ran after Derek, who had reached the door and was shaking hands with the congregation as they left.

'Derek,' she said, holding her hat on with one hand, 'where's Damaris? Sylvester said something about . . . no, that can't be true. Damaris will see me right. I mean . . . Matthew must have left me something.'

Lily intervened, sharp nose quivering, in a squeaky voice. 'He didn't leave you anything. I should know. I was one of the executors of his will. You might as well go and have a drink with Sylvester.'

Wild-eyed, Goldie turned on the bespectacled man at Derek's side. 'Are you the solicitor? Is this true?'

He stammered. 'Th–this is n–neither the t–time nor place t–to—'

Goldie stamped her foot. 'Well, did he or did he not leave me something?'

'Nothing,' said Lily. She nudged the solicitor. 'Tell her! Go on.'

He shrugged. 'It is as Ms Cunningham says.'

Goldie, accepting the bad news, gave a little shriek. Her companion muttered, 'Told you not to waste money on flowers!'

Sylvester, hiding amusement, took her by the elbow. 'Come along, my dear. Champagne soothes all sorrows.' He moved slowly off on his son's arm, Goldie in tow and her companion sticking to her heels.

The solicitor, looking uncomfortable, fled the scene, followed by the Frasier family in a bunch. Lily Cunningham trod on their heels, calling out after them that she needed a lift.

Piers came out with an arm through that of the woman he'd been sitting next to. He didn't look around for Bea, which she thought was just like him; no doubt his companion had some project lined up for him, in or out of bed. Bea was shocked at how much his attitude annoyed her. Piers had known she was going to be there, and it was extremely rude of him – although absolutely typical – not even to have looked around for her.

As the last few people left, Bea overheard another interesting titbit. A heavily-built man observed to his stick-thin companion, 'Where was Bert? I wouldn't have thought he'd want to miss this.'

His friend shrugged. 'Not like him to miss a freebie, either. Gone into a home, someone said.'

The chapel was almost empty. Bea saw that Gail was mopping herself up in her seat. Overdoing the grief a trifle? After all, she hadn't had any contact with Matthew for years. Or had she? Was there something Gail wasn't telling?

Bea leaned over Gail. 'Are you all right? I thought you'd be sitting with the Frasiers.'

'Do I look a wreck?' Gail put her hankie away. 'These affairs always get to me.' She looked around her. 'Derek didn't understand why I should want to come. I'm surprised Trixie brought her children, but they behaved themselves during the service, didn't they?'

As they reached the door together, Derek bustled up. 'Gail, you've got your car here, haven't you? Mine refuses to start and I'm not calling out the garage to get it towed home, not today. I'll have a go at getting it started again tomorrow. Maybe I'll junk it. It's about time I had a better car. But we've got to get back home straight away because the solicitor's gone on ahead and he won't hang around, will he? Oh yes, and Lily wants a lift, too.'

Gail said, 'It's lucky Mrs Abbot is here, too, isn't it? Between us, we'll cope.'

Friday afternoon

A light drizzle had settled in, which didn't make the Frasier house look any more attractive than before. The solicitor had already arrived and was sitting in his car outside when Bea arrived with Trixie and her two children. Gail, with the Frasiers and Lily, parked behind them.

Bea had welcomed the chance to chat to Trixie, who was as undersized as Derek was plump. Her two children were silent, hooked into iPods and electronic games. One was male, one female. One had dirty blonde hair, the other had an Afro. Two different fathers? Trixie wore a lot of cheap rings, but none on the fourth finger of her left hand.

Throughout the journey Trixie talked about how hard-done-by she'd been through a series of jobs and how every man she ever knew had let her down, and what a relief it would be to move in with Derek now he was finally rid of his posh wife so that they could have some fun together.

'About the only good thing that cow ever did,' said Trixie,

hopping out of the car in front of the house, 'was to make sure her sugar daddy left her some money.' All her movements were quick and sharp. 'Come on, you two! We haven't got all day!'

Bea made sure the car was properly locked up, thinking it wasn't her place to disabuse Trixie about possible riches in store . . . or not, as the case might be.

Once inside, Trixie acted as hostess. She ordered her children to make themselves scarce upstairs. She told the solicitor to sit in the big armchair, while relegating Bea and Gail to upright chairs at the side of the room. She switched on the electric fire, remarking that it would take some time to warm up and what the electricity bill was going to be like, she didn't dare think. They all kept their coats on.

Lily hovered, waiting to be seated, but Trixie ignored her. It was Gail who asked Lily if she would like to freshen up? Lily shook her head, and moved the packaging from the new TV to take a seat in the window. The flowers in the vase on the window sill were completely dead.

Derek produced a bottle and poured sherries all round. Even for Tom, who was told to take his upstairs and not make a fuss about it.

Lily crossed plump legs and sipped, looking bored. In repose her mouth had a downward droop.

Gail refused sherry, as did Bea. Derek gave Bea a glass despite her protest, so she held it in her hand waiting for an opportunity to put it down somewhere safe. Derek gulped down his glass, and poured himself another. 'I don't drink this stuff myself usually, but Damaris always said you gave sherry to solicitors.' He grinned, hoisting up trouser legs as he seated himself beside Trixie. 'So . . . on with the show, right? Let's have it. The old man left everything to Damaris, right?'

The solicitor fingered documents in his briefcase, drawing out a sheaf of papers and leafing through them.

'Oh, get on with it, man,' said Derek. 'No legal jargon. A plain "yes" is all we want. Does Damaris inherit the lot?'

The solicitor nodded. 'Yes, b–but . . .'

'That's all we need to know.' Derek drained his second glass. 'No ifs or buts. Lock, stock and barrel. House and contents. Car. Stocks and shares. Everything, right?'

'B–but—'

'Then we can take possession when we like, eh? Move in tomorrow. Get hold of the car. Do you know where it's kept? Well, never mind. There'll be some paperwork somewhere in the house—'

Lily uncrossed her legs, and lifted one forefinger. 'There's just one little tiny thing you've overlooked, Derek. Uncle Matthew left everything to Damaris, yes. She asked me to be her executor, and of course I agreed. But when she came to think things over, she realized that it wasn't quite fair for her to have everything and leave me with nothing. After all, I was just as much a member of his family as her. The very next day she made a will herself, leaving the house and its contents to me. And that's why she gave me her bunch of keys.'

The solicitor grabbed at his papers, trying to tease one out of the sheaf. 'Yes, I've Mrs Frasier's will here, b–but – if you c–could hold on a moment—'

Derek's blood pressure was rising. He poured himself another glass. 'What trickery is this? You weren't a member of his family, not of his blood, nor—'

'Neither was Damaris.' Lily stroked her wings of hair, left and right, her manner complacent. 'If there was any trickery involved, it was the way she sucked up to Uncle Matthew. You can't deny it.'

'I can, and I will. And if you think you're going to get away with what's rightfully mine—'

'P–please!' The solicitor flapped his papers around. 'P–please! Both wills will have to go to probate and nothing can be touched till then. Is that clearly understood?' In enforcing his authority, he lost his stammer.

Silence.

Lily licked her forefinger and drew it across her almost non-existent left eyebrow . . . and then across her right. 'Understood. But I need something in writing to prove that I'm to inherit. I have bills to meet, my father sold our house over my head and I need to find somewhere else to live. I shall have to get a loan to tide me over.'

'I can provide you with a letter to the effect that you inherit the house and contents, if you'll call at the office tomorrow,' said the solicitor, cramming papers back into his briefcase. And to Derek, 'Mrs Frasier made me executor of her will, and I'm bound to respect her wishes.'

'She wasn't in her right mind when she made that will,' said Derek.

'Nonsense,' said the solicitor, standing up and jerking his jacket down at the back. 'She seemed all right to me. Perfectly in control. Ms Cunningham was there when she made the will, though not a witness, of course, as she was a beneficiary. House and contents only to Ms Cunningham. My clerk witnessed the will, as did a girl from the dress shop next door. If you wish to contest your wife's will, then that is your right, but I cannot see under what grounds you can do so.'

Lily drained her glass and set it down. 'If that's all, I'll be on my way. Derek; don't be such a bad loser. You had nothing and you'll get nothing. So what's new?'

Derek's blood pressure was far too high. He tugged at his tie. 'If I know you, you'll be in that house tomorrow, taking stuff out to sell.' To the solicitor, 'If she's got Damaris's keys, what's to stop her clearing the house and selling the stuff?'

Bea leaned forward. 'Mrs Frasier asked us to prepare an inventory of the contents of the house; for which, incidentally, we have not yet been paid. Mr Frasier, I gave you one copy and I have another here. I can supply copies to all other interested parties. I have the second set of keys, which will be kept in the bank until probate is granted. So, if anything is taken out of that house before that time, we'll know that Ms Cunningham was responsible. Right?'

Lily flushed, an unpleasant sight. 'I'm no thief!'

Derek guffawed. 'Prove it.'

Lily tucked both wings of hair behind her ears, exposing even more of her puffy cheeks and sharp nose. 'If you go around saying things like that, Derek, I'll sue. It's slander, that's what it is. That house belongs to me and I can go in whenever I like!'

'Not yet it doesn't.' Derek swung around to the solicitor. 'Tell her!'

The solicitor was conciliatory. 'Probate can take anything from six weeks to six months or even longer.' He twitched a smile into place. 'Ms Cunningham, as executor, you will want to proceed with all possible speed with probate for Mr Kent's will. If you need any assistance, I shall be happy to . . .' He wafted one hand in the air, clutching his briefcase under the other arm.

Gail got to her feet. 'I'll see you out.'

Lily hurried after them. 'Can you give me a lift to the Tube station? I don't drive and I've not enough money for a taxi.'

Once they'd gone, Trixie turned on her brother, white-faced with anger. 'Derek, you told me it was all done and dusted, that we could move in to—'

Derek jerked his head towards Bea, and Trixie fell silent, chewing her lip.

Bea got to her feet. 'It's about time I was moving on, too.'

'You've got the keys in a safe place?'

'In the office, yes. They go into the bank tomorrow.'

'You said you'd bring them with you this afternoon.'

Bea shook her head. 'It was you who said that. I'm waiting to see how the wills stand up before I hand them over to anyone.'

Derek wanted to take a swing at her. She could see him calculating how far she stood from him. She could read in his eyes how much he wanted to hit her. She stood very still, not exactly daring him to hit her, but letting him know she wasn't afraid.

Gail put her head around the door. 'I'm just going to check on Tom's arm, and then I'll be off, too. It's stopped raining, thank goodness. Shall I see you out, Bea?'

Bea hadn't even taken off her coat, so picked up her bag and went out to join Gail, who had opened the front door and was standing on the doorstep. The fresh air outside was keen, but welcome.

Gail said, 'We haven't had our talk yet. Can you manage the same place as before? Six thirty? You noticed the omission, of course?'

'Don't know how I kept my face straight.'

'Matthew left his whole estate to Damaris, but Damaris only left Lily the house and contents. Which means that—'

'The car, the stocks and shares and anything else he owned outside the house, should still go to Derek.' Bea grinned. 'Now I wonder why didn't we point that out to him?'

'I know I ought to have said something, but . . . he's so greedy, I can't bear to listen to him. Didn't he care about Damaris at all?' She sighed. 'Don't answer that. I don't think he ever did, but he might at least pretend . . . no, he couldn't. I don't think Tom cares, either. Oh, they're both going to feel her absence because she used to do everything for them, but that's not missing someone because you love them, is it?'

Bea shook her head. She knew the difference, too, and it wasn't.

Gail followed Bea out to her car. 'Bea, are you any happier than I am about this? Because for two pins I'd go to the police and say . . . but that's the trouble. I don't know what to say, except that I don't understand . . . well, anything.'

'It stinks, doesn't it? Well, I've got to get back, see what's going on at work. We'll talk this evening, not least about Matthew.'

Gail drew in her breath. 'You know, don't you?'

'I guessed.' Bea drove off leaving Gail, hugging her shoulders, to go back into the house.

Seventeen

Friday afternoon

Bea let herself into her house, prepared to mount the assault course of furniture and carpet, and almost lost her balance. The carpet had gone! The furniture was still piled up in the hall, but the carpet had disappeared.

She stood still, listening.

She could see straight through to the kitchen and the only living thing there was the cat Winston, lying full length on the work surface. There was no sound of radio or TV, or of clashing pots and pans. So Maggie wasn't in.

There was no sound of hammers or drills from below. Only a soothing buzz from some machine or other that Bea couldn't identify. The dust sheet had been let down over the stairs.

The telephone pinged as a call came in, but it was quickly silenced. Someone was attending to it. Oliver? Miss Brook?

Bea turned in to the living room and found it deserted and comparatively tidy. It was clear the Green Girls' team had been and gone for there was hardly any dust to be seen. There was no sign of Max or of Miss Townend, and their piles of files had been stacked to one side of the fireplace. It might be possible for Bea to use the room again, if she avoided the area around the dining table where much of her office had landed up.

She was hungry, having missed lunch and not been tempted by the sherry which was all that Derek and Trixie had thought necessary to provide after the funeral. She foraged in the fridge, finding a plate of sandwiches and some home-made soup left for her by Maggie. What a splendid girl she was, to be sure.

Winston looked up with interest as she put her plate on the table, but she fended him off with one hand while putting the soup in the microwave to warm.

'Thought I heard you.' Oliver appeared in the doorway. 'How did it go?'

'Interesting. Gail is ready to talk now. We're meeting this evening. Things have been happening here? No carpet, no Maggie, no Max?'

'Maggie's at the job down the road, the foreman took the carpet at her instigation, and there's someone sanding and polishing the floors downstairs as we speak. Miss Townend has popped out for some indigestion tablets but will be back shortly. As for Mr Max,' Oliver tried to smooth out a grin, 'Miss Brook got him to remove himself by sheer force of personality.'

'How on earth did she do that?'

'I wish I knew. She said she'd had enough of working in your bedroom and went down to confront him. He went out soon after. I expected her back upstairs straight away, but no . . . she came back ten minutes later, brushing one hand against the other, to announce that she will be working in the front office downstairs as soon as the furniture is replaced. She must have checked out the agency rooms while she was at it.' Oliver switched on the kettle. 'Coffee?'

Bea worked her way back over what he'd just said. 'You mean, she wants to come back to work for us on a permanent basis?'

Oliver stared at the kettle, didn't reply. Shrugged.

Bea stroked her temples. Was she getting another pressure headache? 'I suppose . . . do we have enough work to . . .? Yes, we do, because Maggie is wonderful as a project manager but has no great interest in the day to day agency business. But I'm not sure . . . Oliver, how would you feel about Miss Brook moving in?'

'She's good. Very good. A bit sharp at times, but I don't mind that. She understands that I can do some things better than her and I have to admit she handles people better than I do. Come to think of it, routine bookkeeping isn't exactly my favourite thing. I like puzzles, finding things out. I don't want to do the same thing day in and day out. Oh, by the way, I've run off Matthew's engagements for you.' He slapped some papers down on the table. 'Two months back, you said? I included what he'd got on for a month in the future as well. Lots of hospital appointments, I'm afraid. The big C.'

Oh? Then perhaps he had been depressed about his health?

Depressed enough to commit suicide? Yes, probably. Cancer was a killer. But why kill himself in that bizarre way?

'Thank you, Oliver. I'll look at them in a minute.' He was coming on, was young Oliver. He reached for the coffee jar and Bea noted that he was filling out, his shoulders becoming more solid, his arms and legs ditto. Even his hair seemed thicker, glossier. He'd treated himself to a good haircut, which helped.

He was growing up in more ways than one. A while ago, he'd no more have been able to make her a cup of coffee than fly. He wouldn't stay with her for ever, nor should he. He was rapidly losing the little-boy-lost look which had tugged at her heart when she first saw him, and turning into a good-looking young man. He'd coped with the horrible business of being unjustly thrown out of his home, and he'd been secure enough in himself to write off for a copy of his birth certificate.

'Oliver, do you want to talk about . . . whatever?' She didn't want to force the issue, but surely it wasn't good for him to keep the information about his parents to himself? If what Bea suspected was true, his birth father was not the man who had brought him up and then disowned him. As for his birth mother – she might or might not be the woman he'd been taught to call 'Mum'.

He bit out the words. 'It's OK. It's fine. I'm not bothered about it at all. I mean, lots of people get adopted every day. It's what they make of themselves that matters.'

'True. I believe that nowadays you can discover who really—'

He jerked his head. 'I'm not going down that road. I suppose some teenager got into trouble and the man wouldn't or couldn't marry her. What good would it do to find them? If they didn't want to know me then, I don't want to know them now.'

'I suppose I could readopt you, if you liked the idea?'

He closed his eyes and put out a hand to steady himself. Opened his eyes, stared straight ahead. In a deliberately casual voice, he said, 'You'd have to adopt Maggie, too, and I don't think you can do that because her mother is such a control freak she wouldn't let her daughter go.'

'Er, no. I suppose not.'

Now they were both embarrassed.

He looked at his watch. 'Miss Brook will kill me if I don't

get back soon. Some glitch at one of the embassies who haven't enough staff to cope with a big event this evening. She's dealing with it in her usual efficient manner, but will expect me to field everything else that comes in. Maggie will be in about six. Oh, and Mr Piers rang, said he'd be dropping by this evening.' Without making eye contact again, he withdrew.

Bea pressed both hands against hot cheeks. *Dear Lord, did I mess up, or did I! I am such a fool! Of course he doesn't want to be adopted by an old woman. If only Hamilton had been alive, he'd have known what to say to the lad. I am an idiot! What on earth made me lose my head like that?*

She must turn her mind to something else or she'd die of shame. What should she do next? She couldn't think. Ah, the material Oliver had printed off from Matthew's computer? Matthew's appointments for the last couple of months. She started at the beginning, working out what the abbreviated terminology meant.

'Bert'. That would be his old accompanist, Bert Cunningham. Bert cropped up three times; no, four, always an evening appointment. 'Damrs' for Damaris. So Damaris *had* been seeing him regularly? Also in the evenings. 'Dr' for doctor, obviously. After the second one there was, as Oliver had said, a big 'C' with a query.

'Hosp' – no prizes for working that one out. 'Rehrsl' for rehearsal. Would that have been for *The Gondoliers*? The 'Rehrsl' entries ceased after a couple of weeks. Probably after he'd learned he'd got cancer. Lots of doctor's appointments, lots of hospital appointments . . . a cluster of 'Damrs' entries and then two for 'Soltr'. Solicitor? Was that when he made his will and signed it? Probably.

Then 'Hospital' written out in full, followed by 'Op'. Ah, an operation. Another doctor's appointment followed by three exclamation marks. Why? A few days before he died, he'd typed '*The Gondoliers*' in full, followed by another exclamation mark.

There was an appointment for Bert the night before he died, and further notes for the future which he'd obviously not had time to cancel. Ah well. Pretty clear, then.

She checked on the living room, but all was still and quiet in there. Max hadn't returned and neither had Miss Townend. Bea stood at the window, looking down on the garden which was turning grey in an early twilight, and allowed herself a few moments of grief in which to remember her own dear husband.

She went up the stairs to the bedrooms. Oliver was in the guest bedroom, where Max's things were still piled up on the bed.

Miss Brook put the phone down as Bea opened the door into the master bedroom. 'Another job brought to a satisfactory conclusion. Although of course it would have been better if the client had known exactly what they wanted in the first place. The funeral passed off all right? In my day we hustled suicides out of sight without ceremony.'

Bea sat on her bed, relaxing for the first time that day. 'You should have been there. You'd have appreciated the sub-plots. Ex-wives bobbing up all over the place, grieving stepdaughter unavoidably absent due to a prior engagement with the mortuary, a surprise appearance from a woman who declares herself to be the new heiress, friends up in arms, no organist, no flowers, no order of service. And as for the wake; there wasn't one. At least, not unless you count a cat-and-dog fight over the remains. But there was a lot of genuine grief as well, if not from the immediate family circle.'

Miss Brook said, 'You enjoyed it?'

'In a way, yes. And in another way, no. A sad affair. Cancer. There's a lot I don't understand about the manner of Matthew Kent's death, but I hope to clear up one or two points tonight. In the meantime . . .'

Miss Brook tidied the papers on her desk. In anyone less self-assured, you'd have thought her nervous. 'It seems to me that if Mr Hamilton had still been alive, God bless him, he would have prevented Mr Max from . . . I'm not quite sure how to put this, but—'

'From making such a fool of himself? I agree, Hamilton would have handled the situation better. So, how did you manage to shift him?'

Miss Brook allowed herself a tiny frown. 'I wouldn't have put it in those terms, precisely. I merely suggested that he was not serving his constituency well by having to work from such a makeshift office. At that point he discovered he was going to be late for an important meeting, and left. Which gave me unhindered access to the phone.'

Bea tried not to be disappointed. She'd hoped he'd gone for good. 'Did you speak to Miss Townend?'

'The poor wee soul. She's quite unable to make up her mind what she should do. Her eighty-seven-year-old mother, who lives in a nice flat on the South Coast, is pressing her to stop work and return home to look after her. Only, Miss Townend doesn't feel she can leave Mr Max at such a terrible time. She talked about rats leaving sinking ships and her mother not being able to access the care which she ought to be offered by the council. Perhaps you can help her see where her duty lies?'

Bea regarded Miss Brook with awe. 'You certainly have a knack for dealing with people, Miss Brook.'

'You would have been able to do the same, if you'd had the time to give to the matter.'

That was a dig at Bea for getting involved with Matthew Kent's demise, but she didn't take offence. After all, it was very true. 'Have you any ideas about dealing with Max's files? Can we send them somewhere to have the information put on memory sticks?'

'All in hand. And if you can convince Miss Townend of the benefits of retirement, I have drawn up a list of possible new secretaries for him.'

Bea almost laughed. 'You think of everything.'

Miss Brook smoothed her back hair up into its dated but elegant French plait. 'I must admit to enjoying myself, back at work. Early retirement did not suit. My friends always said I would be bored at home, and they were quite right.'

She gave Bea a quick look, almost a plea.

Bea responded, 'Would it be too much of an imposition to ask you to return to working at the agency part-time? Oliver is a good lad and has many talents. He has really been carrying the agency recently, but we are getting so much work now that he can hardly cope by himself. And Maggie is—'

'A delightful child; give her anything practical to do and she is in her element, but I fear she hasn't the tidy mind needed for paperwork. Perhaps we could have two desks in reception in future, one for me and one for her? Three days a week would suit me admirably. Thank you.' Miss Brook switched off the computer, and got ready to leave for the day.

Bea knew when she was being dismissed. She went downstairs to see if Miss Townend had returned, which indeed she had. The poor creature was engaged in picking up pieces of paper in aimless fashion, wandering around, and putting them down again.

'Miss Townend, I'm so glad I caught you. Such a difficult time for my son, and I can't imagine how it must be for you, who has been his right hand ever since he was elected to Parliament. And to crown all, Miss Brook told me of your own personal problems. You must be feeling so torn.'

Miss Townend made a helpless gesture, files in both hands. 'Of course I can't leave him now. Mother doesn't understand how things are, how necessary it is that I stand by him. Only, at her age she does get so confused, poor dear, and last night when she told me she couldn't work out which pills she ought to be taking . . . I must confess that I had a little weep.'

'Of course you did, you poor thing.' Bea took the files from Miss Townend and pressed her to sit on the settee. 'What a dreadful decision you have to make. Your loyalty is beyond question, but your mother . . . well, mothers take priority, don't they?'

A handkerchief came out, and muffled the next words. 'Mr Max puts a good face on things, but his constituency chairman keeps ringing . . . that's dear Mr Max's wife's father, you know . . . and he positively shouts at me and I can't think what to say to him when Mr Max isn't here to take the call as he should be.'

'Indeed. It is too much! My son has been under a lot of stress, I know, but that's no reason why he shouldn't consider your feelings.'

'Oh, he does, of course he does!' She blew her nose, wiped her eyes.

'He does?' Bea didn't think he did.

'Well . . .' A half smile. 'Perhaps at this time, it's too much to expect, though I did tell him about Mummy wanting me to stop work some time ago, and he said that he couldn't possibly manage without me. What he doesn't realize is that I served his predecessor at the House, and her predecessor before that. I've worked there for nearly thirty years, and although I'm still in possession of all my faculties, my migraines do seem to be getting more frequent, and I'm just beginning to feel that it would be nice to relax and not bother about work, and see that Mummy takes her pills at the right time, because that's important, too, isn't it?'

Bea nodded. 'After all your years of devoted service, it's only right and proper that you should start to think of yourself for a change, and of course you want to be with your family when they need you. I know my son appreciates everything you've done for him, but I'm sure that, if you're really determined to go, we'll be able to find someone else to look after him. She won't have your years of experience in the job, of course, but she ought to be able to do his routine correspondence.'

'The thing is, you'll think me such a coward, but I've tried to tell him that he should think about looking for someone else, but every time I start, the phone rings or someone calls. It would be such an upset for him, and I do understand why he can't deal with it at the moment. You wouldn't like to tell him for me, would you?'

'My dear, of course.'

Miss Townend seemed to shed ten years. She looked at her watch. 'Do you think I could go home now? I don't like to leave things in such a mess, but—'

'I'll take care of it.'

'I feel a different woman. I'll go home now and give my landlady notice. Then I can ring Mummy with the good news before she watches *Coronation Street*.'

Bea left Miss Townend getting ready to leave, and went upstairs to shower and change. Miss Townend's mother would probably be as hard a taskmaster as Max, and bully her daughter into an early grave, but some women are cut out to be carers, and there isn't anything much you can do about that.

She tried Max's mobile phone, but it was engaged. So she left a message to say that Miss Townend had felt it time to retire and look after her elderly mother, and that the agency would find him a temp next week.

As she shut off her phone, her landline rang. It was Piers. 'So you're back at last, are you? Sorry I couldn't stop to talk at the crem, but something rather interesting came up.'

Bea wanted to reply that she hadn't been at all upset since she hadn't even noticed he was there, but held her tongue. With an effort. 'I saw you leave with a woman.'

'Yes.' He sounded unsure of himself. 'Matthew's doctor. I

didn't know her from Adam but she obviously wasn't one of the widows. What a turn-up, that Goldie woman! But Sylvester dealt with her beautifully, didn't he? Though I wasn't the only one who thought he was looking decidedly rocky.'

'Yes, Piers? You chatted his doctor up, I suppose, seeing she was by herself. And what did you find out?'

'You know, Bea, if it weren't for that suicide note, I'd be inclined to think that the coroner's verdict was wrong. But then again, these highly-strung types, up one minute and down the next . . . what else can one think?'

'I'm being very patient, Piers. What did she say about Matthew?'

'Oh, she couldn't. Patient confidentiality, and all that.'

'You got something out of her, though?'

'She said she was shocked to hear of his death. Which leads me to think that he'd no particular health problem when he died. It's a something and a nothing, isn't it? You can look at it either way.'

Well, Piers didn't know about the hospital appointments on Matthew's appointments schedule. The big C and all that. With one hand, Bea pulled down the zip on her skirt. 'I'll be in a better position to talk to you about this tomorrow. I'm having supper with the widow tonight.'

'Not Goldie?'

'No, not Goldie.' She put the phone down. Was this another piece of the jigsaw, and if so, what did it mean?

Eighteen

Friday evening

Gail got to the restaurant before Bea, who'd been held up in traffic.

'Do you mind if we eat before we talk?' Gail pressed her hand to her waist. 'I don't seem to have eaten properly for ages, and I know I'll start crying when . . . do you mind?'

'Of course not.'

So they talked of holidays abroad and books they'd read and television programmes they either liked or hated.

'No coffee,' said Gail. 'I'll make some back at my place, if it's all right with you?

Back at Gail's flat, coffee made, curtains drawn, comfortably seated, Bea waited.

Gail made a curiously helpless motion with her hands. 'Of course you've realized that Matthew and I, quite recently . . .' She stopped, pressed her lips firmly together. 'To begin at the beginning, if there is one. Matthew had a weakness for Gilbert and Sullivan and he was an enthusiastic supporter of the local amateur light opera group. He'd even take the alto part, if his engagements permitted. He was tremendous.

'A couple of years back some friends asked me to make up a party to see one of their productions and after that I went to every one. It seemed so silly not to when they were so enjoyable. I mean, it wasn't as if Matthew and I were ever going to meet. He wasn't in the last one so, as we went to the bar in the interval, I asked my friends if they knew why. They said to ask him myself so I turned around, and he was standing right behind us. He'd been in the audience, not on stage.

'We said the usual things; how are you, how've you been doing, what would you like to drink – only he couldn't have alcohol because he was on antibiotics. I said I'd retired, and he said likewise, that he'd been under the weather, they'd thought he'd got cancer but they'd operated and taken out a kidney with this tumour round it, but he'd just heard it wasn't cancer . . .'

What? Bea did a double take and almost missed Gail's next words.

'And we knew, both of us, that we'd been given a second chance. At least,' Gail said, with care, 'I thought we knew. I knew. Definitely. From the moment he looked at me and smiled. I thought he knew, too. The bell rang for the end of the interval, and he hesitated, and I did, too. Then he said, "Seize the moment," and took my hand and we went to sit in the foyer, because he was pretty weak still after the operation. He joked about it, saying he really needed a stick to lean on at the moment, and I said would he like to borrow my father's old stick with the silver knob. He said that would be good, fend off muggers and help him get a seat on the Tube. We talked about how I felt, being retired. Which was quite good, actually, if a bit boring, though I was doing all these community support things. He said he'd had a pretty bad few months thinking he was going to die, and his old accompanist was failing fast, going into a home, but that he, Matthew, had been encouraged to write some stuff for the telly and he was looking forward to doing that.

'It was a surprise when the audience came out. The time had gone so quickly. He said he'd get a taxi and take me home and I said no, that I had my car nearby. I wanted to say, "Come home with me." I wanted . . . I didn't know what to say. It was too quick, I needed to think. It was so wonderful, and yet so unexpected. He said could he take me out for a meal, if it were local, as he wasn't up to much at the moment, and I remembered that the next day I was booked to go away with friends for a week, visiting gardens in France.

'I thought of cancelling it, but then I thought I was being stupid and that if he really meant he wanted to see me again, a week wouldn't matter. I said I'd drop my father's stick around to him early next morning before I left for the airport, and he said that would be good, and to shove it through the letterbox if he wasn't up, because he was taking his time getting up and down stairs at the moment.

'He took my mobile phone number and gave me his card.

I could see he was getting tired, but he was happy, he was! I wasn't wrong about that, was I? He said he'd phone me when I got back and we'd have a quiet dinner together. I said that he must hurry up and get strong again, and he said he would.'

She let the tears fall and didn't try to check them. 'I thought of him all the time we were away. I imagined how it would be when we got back. I thought that Damaris might be jealous, and I was sorry about that, but for me . . . it was just great. He phoned me every night to ask how I was getting on, and to report on his own progress. We just chatted, about this and that, nothing important. He said he was using my father's stick and it was a great help, that on my last day there he'd even managed a walk in the park.

'When I got back, there was a message on the answerphone saying "Welcome home" and that he'd ring me the next night when I'd recovered from the journey. Only, of course, he didn't. I waited in. I rang his number the next morning, but he didn't pick up. I didn't know what to think. The following evening I rang my friends to see if they had any news of him, but they hadn't. I thought he might have had a relapse, been taken to hospital. The third day I actually rang around the hospitals, can you believe? The fourth day, Sylvester rang and told me he'd committed suicide. And I still can't believe it.'

Neither could his doctor, because the operation had been a success. The doctor had known it, and so had Matthew. Presumably Damaris had known about the cancer because she'd arranged for him to make a will. So when had Matthew told Damaris that he was in the clear and not going to die soon? And what had Damaris's reaction been to the good/bad news? Blind rage? What about that blood on the carpet? Had that been Damaris lashing out? But . . . no, if she'd killed him that way, surely the pathologist would have spotted it?

Bea tried to assess how much more Gail could take. Her behaviour recently had indicated a woman on the verge of a breakdown, but she'd been a teacher in the state school system, had risen to be head. There was a backbone somewhere in there. If they were going to solve this mystery, then Gail had to prove that she still had that backbone.

Gail sniffed, got out a handkerchief, blew her nose, wiped her eyes, straightened her back. 'I seem to have done nothing but cry and throw up for days. Enough! Matthew's gone and so is Damaris. I tell myself that worse things happen at sea, I'm the fortunate owner of a nice flat, I have plenty of friends, and enough interests, helping in the community and so on, to pass the time till I die. I'll survive.'

She took out a make-up bag, and attended to her hair and lipstick.

Bea waited, watching, assessing.

Gail took a deep breath. 'Why are you looking at me like that?'

Bea was cautious. 'Tell me, did Bert Cunningham smoke?'

'Like the proverbial. Awful man. I could always tell when Matthew had been with him, because his clothes stank of nicotine. Why?'

'Matthew kept a list of his appointments on his computer. He was due to see Bert the night he died. I found an ashtray under a chair by the fireplace and a trail of cigarette ash on the carpet on the morning I first went to the house, but it was cleared away by the time I returned the next day. I wondered who'd been there. I thought it might have been Bert.'

Gail frowned. 'I wondered why he wasn't at the funeral, but Matthew told me Bert was cracking up, going into a home somewhere.'

'I'm sorry to touch a sore spot, but have you been told the exact circumstances surrounding Matthew's death?'

Gail shuddered. 'I asked Damaris and she said it had been painless and he'd left a note. She said I didn't need to know any more than that, and of course I don't.' She grimaced. 'He must have heard from his doctor that it really was cancer after all. It's the only thing that makes sense. I suppose he put his affairs in order, paid all his bills, left instructions for his funeral, a donation to the church, I expect. Then he'd leave notes for the coroner and some of his friends – for Bert, I suppose; Sylvester, of course. I'd have thought he'd have left one for me but . . . no, I am not going to cry again. He didn't, and so I have to accept that he didn't feel as deeply towards me as I did towards him.

'I can see him taking one last walk around the house – he loved that house, you know; it had belonged to his parents and still had a lot of their furniture in it – and then he'd make sure he wasn't disturbed, take the pills, perhaps play some music? Would he have gone to sleep in his bed? Yes, I think he would.

Wearing his best silk pyjamas. He loved the feeling of silk. Yes, that is how he would have done it.'

It was a shame to disabuse her. Bea wondered if it wouldn't be kinder to leave things as they were. Yes, why not leave things as they were? It would only hurt Gail more to learn of his bizarre end.

The flat lay quietly about them, the double-glazing cutting out the sound of traffic below. A plane droned overhead.

Gail got up and switched on all the lights. 'Out with it, Bea Abbot. A teacher can always tell when a pupil's hiding something.'

'Do you really want to turn over stones? There may be some nasty creepy-crawlies under them.'

'No, I don't. Not at all. But I don't like unanswered questions, either. All right, let's look under some stones. I've given you my fantasy version of how Matthew died. What really happened?'

So Bea told her. Sparing her nothing. The dress, the painted face, the wig, the note next to the empty bottle of wine, the painkillers. Kasia, running away, terrified. Bea drawn on to the premises by Kasia's defection.

Gail sat still, eyes never leaving Bea's face. Growing paler by the second. Was she going to throw up again? Weep?

Bea finished her tale.

Gail blinked. 'I don't believe it. None of it. Oh, of course I believe *you*, but . . . he wasn't one for histrionics in real life. If he'd wanted to use one of his own costumes, well, I suppose I could just about understand that, but to use a hired one that would need cleaning before it could be worn again? No! And he wouldn't have let that poor girl Kasia find him like that, scaring the life out of her. He was fond of her. He told me how she'd been helping him out with extra time while he was convalescing, getting in shopping for him.'

'Yes, the fridge was well-stocked.'

'Suicides don't do that,' said Gail. 'Stock the fridge, I mean.'

'And the red dress and shoes? They were hired for a part in *The Gondoliers*? A part he had to decline because he fell ill?'

'That's right. They'd gone ahead and hired a costume for him, hoping he'd be all right. I think he'd wondered if he might be able to tread the boards one last time but of course he couldn't and they had to get someone else in at the last minute, a woman, she wasn't bad. When he was on the phone to me in France, he said he was worried about getting the costume back because the box was heavy and he couldn't lift anything yet, and I said I'd get it back for him and he said no, he'd get a cab to take it back and that I wasn't to bother. I'd forgotten about that.'

She stood up, walking around, hands kneading the back of her neck. 'He wouldn't have done what you said he did, Bea. He was a most thoughtful man. And a believer. He really was, you know. All this that you're telling me . . . the fact that he had such a strong belief in God, that he was recovering so well from the operation, that he had work to look forward to . . . I just can't reconcile the facts with what I know of the man.'

'Nor what you know of Damaris's death?'

'What! What was that? Oh, you mean why she was on that platform?'

'I mean, why did she leave Matthew's house to Lily, and how has Lily managed to acquire a set of keys to the house if she didn't get them off Damaris before Damaris was killed?'

Gail turned a greenish colour, but didn't collapse.

Bea waited.

Gail whispered, 'I saw it, and refused to see it. I'm not sure I can cope. What in heaven's name is going on?'

'I think Matthew's death has more suspicious circumstances around it than a fatal "accident" to a cheating wife.' For a moment Bea thought Gail was going to collapse, but she didn't. Instead, her head went up and back.

'My daughter did not kill Matthew. Believe me, she loved him, in so far as she was capable of loving anyone. Lily? Well, she was always the odd one out. But . . . no, no, no! That can't be right.'

Bea waited some more.

Gail closed her eyes, breathed deeply. In and out. Finally she opened her eyes again and sat down, composing herself neatly, ankles and knees together. 'You have no proof. He's been cremated. End of story. There's nothing we can do about it.'

'Well, we could ask some questions.'

'Such as?'

'Where's the silver-knobbed cane you lent Matthew? That's what you came looking for that first day, wasn't it?'

'As a matter of fact, I'd forgotten all about it. I wasn't thinking straight. I'd just heard and couldn't believe it. There you all were acting as if it were a normal day and all I could think about was that I couldn't throw up in front of you all. You must have thought me mad. I remember taking the photograph but the stick . . . I suppose it's in the hall there. I'll have to ask Lily if I can have it back, because it was my father's.'

'It's not in the hall. It's not anywhere in his house. Look.' Bea laid out the pages of the inventory for Gail to see.

Gail ran her finger swiftly down the pages of the inventory. An experienced checker of children's homework, she didn't miss anything. Bea half expected her to produce a red pen and correct a misspelling. She finished reading. 'I expect it fell down at the side of the bed, rolled under.'

'We looked under the bed, because that's where the box from the costumier's landed up.'

'Matthew told me he'd left the costume in the hall, because it needed to go back. I don't understand.'

'Here's another question that's going to be difficult for you to answer. How did Lily get hold of Damaris's keys? Damaris definitely handed them over to Lily, didn't she? Which means they must have met somewhere early that morning before Damaris jumped in front of a train. Did they meet at Ealing Broadway station, perhaps? The only person reportedly standing near Damaris before she jumped was a Muslim woman dressed all in black. Lily was wearing a long black coat for the funeral, wasn't she? Suppose she'd tied a black scarf closely round her head to hide her hair. Wouldn't she look like a Muslim woman then?'

Gail did some more deep breathing. In a small voice, she said, 'You think there was a conspiracy, that Lily and Bert were scheming all along to get hold of Matthew's house? No, Bert wouldn't, would he?'

'I think it might be a good idea to ask him a few questions though, don't you?'

Gail shivered, clutching her shoulders. 'I'm trying to picture Lily pushing Damaris under that train. My gut reaction says that yes, she's capable of it. If only I didn't feel so tired!'

'Emotional trauma. Can you also picture Lily dressing Matthew's body up the way I saw it?'

Gail closed her eyes. 'Ouch.' Nodded.

Bea stood up. 'Have you had enough for today?'

Gail nodded again.

Bea picked up her jacket and handbag. 'I'll see myself out. Ring you in the morning, see if you feel up to paying Bert a visit. You don't know where he's gone, do you?'

Gail shook her head. 'We'll have to ask Lily. Only, if there was a conspiracy, she won't want us descending on him with a lot of questions, will she? Is there any other way we can find out?'

'There might be. Let's try her first. Do you have their address?'

'I can get it from Derek. He'll have it.' She went to the phone, and in a moment was through. 'Derek, Gail here. How are you . . .? Yes, I'm sure, but . . . Yes, Trixie is very kind to move in and . . . Yes, yes. But what I wanted to ask you is, do you know Lily's address? It was some place out near Gunnersbury Park, I think, but they might have moved, I suppose . . . No? Still there? . . . Well, could you look in Damaris's address book, as I think they may have been in touch lately . . . yes, I'll hang on.'

A pause, during which she nodded to Bea. 'They're still there.' Then Derek's voice could be heard to which she replied, 'Ah, yes, I remember. Chartwell Avenue? Yes, I went there once with Matthew to pick up some music. Have you a phone number?' She listened and wrote it down. 'That's most helpful, Derek. Thank you. Is Tom's arm all right? Oh, good. Well, I'll try to ring you again tomorrow, see what Trixie's arranged. Love to . . . yes, yes.'

She put the phone down. 'They're still there. I seem to remember it's an old house, a bit of a tip, which Bert bought way back when he'd got some money, orchestrated some music for the theatre, something like that. Three storeys, with a holly hedge in front. He used the back room as a studio, devising and recording jingles for adverts, that sort of thing. Not sure what Lily does.'

'I'll pick you up at ten and we'll pay them a visit.'

Later Friday evening

Bea was restless. She parked the car and decided to go for a walk, pound the pavements, try to make sense of the questions endlessly circling in her head. She found herself at

St Mary Abbots church at the bottom of the hill, pushed open one of the heavy doors and went inside.

Dusk was settling early, but there was still enough light coming through the stained-glass windows to guide her to the small chapel to the right of the main altar. There were usually one or two people sitting there, quietly. Either resting or praying. Or perhaps doing both.

She slid into a chair at the back of the chapel, and let herself relax. She'd been tense for a long time. Too long.

Hamilton had often dropped into this very chair in the chapel, resting or praying for a while. Both, knowing him.

She wondered if Matthew had liked to do the same. She wondered if they'd ever met here in this church, or perhaps passed by one another without knowing that one day Hamilton's wife would be trying to find out the truth about Matthew's death.

She wondered what the truth really was.

Dear Lord, I'm not good at crossword puzzles and conundrums and I wouldn't be able to do Sudoku if my life depended on it. You know my limitations better than I do. What I'm thinking . . . fearing . . . wondering about . . . could it possibly be true? Because if so, it's the worst possible crime that I can think of, and the mind that was capable of doing it . . . If I try to unravel the mystery, I'm going to have to go very carefully. Considering the personality involved, I'm going to need your protection to deal with this. Please.

She came to with a start as someone switched on the lights in the main body of the church and lights came on in the chapel. People were arriving in droves for some service or other, or perhaps for a concert? She stumbled to her feet, and fled, not feeling up to making small talk, or of sitting through a formal service.

Nineteen

Back at the house, Bea noticed that the curtains and blinds had been drawn against the gathering darkness and, as she let herself in the front door, she was greeted by sounds of radio, television, and crashing of pans. Maggie was home and baking something spicy.

'Blessings on you, child,' said Bea, dropping on to the nearest seat in the kitchen. 'What a pleasure it is to come home to your bright face. But what are doing, cooking at this hour of night? Is Oliver home?'

Maggie was dressed in a bright orange sweater over a short, embroidered blue denim skirt. She had gelled and brushed her hair up and her nail polish matched her skirt. 'I'm just throwing some biscuits together while waiting for Oliver to come back from the gym. He's taking me out for a drink. I don't really fancy going into a pub by myself.'

Bea wanted to ask about her failed affair with the plumber, but refrained. Let the child tell all, or keep her own secrets. She was old enough.

Maggie used oven gloves to take a tray of biscuits out of the oven. 'Don't touch. They're hot. And don't let Winston get at them. He's no sense at all and will burn his nose.'

Winston had just jumped up on to the table, so Bea picked him up and gave him a cuddle. 'We'd best get him checked over by the vet.'

'Mm. Oliver says you offered to adopt him.'

Bea blinked. Now there was a nice change of subject! And how did Maggie feel about it?

Maggie's arms went akimbo. 'That meant a lot to him. He said you'd like to adopt me, too, but of course that's just not practical.'

Bea shook her head. No, it wasn't.

'But nice,' said Maggie, with one of her sudden, wide smiles.

'We appreciate it. Both of us. But you won't be upset if he says no, will you? He's got to work this out himself. I told him I'd like to stick pins into a wax image of his father, and he said he'd like to do the same to my mother, but really neither of them can help what they are, can they?'

Bea shook her head. No, they couldn't.

Maggie started transferring the biscuits to a rack. 'Totally inadequate personalities, both of them. My mother's a selfish, narrow-minded old crone, locked into the last century, and his father's the same only worse. The thing is, we don't have to use them as role models.' She held out a biscuit on a spatula. 'Want to try one? Careful. Still hot.'

Bea took one, pushing Winston's nose away as she did so. The biscuit was good.

'I'm so glad you agreed we could sand and polish the floors downstairs. No more carpets, lots of light, lots of white or off-white paint, though not Magnolia, I think.'

Bea nodded again, hearing footsteps behind her.

Oliver with his gym bag, fresh from the shower, and dressed casually for a visit to the pub. 'Evening, Mrs Abbot. Ready, Maggie? Are those cinnamon biscuits?'

Maggie slapped his hand away. 'Give me a minute to get my jacket. You can have a biscuit when they're cooled down, but don't let Winston get at them. He'll have to go on a diet if he's not careful, never stops eating.' She pounded off up the stairs.

Oliver dumped his smelly gym clothing into the washing machine. 'Got any further with the Matthew Kent affair, Mrs Abbot? It's been on my mind all day. He was murdered, wasn't he?'

'Something very nasty happened, I agree. But murder? I'm not sure.'

'Of course he was murdered. That scene on the bed was staged to put us off the truth.'

'Yes, I think it was, but—'

'What it is, you know this friend who helps me with computer stuff? Well, he happens to be the sort of expert who gets called in by the police sometimes.'

She ought to have guessed that.

'I've told him what a puzzle this thing with Matthew Kent was, and he said . . . of course you don't have to . . . but he said that if ever you wanted to talk to someone about things that were bothering you, well, he might listen.'

'Thank you, Oliver. That might be exactly what we need. I'm going to try to find the answers to one or two questions tomorrow and then, if I'm lucky, you can give me your friend's telephone number.'

'You don't want to talk to him tonight?'

'Not enough information yet. Tomorrow.'

That would do, wouldn't it?

When Maggie and Oliver had banged the front door shut on their way out, Bea carefully put the newly-baked biscuits into a tin that Winston couldn't open, and switched the washing machine on. Oliver could make a computer dance a fandango, but hadn't yet mastered the art of turning on a washing machine.

The house was unusually quiet. She liked that. She went down the stairs, from which the builders' sheet had been removed, and inspected the gleaming floors of the agency rooms, which looked ghostly in this twilight world. The reception room had already been repainted, but the other rooms still had plaster drying out on the walls. The electrician seemed to have finished, with new power points everywhere, and new light fitments.

She remembered how it had been when she and Hamilton had run the agency between them, with one-day-a-week help from Miss Brook. Yes, the place had become slightly dingy over the years and yes, the plumbing and electricity had needed to be overhauled, but it gave her a nostalgic twinge to think of the way it had been for so many years.

Oh well, we all wear out in time, don't we? The future lay with Oliver and Maggie and the indestructible, ageless Miss Brook. Of course, Maggie was right, and the new flooring, lighting and plumbing were an improvement, but Bea hoped Maggie wouldn't start to replace the furniture next . . . although, come to think of it, her old office chair – which had once been Hamilton's – could do with a facelift.

Winston explored with her, his claws clicking on the wooden floors. With his tail waving, he peered out of the French windows into the darkness of the garden, and then followed her up the stairs, where he bounded on to her bed in order to give himself a good wash.

Bea read a little, dozed a little, prayed a little. Turned off the lights. Heard the youngsters return. Fell asleep. Woke at half past four with the feeling that something was amiss. The landing light was still on. She struggled out of bed and went to turn it off. Saw that the guest bedroom door was ajar. She pushed the door wider open and discovered that the bed was empty. Max had not returned. Was that a good thing? She hoped it was. Went back to bed with Winston lightly snoring at her back.

Saturday morning

There's nothing like oversleeping to give you a muzzy head. Bea woke at nine to find the curtains open and her early morning cuppa cold on her bedside table. Bother.

She hauled herself out of bed, grimacing at the thought of what she had to do that day. Suppose she couldn't get any information out of Lily? Suppose Max had had a relapse and spent the night in hospital?

Well, it was a Saturday, so Miss Brook wouldn't be arriving to quiver her nose at a boss who overslept. And there would be no Miss Townend. Good.

Yawning, she went to check on the guest bedroom and found the bed still undisturbed. So Max definitely hadn't come home last night. He should have phoned and left a message to say he was detained elsewhere, of course, but hadn't thought of it. Unless, of course, he was back in hospital.

When she went downstairs, there was only Maggie to be seen, shoving packages into the big, brightly coloured fabric bag in which she toted her belongings around. Maggie had also chosen some brightly coloured clothes; scarlet and emerald. Ouch. Hard on the eye.

'One message for you,' said Maggie, 'Sylvester, his office, not his home number. Will you ring back when you can. I'm off to Brighton for the day. Never been. Sightseeing with a friend. Not Oliver. He's gone to some computer exhibition or other, something new and mind-bending. Oh, and he left you this telephone number . . . where did I put it? Oh, here it is.' She produced someone's business card on which he'd written a mobile number. 'And by the way, I meant to say yesterday, don't go down into the basement yet, the polish needs time to dry before we walk on it, or it'll have to be done again.' Off she went, banging the door to behind her. Naturally.

Not walk on the basement floors? Oh. Too late. Bea grimaced. Why hadn't the child left a prominent notice to that effect where Bea could have seen it before she went down there? Oh well, if it had to be done over again, it did.

Bea made herself some black coffee. Dialled the number of Sylvester's office. 'Sylvester rang me a while ago.'

The voice at the other end was not that of Sylvester, nor of his son. 'I'm sorry to tell you that Mr Sylvester passed away yesterday afternoon. Suddenly, after the party he'd been giving. It was very quick. He sat down to rest, and they couldn't wake him up. He left a list of people he would like to be advised . . . we will be in touch soon about . . . details to come.'

'Thank you,' said Bea, and put the phone down with a hand that was not at all steady. She reached for the box of tissues. She was alone in the house and it was all right to cry. Sylvester dead? Of course she'd noticed the signs. They'd even joked about it. He'd been around in the background of her life for ever.

It was all right to cry for an old friend. She knew she was not crying for him, but for herself, who would miss him. She hoped he would get a sympathetic hearing when he arrived Up Top, and that his sins would be far outweighed by his intrinsic goodness. A generous heart.

The landline rang when she was putting on her make-up.

Max, speaking a little too loud and fast. 'Mother, are you there? I thought I'd better give you a ring, tell you what's happening.'

'Where are you?' She could hear background noise. Something rhythmic.

'We're in the train, of course. Nicole didn't fancy the journey in the car. Going up to tell the old folk the good news . . . hang on a minute . . . no, darling, I know I said we wouldn't tell anyone else just yet, but . . . Mother, are you there still? We'll be back on Monday, come in to see you then, right?'

'Yes, right.' So Nicole had actually taken her advice and told him she was pregnant? And her parents, too?

Oh. Bea wasn't at all sure what she ought to feel about this development. Of course she would be ecstatic if Nicole really were pregnant. Or would she? No, she wouldn't. She'd try to be pleased, of course. When she'd thought about it long enough she probably would be pleased. Her first grandchild. Nice thought.

If Nicole were not pregnant, but just pretending . . . how long could the girl keep it up? And was it desirable that she should?

Bea groaned. *Dear Lord, I am such a fool. I rush in, making all sorts of suggestions that I should never even have allowed myself to think about, and this is the result. Ouch. Please Lord, whatever the case really is, can you look after Nicole and Max . . . if that is your will.*

I'm in such a muddle I don't know what to think.

The last thing Nicole said to me indicated that she might indeed be pregnant but hadn't noticed. In which case, am I less or more to blame?

She shuddered.

She noticed the time and realized she was going to be late to meet Gail if she didn't hurry up. Where had she put the card Oliver had left her? With a bit of luck, she might need it later on today. Come to think of it, she might as well take the inventory and the photographs and, well, everything that she had managed to put together about Matthew.

Bea collected Gail and they drove through the traffic to Chartwell Avenue. A pleasant, tree-lined street, a mix of three-storey Edwardian and two-storey-with-a-loft-conversion houses. The holly hedge was still there.

What was new was a 'Sold' sign nailed to the gatepost.

'This begins to make sense,' said Bea. 'You know what to do? Look for anything that could tell us what Lily's been up to, and in particular where we can find Bert.'

They got out of the car and eyed the red-brick façade. It was a large house, but not a welcoming one. The holly hedge was a darkening influence on the tiny front garden, but the faded paintwork was also dark. A bad choice. The tiled pathway was not in good condition, but the gutters were functioning and the down pipes vertical.

Gail pointed to a dingy brass plaque on the gatepost. 'Cunningham, piano lessons. Was that him or her?'

Bea rang the bell inside the porch. More tiling. Stained-glass panels in the heavy old door. A worn doormat. A pile of circulars in the green recycling box. A faint but persistent smell of . . . dry rot?

Lily opened the door halfway and blinked. 'What do you two want? Can't you see I'm busy? Oh, I suppose you've brought back the things you stole.'

Bea raised her eyebrows. 'You mean the little silver jug and the china shepherdess? Mrs Frasier allowed Goldie to take them. Now, what we wanted—'

'Oh, did she, indeed! I'll have to have a word with Goldie. So, what did you want, then? Ah, you've brought me the keys? Or have you given them to the estate agent already?' She opened the door wider.

'No, I've still got them,' said Bea, brushing past Lily into the cavernous hall. More tiling, cleared spaces where large pieces of furniture had once stood, dust in the air. An old coat-stand with female articles of clothing on it. Prominent among them was a long black coat, and a black scarf. Suitable for a Muslim woman.

There were no men's clothes hanging up, but a number of black plastic bags gaped open on the floor, containing what looked like men's shirts and jackets. So Lily was having a clear-out of her father's things already? And some of the furniture had already gone to the sale room, or wherever Lily intended to live?

Bea said, 'There's a couple of things I wanted to check with Bert before I hand the keys over.'

Gail almost stepped on Bea's heels in haste to get in before the door was closed on them. 'May I visit your loo?'

'Oh, I suppose so. What do you want with Bert? It's me who inherits.' Lily closed the door on the outside world. There was only a dim light bulb in the hall and the air was chilly. Bea stepped through a door on the right, closely followed by Gail. They were in a large front room with a high ceiling and squared-off bay window. More dust. Drooping maroon curtains. Lighter patches on the wallpaper showing where more furniture had been removed. A grand piano was still there and a couple of glass-fronted bookcases, their doors hanging open, their shelves half empty. Stacks of sheet music. Cardboard boxes, half full of books.

Communicating double doors led from this room into another equally large one at the back of the house. Bea pushed one of the doors wide open to reveal a combined sitting room, recording studio and office. There was a small armchair sitting in front of a television set, and spaces where a settee and other furniture had once stood.

'Through here?' Gail slipped into the second room.

Lily made as if to stop Gail, but Bea took her by the arm and turned her away towards the piano. 'Leave her be. She'll find the loo. Is this where you give music lessons, Lily?'

'What if I do? All that's finished.'

'You're moving, I see. Where are you going?'

'None of your business.'

'And Bert? I really need a word with him.'

'What for? Forget him. His mind's gone, He's totally lost the plot, not making any sense since Uncle Matthew died. The shock sent him all funny.'

'So what will you do? You can't get into Matthew Kent's house, can you? Your solicitor seems honest enough, if not the brightest knife in the drawer. He's confused, what with two wills and two families wanting to move into that valuable property. He's made it clear that nobody moves anywhere until probate is granted, right?'

'No need to worry about me, I have a bed-sitter all lined up, but I won't be there long. Half the furniture's gone already, the rest goes Monday morning, except for the stuff the new people are going to buy. They move in Monday afternoon. So what do you want?'

'I worry about you, I really do. You've lived here all your life. You've struggled to earn a few pennies by giving piano lessons. You've never married. It must have seemed that the world had fallen apart when your father said he was selling the house to move into a home. If he was your father.' She knew that was a cruel thing to say, but she believed that what Lily had done was more than cruel, and it might provoke her into saying something unwise.

Lily's lower lip came out. 'He was my father as long as it suited him, so long as I slaved for him, cooked and cleaned and ran all his errands, took him to the doctor's and dentist's and dished out his medication and got up in the night to help him to the toilet and back. Oh, he called me his lovely daughter then,' said Lily, tucking her hair back behind her ears. 'But do you know how he repaid me? He went behind my back to find a company which would give him an annuity in exchange for this house, arranging to hand it over to them for sale when he felt ready to go into a home. And he didn't tell me until six months ago. Now I'm homeless and he's in clover for the rest of his life. Is it surprising that I'm bitter?'

'No, it isn't. Tell me, when did you meet up with Damaris again? I know you used to play together when you were children, but . . .'

'Damaris?' Scorn in her voice. 'What a waste of space. Never could see beyond the end of her nose. Bert told me about it as soon as she started making regular visits to Uncle Matthew, and she only visited him because he'd got cancer. Bert could see what she was working for, and so could I. He thought it was amusing that she was going to get Matthew's house and money, and that I was going to be left with nothing. That's the kind of person Bert was.'

'So you decided to look Damaris up?'

'I went into the shop where she worked and asked her to have lunch with me for old times' sake.' She lifted her upper lip in a gesture of contempt. 'She talked of nothing but how life was coming right for her at long last.'

'She arranged for Matthew to make his will, and asked you to be executor. Why was that?'

Lily reared back her head. 'Why not? We went back a long way. She trusted me. She wouldn't have asked that useless husband of hers, would she?'

'Point taken. So she was looking at a bright future, and you were looking into the abyss. How did you get her to play your game?'

'What game? There was no game.'

'If there was no game, if you didn't have any hold on her, then why did she leave Matthew's house to you?'

'She felt sorry for me, that's why. Now, if you don't mind, I've got a lot to do.' She looked at the door into the other room. 'Has Gail got lost?'

Bea was soothing. 'She's had a gippy tummy for days. So, where am I to send the keys on to – after probate has been granted, I mean?'

'I'll let you know.' Lily was getting suspicious. She kept looking at the door to the inner room. 'The loo is upstairs.'

'And which home is Bert in?'

'No business of yours. Anyway, it wouldn't do you any good to see him now. I told you, he can't remember how many fingers he has on each hand. Now, if you don't mind, I'm asking you to leave, both of you.'

'Oh, very well.' Bea called out, 'Gail, are you all right?'

Gail appeared in the doorway, looking flushed. 'Sorry about that. Can't seem to keep anything down nowadays.'

Lily practically shoved them out of the door.

Lily slammed the door behind them. Interfering old women! Had they come to gloat? One thing; they'd never learn the truth about what happened to Matthew from her. And they couldn't prove anything.

She seethed with frustration. All that scheming and she still hadn't a penny to bless herself with.

Back to work. Some of the furniture had already gone to the saleroom. Some the new owners were going to buy. It would be enough to keep her going until probate was through and she could lay her hands on Matthew's house.

Bea and Gail walked in silence to the car and got in. Gail produced a wad of paper from her handbag.

'These were in the shredder. It had jammed because she'd put in too much at once. I used the reverse switch to get them out. They're some flyers showing Matthew in costume, with Bert at the piano beside him. They're way out of date. So why is she shredding such old stuff?'

'It's a puzzle, to be sure,' said Bea, who had a pretty good idea why. She looked at the flyers. They showed Matthew caressing a microphone and smiling into the camera. A slightly built man with a heart-shaped face sat hunched over a keyboard at his side. He didn't look anything like Lily. Bea said, 'It's definitely Bert at the piano?'

'Sure. Poor Bert.' Her sympathy was perfunctory.

Bea nodded. This was the last piece in the jigsaw puzzle. She had a pretty good idea now as to what had happened. She stowed the flyers in her bag. 'Did you find an address for the retirement home?'

'I looked through her address book by the telephone. Nothing. Just as you called to me, I spotted her handbag on the floor and there was a brochure sticking out of it. I could only see the first few words. Green something, and a picture of a big house. Do we really need to question Bert? If he's really lost it . . .'

'Bert sold the house and bought an annuity to cover his bills at the home, which meant Lily will never get anything, even if he dies tomorrow. I feel sorry for her, almost, because she's lived there all her life and she's not only going to lose her home but also her place of work.'

Gail looked at her watch. 'I see what you mean. Even if he wasn't her real father, she deserved something, didn't she? Time's getting on and I'm chairing a committee meeting this afternoon.'

'There's a post office across the road. I'll pop in there and ask if they know of a retirement home around here called Green something.'

Without waiting for Gail's reply, Bea got out of the car and darted across the road. She was out in under five minutes but went into an adjoining shop before returning to the car with a bunch of flowers. 'It's not far away. Green Gates Retirement Home.'

'I'm not sure I can cope with Bert today, especially if he's lost it. Too sad.'

Bea rounded the corner and parked the car outside a large house. 'I need a witness. Please, Gail. It won't take long.' The front door was locked. Bea rang the bell. It was a large, imposing Edwardian villa in its own grounds, but it didn't seem that the inmates were allowed to roam at will outside the house. There was a three-storey modern extension at the side, well maintained.

Bea looked through a window into a large sitting room. An arrangement of dried flowers in a vase. High-backed chairs ranged around the room. Various elderly people sitting in the chairs staring at a huge television. No Bert.

Gail followed Bea to the door. 'Not exactly lively, is it?'

A pleasant-looking woman opened the door. 'Sorry, short-handed today. I didn't hear the bell.'

'We're old friends of Mr Cunningham's, just been told by his daughter Lily that he's moved here but is not very well. We'd like to see him for a few minutes if we may. We promise not to tire him.' Bea held up the flowers she'd just bought.

'Well, that's nice of you. His daughter hasn't been to see him since he was brought in. Such a shame. Er, you do realize that he's pretty confused at the moment? We've had to sedate him a couple of times, for his own safety. Follow me. I think he's in the sun lounge at the back.'

They followed the woman across a brightly polished hallway and down a corridor. Sounds of tables being laid came from a dining room and savoury smells made Bea think longingly about food. She hadn't had any breakfast.

The sun lounge had been built on to the back of the house and was bright with pot plants and bamboo furniture. Four people were playing dominoes at a table. Two more were reading newspapers. A woman was knitting in one corner, hooked up to an iPod.

A tall, slim man dressed all in grey, was sitting in a chair looking out over the garden. He was leaning forward, both hands resting on a stick. There was a half-healed cut on his left temple, with a yellowing bruise around it.

His hairline was receding, but he was a good-looking man for all that. He had a strong face which wore an expression of patience. Even, of suffering.

He didn't move or even see his visitors until Gail exclaimed, 'Oh!'

He turned his head. His eyes focused on Bea. He had cornflower-blue eyes. He didn't recognize her and his remote expression didn't change. His eyes moved past Bea to Gail. He recognized her.

His face came alive. He stumbled to his feet, dropping his stick. His silver-knobbed stick.

Gail bent to pick it up.

'Oh, Matthew,' she said.

Twenty

A clock chimed twelve somewhere in the depths of the house and a slow surge of residents headed from various places towards the dining room. In the sun lounge everyone watched with varying degrees of curiosity and interest as Gail flung her arms open and Matthew stepped into them. They held one another fast, eyes closed, tears on their cheeks.

Matthew said, 'I prayed you'd come.'

Gail could only repeat his name, over and over. 'Matthew, Matthew, Matthew!'

'What's going on?' Ice in her voice, authority reasserted itself.

Bea grinned. 'Nice to see lovers reunited, isn't it?' She understood now why these two people from such disparate backgrounds had ever got married. Sex, that's what. Matthew and Gail had taken one look at one another when they first met, and that was that. As it was now.

Authority was not pleased. 'I think you owe me an explanation. Why is that woman kissing Mr Cunningham?' Recollecting that they had an audience, she turned on the other residents of the room, frozen into various attitudes of surprise. Authority produced a professional smile. 'Now, then. Off you go. Lunch will get cold otherwise, and we don't want that, do we?'

Force of personality swept them – if reluctantly – out of the room. By which time Matthew had collapsed back into his chair, laughing, still holding on to Gail . . . who wasn't about to let go of his arm, either.

'Now!' Authority meant it, too.

Bea produced a card. 'My name is Bea Abbot of the Abbot Agency, domestic only. My friend here is Mrs Gail Kent, who is—'

'Matthew's ex-wife,' said Gail.

'My fiancée,' said Matthew, laughing. When animated, his face was that of an actor, mobile, expressive. 'In fact, in the eyes of the church—'

'We're still married, hurray!' Gail touched the bruise on his temple with a forefinger, and then kissed it. Lightly. 'How soon do you think we can make it legal again?'

Authority closed the door into the corridor and folded her arms at them. 'I would like an explanation, please. Mr Cunningham here is my responsibility and—'

'He's not Mr Cunningham,' said Gail. 'He's Matthew Kent. Oh, Matthew, I'm so glad you're not dead!'

Bea produced a card from her bag. 'He's Mr Matthew Kent and this is one of his cards. You see the website at the bottom? If you access the site, you'll see his picture. And here,' she produced one of the leaflets which Lily had been trying to shred, 'is a picture of Mr Kent in costume, with his accompanist, Bert Cunningham.'

'I told them,' said Matthew, 'but they didn't believe me. They said I was confused. And indeed, I was confused. It's been a nightmare.'

'I think,' said Authority, 'that you two ladies had better leave. You are upsetting my charge, and we can't have that or he'll be ill again. Meanwhile, I'll ring his daughter and ask her to visit, to calm her father down.'

'His daughter's dead,' said Bea. 'Sorry, Matthew; but she is.'

'Damaris dead?' He registered shock, and then something else . . . a slow realization that there was worse to come. 'I don't understand . . .'

Authority snapped out, 'See how you are confusing him. His daughter's name is not Damaris. It's . . . it's on the tip of my tongue . . .'

'Try Lily,' said Bea.

'That's it! Lily Cunningham. She brought him in just over a week ago, a little earlier than we'd expected, but he'd had a fall and needed rest. He had a slight concussion and we kept him in bed for a while, just till he recognized his own name. It's not unusual for people of his age to become confused after a fall.'

'Nobody's blaming you,' said Bea, realizing the woman was afraid for her position. 'I'm sure you acted with the best of motives and looked after him as well as possible. Tell me, how did Lily bring him in? She doesn't drive.'

'In a taxi, of course. He was not a well man; anyone could see that. So we put him to bed and had our doctor see to him next day.'

'We understand that Bert Cunningham had made arrangements for himself to come here some time ago, suffering from arthritis. He must have visited this place before deciding that it suited him. Granted that the two men are much of a height, did nobody recognize that this was not the same man?'

'I . . .' The woman reddened, clasping and unclasping her hands. 'I've only been here three weeks. The lady in charge before me . . . she's moved on somewhere else. I'm afraid there's been a lot of personnel changes recently.'

'If you consult your records, you'll find a description of Bert's physical problems. Do they match those of our friend here? What of the scar from his recent operation? What of his need to take antibiotics still?'

Authority wasn't happy. Her eyes switched to Matthew, to her watch, and back to Bea. 'I think I'd better ring Mrs Meadows, the owner. In the meantime—'

'Yes, in the meantime, perhaps we could all transfer to your office? I myself would like to make a phone call to someone who might help sort this little muddle out . . .' But not Sylvester. Never more Sylvester. ' . . . And then we can look up your records and do some checking, right?'

'I really think it would be best if you left. I cannot have Mr Cunningham upset like this. I am a qualified nurse and I can see he's running a temperature.'

'Probably needs his lunch,' said Bea, without sympathy. Matthew was somewhat flushed, it's true, but that was more likely due to excitement and happiness than to a fever. 'Which reminds me; you couldn't find us a sandwich or two, could you? I'm famished.'

'So am I,' said Matthew, with a slow smile at his beloved. 'In more senses than one.'

'Well, really!' Authority was not pleased.

However, she did lead the way to an office off the main hall. There she telephoned her boss, while Bea found the business card Oliver had given her and got out her mobile.

Once through to a gentle-sounding voice, Bea said, 'You won't know me, but Oliver gave me your name. I'm Bea Abbot, and you are—'

'Mr Cambridge. Are you ringing about the red shoes? Oliver has been amusing me with the details. You have some evidence to show the suicide verdict was wrong? You need some advice?'

'How does one extract a person wrongly incarcerated in a retirement home? Do I need a writ for *habeas corpus* and how do I obtain one? And how do I arrange for someone to be arrested for murder?'

'I think I'd better come out to you. Give me directions.' His voice sounded a lot less gentle than before.

Meanwhile, Authority had rung the number she'd been given for Mr Cunningham's daughter. 'Ms Cunningham . . .?' The phone quacked indignantly, and Authority frowned. 'Yes, I've been given this number for Ms Cunningham. Her father is . . . that's not the number for Ms Cunningham? Yes, I have dialled correctly. Who did you say you were? Derek . . . Fraser? Frasier? Well, isn't Ms Cunningham to be found at this number? She isn't. Oh. Well, do you know where I can find her? Yes, I'll hold on.' She held on, while Bea smiled down into her hands. So Lily had given Damaris's number as a contact?

'Yes, I've got that,' said Authority, writing down a number. She put the phone down, and punched more numbers. The phone rang and rang. An answerphone clicked in. Authority put the phone down. More frowns.

Bea and Gail exchanged looks. Lily had gone out. Or . . . fled? 'Coffee and a sandwich?' asked Bea.

'I hardly think . . . well, perhaps. I'll see what I can do.' Authority produced both. Good for Authority.

Lily stared at the phone. She had a bad feeling about this call. If it was important, they could leave a message. But suppose . . .?

No, ridiculous! Nothing could go wrong now. Could it?

Only, why had Gail taken the leaflets out of the shredder?

Oh, as a memento. Of course. There was nothing to worry about.

The phone stopped ringing. They hadn't left a message. The call hadn't been important.

But, just in case, she would take her black scarf out into the garden and burn it. No need to take chances.

Oliver's contact, Mr Cambridge, arrived at the same time as the home's owner, Mrs Meadows. She was alarmingly loud, fiftyish and strongly-built. He was as quiet as smoke, a tall streak of a man with the face of a patrician, who introduced himself in a murmur and drifted across the room into a chair, bestowing a faint smile on all and sundry. Bea trusted him on sight.

'Well? What's the problem?' Mrs Meadows tried to be affable but didn't succeed.

Bea put down her empty cup. 'I'll start, shall I?'

Matthew pointed at Bea. 'Apart from being an angel in disguise, who exactly are you?'

'My name is Bea Abbot and I run a domestic agency. Ten days ago your cleaner discovered a corpse on your bed, dressed and made up to look like you in costume. She yelled for help and when I arrived—'

Matthew looked from Bea to Gail and back again. 'What? But who . . .? You don't mean . . . Bert?'

'Yes, I'm afraid so. I sat with the corpse till the police arrived. The next day I was asked by your stepdaughter Damaris to prepare a detailed inventory of the contents of your house. Circumstances made me think all was not well, I met Gail, and over the following days a strange story began to emerge.

'Correct me if I'm wrong, but early this year I believe that you and your old friend Bert both received bad news about your health. Bert was afflicted by arthritis, and a heavy smoker. The prognosis was not good. About the same time you, Matthew, were informed that a growth was affecting one of your kidneys and that it looked like cancer. You shared the news with one another, but responded in different ways to the situation.

'You, Matthew, had no close family except for your adopted stepdaughter Damaris. Damaris suggested you make a will in her favour and you agreed to do so. Why not? You thought you only had months to live.

'Bert, on the other hand, decided to purchase an annuity to cover the cost of his moving into a retirement home, using his house as collateral. Living with him and looking after him was the woman known as his daughter, Lily. What he'd done to ensure a comfortable future for himself automatically left Lily without anywhere to live or any place to give piano lessons, but he didn't seem to care about that.'

Mathew said, 'He never believed she was his, and she wasn't kind to him. I don't blame him for what he did.'

'Maybe not, but when Lily found out that you were going to leave everything to Damaris, while she'd be left with nothing, she started to make plans of her own. Lily and Damaris had often been in one another's company as children so now Lily renewed her acquaintance with Damaris, who accepted her at face value as an old friend. Damaris introduced you, Matthew, to a solicitor known to her family, and you duly made a will, making Lily one of the executors. Why not? You'd all known one another for ever, and who would you trust except your oldest friends?

'But then everything went wrong for Damaris. Your surgeon operated to remove the affected kidney, and it was discovered that the growth was benign! You felt you'd been given a new lease of life. Quite by chance you met up with Gail – your ex-wife – again, and were offered some new and interesting work. Naturally you shared your good news with your old friend Bert. Who told Lily.

'Now both Lily and Damaris were looking at a bleak future. I don't know which of them actually came up with the idea, but when Bert next visited you he took with him a bottle of wine which had been drugged with sleeping pills. But it all went wrong. Over to you, Matthew. What happened next?'

Matthew held Gail's hand to his lips for a moment. 'The first part of the evening is clear enough, but it gets a bit fuzzy. Bert usually arrived at my place in a taxi, which I'd pay for. This time Damaris and Lily brought him in Damaris's old car. Lily doesn't drive and neither does Bert, nowadays. Anyway, the girls said they were going on to the pictures and would collect Bert later.

'Usually I'd give Bert some of my own wine, but that night he said he'd gone to a lot of trouble to buy a bottle of wine himself, to repay my hospitality. I was on antibiotics, so I only took a mouthful. It tasted awful, but Bert didn't seem to notice. He was such a heavy smoker, I don't think he'd any taste buds left. I made an excuse to go to the kitchen, where I tipped my glass down the sink. He poured me another glass, I put some traditional jazz music on, we started talking about old times, he began to propose toasts . . . so to please him I did take the odd gulp. Maybe half a glass.

'After a while I noticed he'd fallen asleep, was snoring. I felt sleepy, too. I was woken by something . . . the telephone, maybe? I remember starting to my feet, my glass of wine going over. I think I must have hit my head on the mantelpiece and knocked myself out.' He passed his hand across his eyes.

'I woke up here, in bed. Concussion, they said. Everyone talked to me as if I were Bert. I wasn't sure at that point who I was. It took time for my head to clear. There was a suitcase full of clothes which fitted me, and the stick . . . but no mobile phone, or money, credit cards, keys. Nothing. I was unsteady on my feet, and my head ached abominably.

'It took me a couple of days to remember that I was Matthew Kent. I told them my name and they shook their heads, said it was the knock on the head that had affected me, and that I mustn't get upset or they'd have to give me something to calm me down. I asked them to contact Damaris or Sylvester or my own doctor, to prove I was really Matthew Kent, but they didn't believe me. They sedated me. I tried to borrow someone else's phone, or some money, but everyone had been told I was confused. And in fact, I was. I almost came to believe that my mind had gone. The only thing that kept me sane was the stick Gail had lent me. For some reason Damaris had been kind enough to let me keep it.' He put Gail's hand to his lips again. 'I prayed that you'd come, and you did.'

'What an extraordinary story,' said Mrs Meadows, in a tone which meant she didn't believe a word of it. 'Whatever next?'

Bea said, 'What happened next is that the two women had one dead body and one unconscious body on their hands, and it was *the wrong way around*! You see, it wasn't going to benefit them if only Bert died. He'd put everything into an annuity and died straight away. They'd set everything up for a double suicide, two old friends, both ailing . . . why not? True, Matthew had been given the all-clear by the hospital, but everyone knows performers get their melancholy moments. An old friend's death might well have tipped him over the edge into suicide.'

Matthew wasn't buying it. 'So why didn't they put a pillow over my head and kill me, too?'

'Lily might have done so, but Damaris? Maybe it was she

who couldn't bring herself to kill you. Maybe they didn't think the bump on your head could be passed off as a part of a suicide attempt. There was one alternative. If they could only turn Bert's corpse into Matthew's, then they'd hit the jackpot. They could easily explain Bert's absence by saying he'd gone into the home as he'd planned all along to do. And in fact that part of the plan worked well; people did ask after him, and were satisfied when told he was in a home.

'So they took Bert upstairs to Matthew's bedroom and laid him on the bed. They wanted to make him unrecognizable to a casual eye, and they succeeded by making him look like a pantomime dame. He was stripped to his underwear, his face was painted, and he was covered over with the first dress that came to hand, which happened to be one which Matthew had left in a box in his hall. This had been hired from a costumier when the local amateur theatrical company planned that he play the duchess in the comic opera, *The Gondoliers*.

'The dress was a trifle too big for Bert, but that didn't matter because Damaris was going to identify the corpse as Matthew and with his face made-up in that ludicrous fashion, no one else would be able to recognize him. A wig was set on the table nearby, with the empty bottle of wine, the packet of pills, and a brief suicide note which one of them either concocted there and then . . . or maybe it was a note Bert had written before to explain something, apologizing for something he'd done or not done? I saw the staged "suicide" and it was . . . quite horrible. Shocking. But as Kasia, Matthew's cleaner, pointed out, the shoes didn't fit. It was the fact that the shoes didn't fit that really set me thinking.'

Matthew murmured, 'Poor Bert really did die?'

'I don't think he meant to kill himself or you. But yes, he died, poisoned by the drug in the bottle he'd brought with him to celebrate your reprieve from death. With Bert dead but you still alive, where did this leave the conspirators? Damaris was going to be fine as she was all set to inherit everything but Lily was still going to be homeless. Neither could afford to give the other away, so they worked together to set the scene. Lily took Matthew off in a taxi and delivered him here, saying he'd had a fall and was very confused, couldn't be left by himself, and would they take him in, please . . . which they did.

'Then Lily went back to help Damaris and together they cleared away all evidence of your and Bert's collaborations over the years, such as snapshots and flyers of the two of you working together. They tidied away evidence that Bert had been due to visit you that night. They deleted files on your computer . . . but not the hard drive, which we were able to copy, and which helped us to piece together what the last few months of your life had been like. The funeral went ahead, if not quite as they had planned—'

'Funeral!' Matthew was horrified.

Gail soothed him. 'Yes, dear one. And very well attended it was, too.'

'But . . . you mean they buried Bert instead of me? But anyone who knew us would realize—'

'Damaris identified the body as you. She got the death certificate, which accurately stated that the deceased had died of an overdose.'

'It was a cremation,' said Gail. 'We'll get a proper plaque put up to Bert at the cemetery, letters to the papers, all that.'

'That's horrible!'

Bea nodded. 'Yes, it was bad, Matthew. But remember; the nightmare stops here. Getting back to Lily and her dilemma. We know that a couple of days after Bert's death, Lily persuaded Damaris to make a will in her favour, leaving her your house and its contents. A surprising move because Damaris's family was also in need of money . . . until you realize that Damaris was paying Lily to keep quiet. In effect, the two women had murdered Bert and kidnapped you, stealing your identity, but were no nearer accessing any ready cash. They tried to sell your car through my agency, but . . . oh, where is your car, by the way?'

'In for a service. I suppose it's still at the garage.'

'They didn't know that, so the car must still be there. Another problem they had was that of keys. Damaris took possession of your set of keys, Matthew. When she asked the agency to do an inventory on the contents of the house for her, she gave me Kasia's set, which I've hung on to for one reason and another. The conspirators didn't seem to be able to lay their hands on a third set. But with Damaris due back at the shop, and clearing up still to be done at the house, she arranged to pass her set on to Lily, who wasn't working, remember. Matthew, you did have a spare set somewhere?'

Matthew said, 'A neighbour has a set, but she's away visiting her son in Canada. There's been a number of thefts of keys left on a table in the hall by people hooking them out through the letterbox, so I keep my spare set in the pocket of an old coat that hangs on a hook by the door.'

'That explains it. They were well hidden. But Lily is a resourceful character. On the Tuesday morning Lily duly turned up, late, at the house with Matthew's keys. She acted very shaken by a fatal accident at Ealing Broadway station, an accident in which Damaris "fell" under an express train and was killed.'

Matthew's face was without colour. 'No, I don't believe it. How?'

Bea said, 'I can't prove this, but the only person anyone saw on the platform near Damaris before she fell was a Muslim, dressed all in black. Lily possessed a long black coat and black scarf which she could have wound round her head to make her look like a Muslim. The clincher is that Lily admitted to being on Ealing Broadway station when Damaris "fell" to her death, and she was in possession of Damaris's keys by the time she arrived at your house. Conclusion: they must have made contact with one another at some point that morning.'

Everyone was silent, eyes wide with horror.

'Yes,' said Bea. 'Poor Lily, as you say. She'd gone through so much, committed at least one murder, and still had no money to put into her purse. The solicitor wouldn't let her move into Matthew's house until probate was granted – and that was another can of worms, wasn't it, since Derek Frasier decided to dispute the validity of Damaris's will? Poor Lily. I hope she's still at home, but I don't count on it, though where she'd go . . .' She shrugged.

More silence.

The pale man in the corner took out his mobile phone. 'I think this is where I come in. Mrs Abbot, may I have Ms Cunningham's address?' Bea wrote it out for him, and he excused himself from the room.

No one moved. Bea closed her eyes. The morning had taken a lot out of her. And one small sandwich had hardly touched the sides. She was hungry. She took the last sandwich on the plate, and checked to see if she had any coffee left in her cup. She hadn't.

Her movement seemed to release the others from a trance.

Mrs Meadows said, 'You'd better go and pack then, Mr . . . er . . . whatever. I'm sure you'll agree we've looked after you very well while you've been in our care, and your bills will be covered by – er – our solicitor will attend to all that.'

Matthew looked dazed. 'This is . . . I can hardly believe it.'

Gail put her arm through his, and handed him his stick. 'Don't worry, darling. It's going to take a bit of sorting out, but I'll help you. Let's go and pack. The sooner you're out of here, the better.'

Mrs Meadows took a deep breath. She turned to her computer. 'Which means we have a room free. Now who's next on the list and are they able to come in straight away?'

Two weeks later

Bea upended her handbag on her desk. The sun shone brightly into her office, the smell of new paint had disappeared, she had almost become accustomed to the lack of carpet, and she'd probably get used to having new furniture in due course. Winston had taken over the new black leather chair in the window, which gave him a good view of bird activity in the garden. It also gave him early warning when Maggie was cooking upstairs.

Bea's favourite pen had gone missing. It wasn't anywhere in her desk, but the lining of her handbag was a trifle loose and things did lose themselves at the bottom. Keys, for instance. Or a lipstick. So she upended her handbag and gave it a shake.

A flurry of papers settled on the surface. Oliver fielded a couple and handed them over. 'Ahha. I told you that murder pays. Matthew's been generous, hasn't he? One decent-sized cheque to cover the inventories we made, and a huge one for saving his life.'

Bea had been one of the two witnesses at the Kents' civil wedding ceremony the previous week followed by a blessing at St Mary Abbots afterwards. Gail had dropped in only the day before, to thank Bea personally for everything she'd done and ask her – somewhat diffidently – if they might continue to meet.

'I really need you as a friend who can tell me where I go wrong. Matthew seems to think I'm perfect, but I know I'm not. If only I can avoid the mistakes I made first time round!

I've asked him to be firm with me if I start behaving badly, but I'm not sure he will. He's such a kind man.'

Bea stifled a moment of envy. How wonderful to have a second chance at love with a kind man. Oh, if only Hamilton . . . but there it was, and one had to make the best of things. 'You'll be just fine.'

Gail turned pink. 'I'm trying to make it up to him. I've asked him if he'd do a turn at the big charity event I'm organizing next spring, and he hasn't said no.'

'Good for you, girl.'

'I'm selling my flat, of course, and I'm covering everything that Derek spent when Damaris died. I've also paid for her funeral, poor dear. I will try to keep in touch with Tom if he'll let me, but I'm not sure he will.' She shrugged. 'I'll do what I can and that's all one can do, isn't it?'

Bea had given Oliver and Miss Brook a bonus for their part in solving the mystery of the red shoes. Maggie had received a bonus, too, on the successful conclusion of the make-over she'd done at the flat down the road. She'd already been asked to take on a similar job; perhaps this was her future?

Looking around the refurbished room, and knowing how busy Maggie was, Bea made a note to find someone else to do the cleaning for the agency in future. She much regretted that Kasia hadn't registered with the agency and got herself a permanent job. But there, you couldn't organize everything and everybody in this imperfect world.

So, back to the present. Bea picked up another piece of paper, which turned out to be the order of service for her old friend Sylvester. 'I'll miss him.' She'd read one of the lessons at his funeral, just as he'd wanted.

'Why do women carry so much around in their handbags?' Oliver teased out a business card from the pile on the desk. 'I see you've kept Mr Cambridge's card. What do you think of him? I like him. He says that as the law stands I can call myself any name I like.' He frowned, straightened his shoulders. 'Well, what's in a name, anyway?' He was coping pretty well with his problem.

Bea shoved make-up back into a side pocket of her handbag. 'As you say, what's in a name? The great thing is that he knew who to contact in the police, and how to get Lily arrested. Poor girl. What she did was dreadful, but I can't help feeling

Bert was largely to blame.' She put Mr Cambridge's card back into her handbag, telling herself that she hoped never again to get involved with a murder, but that if ever she was in trouble, perhaps . . . well, it did no harm to keep his card, did it?

Oliver said, 'I'm not touching those used paper tissues of yours.'

Bea laughed and dumped them in the bin. A note from Piers was returned to her handbag. He'd invited her to a new gallery opening next week. She'd go and enjoy the evening in a way, but really they had nothing in common, did they? They certainly weren't going to jump into bed with one another, as Gail and Matthew had done.

Bea picked up an expensive card with an enclosure; the card was from Max and Nicole, while the enclosure was a copy of the scan for her baby. Ugh. 'I'd better put this on the mantelpiece upstairs.' Bea thought that in her day such things were kept private, and were certainly not handed around for everyone to gawp at. But Nicole would expect to see it when she and Max came over next.

Finally, she spotted her pen. 'There it is. Now where are those letters for me to sign?'

Oliver was smoothing out one last piece of paper. 'What's this?'

Bea grimaced. 'I used it to write down Matthew's address, the day it all started. It must have been in my bag ever since. Is it anything important?'

'Someone wants us to investigate the death of her brother. She says she's sure he was murdered, but the police won't take her seriously.' He frowned, then laughed. 'A nutter. She thinks the CIA did it.'

'Tell her we're a domestic agency, pure and simple. We don't do murder.'

'As you say,' said Oliver, laughing. 'As you say.'